MORTAL

FOE

MARTY

ROPPELT

Mortal Foe

Marty Roppelt

ISBN: 978-0-9990692-1-9
Dragon Breath Press, LLC
Ridgeland, Mississippi
dragonbreathpress.com

DEDICATION

To my darling wife, Becky, for her unwavering support, and for the encouragement that sometimes manifested itself in a necessary, if gentle, kick in the pants. Thank you for "doing life" with me, and for helping bring *Mortal Foe* to light.

And to our Creator, without Whom nothing is possible.

ACKNOWLEDGEMENTS

A number of people should be mentioned here, folks who have either influenced this story, or who have otherwise been instrumental in its publication.

First, I would like to thank John Thomas and Laura Thomas, longtime friends, for their encouragement and support from the time I first began writing short stories in the early 1990s. Thanks to my family, who back me whether they fully understand what I'm doing or not. And though I've already dedicated *Mortal Foe* in part to my wife, Becky, she deserves my undying thanks as well.

Another thanks goes to Christopher Chambers for his cover concept—Grandpop's darkroom. He can be reached at chris@juroddesigns.com.

Finally, Janet Taylor-Perry had enough faith in this work and the courage to publish it as one of the very first Dragon Breath Press publications. Thank you, Janet!

DISCLAIMER

All entities depicted in this novel are fictitious. Any resemblance to any person living or dead is coincidental.

MORTAL

FOE

Mortal Foe   *Marty Roppelt*

For we wrestle not against flesh and blood, but against principalities, against powers, against the rulers of the darkness of this world, against spiritual wickedness in high places.

Ephesians 6:12

CHAPTER 1

My eyes snap open wide.

A shadow faces me from beyond the foot of my bed. I shiver, holding my breath. The tall, bulky intruder seems oblivious. My sleep-hazy mind tells me to lie still. I'll make myself smaller that way, so the invader won't see me.

I'm making myself small...

My brain stirs slowly. A minute passes, then a few more. My eyes take their time adjusting to the darkness. Across the room, the sinister hulk takes the shape of my antique cherry-wood armoire.

My girlfriend, Kelly, lies next to me, undisturbed. She faces away. Her chest rises and falls with each breath, her body radiating warmth.

I don't move. Dread still freezes me in place. A voice in my head, my own voice, whispers a warning to me. The warning is so primal it would wear a bearskin if it had a life of its own.

Don't show the darkness any fear, any weakness.

A familiar neon green beacon, my alarm clock, demands my attention. A quarter past midnight. The glow helps me shake off the drowsy panic. My eyes scan familiar, dark shapes around me—the armoire, the dresser, the doors to my closet and to the hallway, the rumpled down comforter covering my girlfriend.

Despite the need for rest, my eyes won't stay closed. This irritates me. The frustration of not being able to sleep keeps me awake even longer. I can deal with the frustration. But I can't shake this sense of dread.

A dream. Just a weird, stupid dream.

The clock's digits change without remorse, mocking and exasperating me. Twelve forty-seven, eight, nine... *Tomorrow won't be good.* I risk coming off like a yawning zombie. Twelve fifty-five... I consider pummeling my pillow. My legs swing out of bed instead. The cold of the hardwood floor against my bare feet chases away the last of my drowsiness.

I amble into the kitchen. Sitting in silence in its cradle on the kitchen counter, is my cordless phone. My eyes lock on the handset. An urge brews up to call someone close to me, but who should I call? My mom, my dad? Neither of them would answer at this hour, for different reasons, and neither should, of course. Now I expect the phone cradle to light up and ring, as my roused senses try to decipher the dream that woke me, that somehow signaled to me something is wrong...

A dream has me waiting at a ridiculous hour for a phone call from someone in my family.

I grumble to myself, "This is nuts."

The opened refrigerator bathes me in a sudden glare. Unguided hands fumble past paper bags and Styrofoam containers of restaurant leftovers. I finally find a bottle of beer. My fingers close around the long neck, I twist off the cap, and I take a swig. The light cord of the ceiling fan dangles near my head. I ignore it. Something about the darkness is important. Not comforting, but...

But what?

Raising a cigarette to my lips, I open the window a few inches, then sit at the table. My old Zippo lighter's top pops open with a metallic clink, the flint makes a quick, scraping rasp, and the flame whooshes to life. I cringe. *Did the noises rouse my neighbors from their own troubled sleep?*

My gaze wanders past the flame.

Don't show the darkness any fear.

Darkness dominated the kitchen only a moment ago. This flame, this puny, solitary sliver of light defeats the darkness. My Zippo can't signal ships at sea. My fridge probably could. Both lights can expose shadowy shapes, however, and the night cannot overcome either light. The only thing that can extinguish the light is me.

Don't show it any weakness.

I light my cigarette and kill the glow of the Zippo.

"Join you?" A voice, half-awake, issues from the doorway behind me. I hope I didn't jump too high.

"Sure. Beer?"

"No. You can fire up a smoke for me, though. Thanks."

Kelly glides past. A wisp of vanilla, musk, and flowers, Chantilly, her favorite perfume, follows her. She sits opposite me and takes the lit cigarette I offer. "Should I turn on the light?"

"If you like."

She slips into her seat, apparently liking the darkness better.

I jerk my chin toward the open window. "You want me to turn the heat up?"

"I've got my robe on."

I chuckle. My own total nakedness doesn't concern me. Kelly, on the other hand, wears her gauzy emerald green "robe" only, untied. She might as well be naked, too. I understand, of course. The sheer silk garment's function was never to keep the wearer warm, but to light a fire in someone else.

Kelly toys with her cigarette, rolling it between her thumb and fingers. "Worried about tomorrow?"

"About my department head? He's audited my classes before."

"So, why the stress?"

"I'm that transparent?"

Her laugh drips playful sarcasm. "You light up every hour and a half when you're awake. You only smoke more at a bar, when you're bored, or when you're stressed. We're not at a bar. And when I do things right you're definitely not bored." She leans over the table. Her lips pucker into her best Marilyn Monroe pout. "Didn't I do things right tonight?"

"Oh, yeah."

Several hours ago, Kelly left her Downtown Cleveland office after work to meet me at an upscale bistro on the west bank of the Cuyahoga River. A glass each of Chianti Classico turned into a whole bottle. She asked after glass three if I could spend the night with her. I toyed with the idea. After a few minutes, I finally decided to beg off.

But Kelly doesn't often take long to get what she wants from me. Tonight was no exception. The wine shot straight to my head. The low lights hid the dainty foot that nudged and rubbed my calf under the table. The aromas of Italian cooking mingled with Chantilly in an irresistible wave of sensuality. We passed on dessert. Kelly promised something much more stimulating at my apartment.

Now she sits back in triumph, blowing two perfect smoke rings toward the ceiling. "So, this is stress."

"Yes and no," I mumble.

"Nightmare?"

"Yeah."

"I'm surprised."

"Why?"

"It's just a dream. You're a bright college professor..."

"Journalism, not psychology. Who said I put stock in that stuff, anyway? I woke up, that's all."

"What did you dream about?"

"Funny. Now that I'm awake, I don't remember much."

Why did I just lie to her?

The truth is I remember every detail. The odd nightmare burned itself into my consciousness like a glowing cattle brand.

In the nightmare, my grandfather, photographer Jimmy Cullen, pulled a photo print off the wire that runs the length of his basement darkroom. Grandpop—I've always called him that—held the photo as far from his face as possible. His eyes widened. His ruddy

15

complexion drained of all color. His lips quivered. He acted as if he'd been handed a live hand grenade.

"Grandpop?" My tongue lolled in my mouth with Novocained sluggishness. "What is it?"

A sudden wind blew. Dried fallen leaves scraped across the pavement outside. Our heads snapped in unison toward the sound. The basement's bare cinderblock walls gave the place a fortress's ambiance, but they didn't blot out the rattle of dead leaves. Grandpop stared for a long moment. He froze as if expecting the walls to give way to the leaves, or to worse. The still house seemed to invite the whispery sounds of death inside and embrace them.

Grandpop spoke. But like a badly dubbed foreign movie, the words his mouth formed didn't match the words that came out. "Alone tonight…Darn it, Maureen…Doggone kids' Halloween dance…"

Exhausted by his outburst, Grandpop plopped down on a tall stool at his work table. A complaint? The words, the whining and grousing, were out of character. I had no response for him, which is also unlike me.

"No Grandma?" Invisible marbles rolled around inside my mouth.

Grandpop blinked hard, jumping as if electrically shocked. He jammed the print into a large manila envelope that already bulged with something else inside. The package bore a number written in green ink: nine-eight-five-nine.

Grandpop rose from his stool, a barstool I recognized from my dad's Downtown tavern. He strode toward the walk-in closet at the back of the darkroom. He muttered at the envelope as he passed me.

"Caught you again, didn't I?"

"Caught who?" My voice changed. I sounded like a Munchkin from Oz.

Grandpop disappeared into the closet, leaving me in the darkroom alone. I couldn't bring myself to move. My curiosity was the kind a child suffers when he's told never, ever to do a certain thing. The curious kid in me wanted to see what was going on. The adult in me feared for life and limb. My fear rooted me to the spot.

A "pop" and loss of light announced the death of one of the darkroom's two light bulbs.

"I don't spook so easily!" Grandpop hollered.

A car cruised up the driveway. The engine's hum filtered through the fortress walls. The side door to the kitchen creaked open and banged closed.

We were no longer alone.

My heart raced, my joints froze. I wanted to run. My muscles fought against me. Stark terror turned my feet to lead. Footsteps headed our way from the basement stairs.

"Jimmy?" my grandmother, Maureen, called.

My heart slowed but I still couldn't move, despite my relief.

Grandpop met Grandma in the doorway and gave her a peck on the cheek.

"How's my Lass?"

"Missed you." She scrunched her face into a silly expression, a kind of mock pout, uncharacteristic for her. "Atlanta? The Series?"

"Too much traffic. The Indians lost. Quiet flight." He gave a one-shoulder shrug. "Missed you, too."

They held each other, their embrace a subtle dance. The surviving forty-watt bulb above us threw weird shadows into the corners of the darkroom. The sounds of our breathing, and the scraping, rustling leaves grew louder in the otherwise silent murk.

Grandma pulled away, giggling. "Cup of hot chocolate and a ghost story for you?"

I almost laughed out loud at her bizarre behavior.

"Nah," Grandpop said.

"I'm going to bed."

Grandpop answered in a melodramatic, fearful tone. "Just a couple more things to do. Then we'll be together again."

His stony expression was the lawyer's before a murder trial, or the soldier's on his way to deadly combat. His demeanor only made his words to Grandma more jarring, more frightful to me.

They kissed. Grandma wheeled and left the

darkroom. We heard the groan of well-worn wooden stairs, first to the kitchen, then further above to the bedroom of their old colonial-style home. Grandpop settled again on his stool. He reached across his work table for his Kodak Medalist 620, the camera he used since his enlistment in the Navy two generations ago.

Every once in a while, a dream becomes so surreal that, despite still being asleep, some distant part of the brain announces "This is a dream!" I remember the exact moment, a sort of "out-of-body" experience. I *became* Grandpop. I sat on his stool and held his camera, but I was still an observer, too, watching myself play his part. I gripped the antique as if shaking a frail old friend's hand. This friend accompanied me—him—through everything from the best of times to the most harrowing hell.

No more experiences would be shared and captured on film. A hot, sharp pain ripped up my left arm. A giant fist squeezed my chest and I gasped in vain for breath. My mind raced away from the Medalist 620 to my grandmother lying in bed, likely dozing while trying to read a book. She would wake, sensing Grandpop was still in the house, and yet gone. She would find him here later. Sadness engulfed me.

I'm sorry, Lass...

I slumped to the work table. As Grandpop, I wanted my last thoughts on earth to be of Grandma, to take the memory of my gentle, devoted wife's face with me on my way to meet

God. But my last glance caught a shadow that was not Grandma's, moving toward me from beyond the darkroom doorway.

Then I woke to the strange shadow at the foot of my bed…

"Yeah, I've had that happen before. It's so frustrating."

Kelly's voice, from behind the glowing cigarette tip, jars me back to the waking present. I shake the nightmare out of my head.

"Had what happen?"

"Dreamed something and then forgotten it only a couple of minutes after waking up. Frustrating."

"Yeah."

Kelly takes a drag from the cigarette and stabs the ashtray with it. She shoves her chair aside, composes herself, and glides back around the table, tracing her finger up my bare arm. Her nail scratches a light reddish trail on my skin.

"Know the best way to get rid of frustration, Buddy Cullen?"

"Tell me."

"Showing's better than telling."

I crush my own cigarette out and glance at the phone. Nothing happens, of course. The phone's not going to ring tonight. Not for this. I rise and lay foolish superstition aside. A colleague at Case Western Reserve University, a science professor, once assured me that to attach meaning to dreams is unscientific, a bogus exercise. Dreams, he theorized, might be nothing more than a mash of random thoughts and memories.

Kelly breezes ahead of me, tugging me by my hand. Her urgency mounts. My gaze consumes her. The wispy robe caresses her perfect form. Her cat-graceful step entrances me. She pirouettes, sits on the edge of the bed, and leans back, pulling me down toward her.

Ghosts and demons and other unexplainable things lose their fascination. I lie far less gracefully beside Kelly. Her lips explore the base of my neck, but I still keep one ear cocked toward the phone. She nips lightly at my ear lobe, with a deep-throated chuckle. In a few short moments, she commands my full attention...

The phone rings. I gasp, irritated by the interruption. I'm dismayed, too. I know what the call is about.

"I have to get that."

"No, you don't." Kelly tangles her fingers in my hair and pulls my face back down toward hers. "That's why God gave us answering machines."

I'm conflicted, keyed up but powerless, able to break free but unwilling to try. The machine answers the call; the phone stops ringing. I feel Kelly's smile in the darkness as her lips brush against mine. I lose myself in her, lose every part of myself.

Every part, that is, except the faraway corner of my mind that wonders if Grandma just woke from the same nightmare and found Grandpop dead in his darkroom.

CHAPTER 2

I would have taken a quicker, more direct route on any other day. But the Indians moved to Jacobs Field last year. I decided it was more fitting to drive past crumbling old Municipal Stadium on the way to Grandpop's wake.

The most magnetic woman I ever laid eyes on sits next to me in my car. *How did Kelly become my girlfriend?* I choose not to try to solve the mystery. She's out of my league. I fear that if I solved the mystery the story would end, and so would our relationship.

We wait at a red light.

Kelly chafes.

She finally breaks a long silence with an impatient sigh. "I-90 would've been faster."

"Lake Avenue's a lot prettier."

Few would disagree. The sun hangs in a cloudless November sky. Lake Erie, steel blue and calm, stretches to the horizon. I appreciate the beauty, especially today.

The light turns. We angle left at Edgewater Park to the West Shoreway.

Kelly fidgets.

She tenses up as we pass the West 25th Street exit. I'd hazard a guess that the exciting, multi-street intersection's design involved too many quibbling city engineers. A mile later, I ignore the West 6th Street Downtown exit.

Kelly squirms.

I try to explain as we pass Cleveland Municipal

Stadium.

"Grandpop took a lot of pictures of the Indians in this old ruin."

She sits back and nods. "Was he their official photographer?"

"You'd think so, but no. He freelanced, took pictures of a lot of things for a lot of publications. Indians games were his favorite gig, by far."

I nudge the steering wheel over. We glide to the East 9th Street exit ramp and thread our way back west, through Downtown's modest skyscrapers. A red light stops us at Public Square. The smallish, hundred-seventy-five-year-old Old Stone Church sits next to us, nestled amongst taller, newer buildings. Several generations of factory soot and car exhaust crust the oddity's exterior. Even Grandpop might never have seen the little black church's original color.

We cruise past the gloomy house of God. I'm glad the funeral won't be held there. Yes, it *is* a church. Yes, I understand why it looks this way. But I never pass by without a sense of foreboding. This time is no exception.

I want to tell these things to Kelly but seem unable.

We park in a public lot on West 6th Street. I wish, despite myself, that Kelly hadn't gotten the day off. I'm uneasy about her joining me. I don't know why. She couldn't miss my discomfort the moment I picked her up, I'm sure. Neither of us has said anything yet. I'll bet she's dying to, however.

We climb out of the car and lock the doors.

Kelly's outburst confirms my suspicion.

"I'm your girlfriend. Your family would expect to see me. Besides, I've never been to an Irish wake."

"It's a pseudo-Irish wake."

"How do you mean, 'pseudo'?"

I steer her toward the lot's exit. "I mean, we won't see Grandpop's body there. At least, I don't think we will."

"Are you serious?" Her step slows.

"Oh, yeah. I've been to a dozen of these. I never knew the difference myself until I did a paper on real Irish wakes in grad school. Traditional wakes in Ireland weren't just about throwing a party and boozing it up. They celebrated the deceased's life in the deceased's presence."

"With the body?"

"In its open box, propped up in a prominent place."

Kelly gasps. "In the middle of a party? Was this right after..." Her voice lowers to a near whisper. "I mean, how fresh was..."

I stifle a chuckle. "The body? Oh, well, the wake didn't happen the day of the death. First, the family's women would wash and dress the body, then would come a day of keening and wailing."

"Keening and wailing?"

"Yeah, an important part of the preparation. The noise was supposed to scare evil spirits away. Then they'd prop the stiff up in the parlor and all get hammered."

"Parlor. So, this isn't a real Irish wake because

it's not at his home and his body won't be in the room?"

"Hope not. And I doubt my grandmother is a keener and wailer."

So, the evil spirits are still here....

We hurry across sun-drenched West 6th Street and find ourselves swallowed by the dank shadows of the Warehouse District.

The designation "warehouse district" does this part of Downtown no justice. The charm of these Victorian Italianate façades might have been undervalued a century ago, I suppose. They were built as warehouses, for that function. We wouldn't put much effort into a warehouse's appearance today. These structures' architects did. They found elegant ways to use the new, efficient processes of making steel and iron. They honored the industries that forged the backbone of Cleveland, a backbone now bent and broken and in search of something to take steel's place.

We head for the Burgess Building. A civic preservation group converted the Burgess from a wholesale grocery into offices when I was in high school. O'Leary's Irish Pub, Dad's tavern, takes up the basement. Stories still circulate about O'Leary's, legends that give the place a questionable mystique. Some say the Burgess's basement was a stop along the Underground Railroad. This is a crock. The grocery was built in 1874, almost ten years after the need for the Railroad ended. No one documented when the basement first became a bar. The rumors I heard growing up about bootleggers and gangsters seem more credible, if less savory.

Dad never confirms or denies anything.

We hustle around the corner from West 6th Street to short, narrow Frankfort Avenue. The odors of urine, vomit, and alcohol linger here. Frankfort is actually an alley with delusions of "avenue." A sign hangs on the Burgess Building's brick wall, above a weathered wooden door. Kelly cocks her head to one side. She stares at the sign and its caricature of a cow kicking at a hurricane lamp.

"I never got the connection. Mrs. O'Leary and her cow torched Chicago, not Cleveland."

"My dad's not big on historical accuracy. The name's unmistakably Irish. It's recognizable, too. I'd bet everyone's heard of Mrs. O'Leary and her cow."

"Brand name recognition?"

"Yeah, an attempt, I guess."

I yank the door open and usher her in ahead of me.

Dad owns and runs O'Leary's, so I practically grew up in the place. I've brought Kelly here a few times, too. Stepping down to the windowless tavern in the cellar unsettles me today, however.

"I get the impression we're climbing into a grave, don't you?"

She ignores me and strolls into the barroom.

A lot of folks are already here. Most of them are old and middle-aged men. Several of them put down their pints and smokes and approach us. They shake my hand, offering their condolences. Then they hustle back to their beers and cigars. I understand. The majority of these men are married.

They all now try to pretend they aren't devouring Kelly with their minds' eyes.

They fail.

She's tall and slender. Black nylons stretch tightly over her long legs. A clingy, black, knee-length skirt accentuates, rather than conceals. Her black silk blouse is unbuttoned maybe one button too many. Creamy-white, heart-shaped face, long, wavy auburn hair, big, sparkling green eyes—Kelly Byrne can bring out the babbling Irish poet in any man, whether he's Irish or not.

"Buddy! Just in time. Bring that fine lass over here!" Dad calls from behind the bar.

We wedge our way through the crowd. Capacity in the little pub is supposed to be a hundred but add a minimum of fifty more. Some of the overflow of mourners hold civic offices. They turn a booze-blinded eye today. Many will deal with staggering hangovers tomorrow.

I sigh. "Looks like they've all been here a while."

We arrive at the battered oak bar. Kelly extends her hand.

"Hi, Mr. Cullen," she says.

Dad takes her hand. His manner and tone irritate me. The sudden spark of jealousy surprises me. He either misses or ignores my glare. "Mike, please. Beer, Kelly?"

"And a Bushmills, please," she says.

Dad's eyebrows shoot upward. "She know what she's doing?" he asks me.

"Almost always."

Dad pours three heavy-handed double shots of Irish whiskey and plunks two bottles of beer down on the bar.

"Need a glass?"

I reach for one of the bottles. "Already comes in one."

"'Atta boy. Kelly?"

She puts her bottle to her lips with a throaty chuckle. Thankfully, Dad makes no comment.

My father is my ideal of a Downtown Cleveland bar owner. He wears his gray-streaked hair tied back in a ponytail, reaching to the base of his neck. Two days' stubble covers his face. No surprise. His mug always shows only two days' worth at any given time. I'd swear he trims it daily. He's dressed in his standard army fatigue pants and beat-up service boots. A black cotton Polo shirt subs for his usual tan one. Dad keeps himself in fair shape. If not for the gray hair, the slight thickening of the waist, and the faint circles under his eyes, we might be mistaken for brothers.

He raises his whiskey. We follow suit.

"To my father, Irish Jimmy Cullen..." He hesitates. Embarrassment clouds his face. No more words come to him. I fail at the moment, too, and a few short seconds stretch into an uncomfortable eternity.

A dozen mourners within earshot raise their glasses. A chorus of, "To Irish Jimmy," sounds through the cloud of beery smoke, to our collective relief. We all drink.

Old, bird-like Tom Jamieson shuffles up to the

bar. "It's a fine wake, Michael Cullen," he croaks.

"A hundred mourners laying waste to a river of beer and a lake of Irish whiskey," Dad says. "It's a fine one, sure."

Strange. The free-flowing alcohol pulls Irish brogues from men who never visited the Emerald Isle, let alone came from there. Dad is not immune.

Jamieson takes a drag from his cigarette and looses a deep, tubercular hack. The irony, the unfairness, raises my hackles. Grandpop never, to my knowledge, touched a cigarette or cigar. Layers of tar crust Tom Jamieson's fingers and lungs, yet Grandpop's clean, healthy heart gave out first.

Then again, being a smoker myself, I have no room to judge. I take a breath, swallowing the irony.

"Where's Grandma?"

"In the far corner booth. Past Frank and Judy Lucas and Dennis Cameron." Dad points his chin toward a knot of people near a couple of booths. "Go check out the body after you pay your respects."

"What?"

Dad's deadpan, poker-faced stare melts into a smirk. "Body of work," he says to me, with a wink at Jamieson. He and the old codger break into laughter.

"Nice, Dad."

Pay respects to Grandma...

An idea resurfaces, one I've already quashed several times today. I bite my lower lip.

Tell her about the dream you had the night Grandpop died. Ask her if she had the same dream.

The memory gives me the shivers. I nix the idea. Again. Why would I bug Grandma with my nightmare, especially today? The weird coincidence could only deepen her wound. Yet here I am, forcing myself to ignore the fluke for the dozenth time today.

No. I refuse.

Kelly and I muscle our way to the booths, bulling through the mob to Grandma's side. I lean over to kiss her cheek.

She gazes up, saying nothing.

The moment strikes me as odd. This is my grandmother, and yet it isn't. I assumed she would be sad, but I couldn't guess how she would handle the loss. My grandparents were young when they married in 1945. Grandma was eighteen, Grandpop turning twenty. They were close from the start, according to family lore. They only grew closer, until each practically became part of the other. To have Grandpop taken away like this must be like having one of her limbs lopped off. Grandma was always sharp as a shark's tooth. She seems dazed now, her eyes empty of everything except shock and disbelief.

Kelly takes Grandma's hand. "Mrs. Cullen, I'm sorry."

"Thank you," Grandma murmurs.

"Hey, Gram..." The Dream Question begins spilling out of my mouth. Grandma gazes up at me. I blink. "Uh, you need anything, let me know. I'll touch base later."

We turn and push our way to the back of the

tavern.

Several large panels stand propped up around a banquet table. A pack of people mill near the set-up. They paw and gawk at Grandpop's favorite keepsakes and memorabilia, given to him by Indians players he befriended over the decades. The old saying goes, "It's not what you know, it's who you know." Grandpop knew Hall of Famers like Bob Feller, Larry Doby, and Lou Boudreau. But the souvenirs don't say anything about Grandpop. Other items interest me more. His citations for bravery from the navy and his Medalist 620 camera grab my attention.

Enlarged photos hang from the surrounding panels. Kelly studies one in particular. She points to the shot, a picture of a Japanese kamikaze pilot in the cockpit of his plane as he takes his dive of destruction and death.

"This one reminds me of some old war movie," she says.

Grandpop showed me this picture when I was in high school. The image made me squirm then and does again now. "The guy's looking right at the camera. Right at my grandpop."

"That's the way it was, Boy-o."

A beefy hand claps me on the shoulder. I turn. The hand's owner climbs onto a chair, then to a table top. He clears his throat with a dose of Bushmills. "Shush," hisses from every corner like hydraulic machinery coming to life. Silence falls. He begins.

"That brave young lad stood on the deck, a

camera in his hand. The enemy fired shot on shot, but missed the boy so grand..."

One of Grandpop's old navy buddies, Bill Mannion, tall and portly and self-important, the Shoulder Clapper, performs for all. He recites a ditty so awkward he must have written it himself, in a hurry. His ode to Grandpop is amateurish and rough. Still, the effort touches me.

A hand more delicate than Mannion's grasps my elbow, then takes my arm. I mumble without turning. "Sorry I didn't say 'hi' right away, Mom."

Her retort drips acid. "A lot of distractions here."

"Mrs. Cullen," Kelly greets her curtly.

"Kelly," my mom replies in kind.

I don't understand the tension between my girlfriend and my mom. Mutual animosity brewed up the instant they met. Nothing has changed. They always behave like two rival cheetahs who surprise each other on disputed turf. Their bodies tense up, their teeth show. They do manage to stop short of growling and spitting. But they eye each other all the while.

"You think Mr. Mannion's making this up as he goes along?" I ask in a too-loud whisper as he continues his oratory.

"Yeah," Mom and Kelly mutter in unison.

The verse Mannion delivers has to do with my grandfather's war service. I start to block the speech out. Mom and Kelly face Mannion with frozen smiles, feigning politeness. I break away from them. The display calls to me. I meander back to the table to nose around a bit more.

Next best thing to having the dead body.

I pick up Grandpop's camera. This heirloom was much more than a mere possession. It was an artist's tool, like one of Van Gogh's brushes or Michelangelo's chisels. The old Medalist was almost a part of Grandpop. I rarely saw him without it.

"The image of his mortal foe, whose face so glum and sullen, was captured for eternity by Irish Jimmy Cullen."

The last line of Mannion's poem refocuses me. I peek one last time at the photo of the kamikaze, the mortal foe. Maybe Mannion will give me a printed copy of his epic. I'll frame and hang it next to the creepy picture somewhere.

Mannion climbs down from the table, to the other drunken mourners' generous applause. Dad rushes to shake his hand. He disappears in Mannion's rib-crushing bear hug.

Dad eventually escapes the Bear's embrace. "Thank you for your words, Bill."

"I tell you," Mannion slurs, "Irish Jimmy was a fine man, and fearless he was. And humble. Never once bragged about his service. He could've. The USS *Enterprise*. The rest of us shot at the kamikazes with a forty-millimeter gun. He shot at 'em with his camera. Unstoppable..." Mannion's voice trails off. He looks down, frowning. Uncertainty and fear cross his face. He is Grandpop's age.

And obviously, Grandpop was stoppable.

"No," Dad says, "besides his family, my father loved talking about..."

"Ah! The 1948 Cleveland Indians!"

I needle Mannion. "The Irish fought the Indians, didn't they?"

He stays stuck in his boozy brogue. "Aye, Boy-o, and they were legends then. But the Irish are a mysterious, fickle lot."

"That we are," Dad says. He raises his glass. "To the '48 Indians!"

Everyone joins in the toast. Most of the older folks in the room had personally seen the last Indians club to win the World Series. My father was just a toddler in 1948. Grandpop did take him to a Series game in 1954, a tremendous childhood experience according to Dad.

The Indians didn't win a single game that Series.

Dad waves his hand at me. "Buddy, let's get a picture."

"Of whom?"

"See the panel to your right, the second picture from the top?"

I locate the war era group photo. Someone besides Grandpop must have taken that shot because he poses in the picture, too.

"Yeah."

"Most of the rest of the guys are here. Let's get 'em together."

"I didn't bring my camera."

"Use the one in your hand. Here." He hands me a paper bag with a dozen antique flash bulbs. I glare at my father. Guilt saturates his grin. He obviously took the bulbs from Grandpop's darkroom.

"Are these the last bulbs?"

"I don't know. Probably. Think of a better way to use them?"

The idea gains traction with me, posing some of Grandpop's friends for a picture at his wake, and using his own camera for the shot. Dad and I struggle to assemble the men we need. We finally arrange Tom Jamieson, Bill Mannion, and three fine Irish lads named Rakocszy, Brochetti, and Schmidt in the same pose as in the old photo. Mannion grabs Dad by the arm to pull him into the picture as well. Dad manages to place a barstool, like the one in the darkroom, in Grandpop's spot.

The Empty Chair.

The gesture brings me close to tears. I put the Medalist up to my eye and snap the photo.

The flash throws a harsh strobe on the group with a loud *"POP."* The dim barroom suddenly appears even darker to me than before. I squeeze my eyes shut. Ghost images float across my closed eyelids, X-ray outlines of the mourners packing the pub. The phantom images have lives of their own. They move and mingle with one another.

I open my eyes. The darkness still seems somehow deeper than usual.

Despite my inability to readjust my eyesight, I manage to spot Kelly sidling up to my grandmother's booth. She sits next to Grandma. I replace the spent bulb with a fresh one, and squint at Dad for a go-ahead signal. These are probably some of the last flashbulbs of their kind.

Dad winks at me. "Make sure I get a print of that one."

I peer through the camera's viewfinder. Kelly crosses her legs demurely. She gives me an attitude far from demure—chin pointed downward, eyes half closed, lips parted and caressed by her tongue...

I know she will be comforting this mourner later.

CHAPTER 3

Today is the polar opposite of yesterday. A damp cold seeps down to the bone, replacing the crisp chill. Ominous gray cloud cover obliterates the sun. Light bathed everything yesterday, a good day to celebrate Grandpop's life.

Today is much better suited for his funeral.

A lone snowflake escapes its dismal prison in the sky. My eyes follow the delicate flake's descent to the windshield. I flick a switch. My windshield wipers dispatch the fugitive snowflake with a single swipe. I wouldn't mind snow. A white blanket covering everything would bring a certain cheer to my surroundings. But I won't be teased.

I park near the front of the gathering funeral procession and climb out of my car. I don't bother with the lock. The neighborhood around St. Ignatius can be iffy, sometimes even during the day. The funeral directors are placing mini flags on top of each car. They guard the vehicles. I put my faith in them. Besides, who would want to steal a beat-up, twelve-year-old Buick Skyhawk?

Mom stands on the church's wide sandstone steps. She gabs with two mourners. One mourner is tall, lanky Rick Jankowski, RJ, my best friend since grade school. I expected to see him. His younger sister, Erika, stands next to him. Her presence surprises me. She's one of my students. Logan Tuttle, a capable graduate assistant, will run my classes for the week. Erika should be there today.

Mom makes no effort to filter her observation as

I approach. "You look awful, but not as bad as your father."

"Thanks, Mom." I shuffle to her. She lets me hug her slight, wiry frame.

RJ smirks. "He's looked worse. Suffering the wrath of grapes?"

I jab an elbow into his ribs. "Barley, hops, and malt. Not that bad. You up for the Come On tonight? A round of darts or two?"

"You mean a hair of the kennel that mauled you yesterday?"

"Yeah, something like that."

"Sure," he says. We're set to meet at the Come On Inn, one of our favorite neighborhood taverns. The agreement draws a stony stare from Mom.

I tug one of the massive wooden doors open for Mom and shoo RJ in next. Before Erika passes me, I pull her to the side.

"Cutting class today?" I ask her a bit sharply.

She answers in a tone as comforting as the warm air in the vestibule. "Your granddad's a legend. My grades won't suffer. Sorry for your loss."

My own attitude suddenly appalls me.

"Excuse me. Thanks for being here."

She gives me a nod, and a genuine smile. "My folks send their condolences from Florida."

"Thank them for me, please."

RJ and Erika sit in the back pew. I want to sit with them. I can't of course. Instead, I lead Mom to the first pew at the front of the sanctuary. Dad and Grandma sit there. Dad and I could have been pallbearers, which would have given us duties to perform. But we granted those honors to Grandpop's shipmates. This leaves me with a disagreeable job, one all too familiar to me.

I plop down on the hard, wooden pew between my mother and my father and act as a buffer.

This has been the family dynamic for as long as I can remember. Some things never change, I guess. But I won't allow myself to think about my parents' broken relationship. Not now. Their divorce brings up a mind-boggling question, however.

How in the world did my grandparents' marriage survive for fifty years?

The obvious response is they lived long enough to do it. The answer strikes me as too quick and easy. Divorce was frowned on in their day, but not unheard of. Yet acceptance steadily grew until divorce became commonplace. Why? At least half of Mom and Dad's generation will not celebrate their fiftieth or beyond with the same mate, not unless they lived a hundred years or longer. Researchers predict even more dismal numbers for my generation. How did my grandparents know they were meant for each other? And if they weren't, how did they get through at least 18,250 days together without either moving into separate bedrooms or killing each other? Their marriage's longevity amazes me.

Are Kelly and I supposed to be together? How will we know?

"The grace of our Lord Jesus Christ and the love of God and the fellowship of the Holy Spirit be with you all."

I recoil at Father Cleary's rumbling voice. No one else in the congregation shows surprise. My full-body flinch annoys Mom. I can tell by the way she bashes my knee with her fist.

"And also, with you," I reply with the gathered while rubbing my knee.

Father Cleary sprinkles Holy Water and drones on about the waters of baptism and eternal glory. My attention wanders to the church's impressive stained-glass windows. They reach from a few feet above the floor almost to the soaring ceiling. On sunny days, the countless bits of colored glass glow like gemstones in a display case. They must have shined that way yesterday. Today, however, the gloom dulls the depiction of the first visitors to the baby Jesus's manger. The event takes on a sense of dread somehow—

"Are you okay?" Mom hisses out of the corner of her mouth.

"Did I nod off?" I whisper, afraid I might have dozed.

"No."

"Then I'm okay."

I wonder if I am, in fact, okay. The day started poorly. Kelly got up and showered. I didn't even move, unable to rouse myself after our erotic all-night wrestling match. I lay sprawled on the bed, naked and exhausted. She took her time pulling on her clothes after her shower, putting on a show, I assume, to torment me.

Once dressed, she turned to the bureau mirror to

apply some make-up. I finally managed to communicate, or, at least, to mumble. "I'll drive you to work. I've got time."

"I'll take the bus. It'll be at the corner in ten minutes."

"I can be ready in ten minutes."

She smiled at me. "No, you can't."

"You're proud of yourself, aren't you?"

"Yes, I am. Sorry I can't make it to the funeral." She sauntered to the bed and gave me a soul-ripping kiss. Then she simply turned and left. Guilt brewed up in me for not making more of an effort for her.

I am no longer sure about my guilt feelings, but something is here...

Bill Mannion, Tom Jamieson, Brochetti, Rakocszy, Schmidt, and another man, a stranger to me, haul Grandpop's coffin down the aisle. Another important moment somehow sneaked up on me. My random reflections must cause this effect, this wrinkling of linear time. These irrelevant musings about marriage and guilt and stained-glass windows take me away from great chunks of what Father Cleary says. The funeral whizzes by. And now a whisper in my head makes matters worse. The whisper urges me to turn and look behind me.

I sense someone's stare on the back of my head.

Someone is scrutinizing me, measuring me. I'm sure. St. Ignatius is packed for the event, so someone will glance toward my family at any given time. We sit at the front of the sanctuary. We would, therefore, be seen from behind.

Except, this isn't just "being seen." This is

something else. A part of me I was never aware of before knows so. A stranger within prods me, urges me.

Turn around.

I don't ignore the whisper. I can't. So, I defy it. In an attempt to not be rude to Father Cleary and disrespectful to Grandpop, I do my best to fight the distraction.

Turn around. Turn.

The whisper gets louder. I shift in the pew. Mom shoots me a sideward glance of disapproval.

Turn around! Do it now!

The whisper grows to full voice, my own voice, urgent and insistent. This crazy stuff isn't supposed to run through my head. Not at my grandfather's funeral.

TURN! LOOK BEHIND YOU!

I bow to the command if only to silence my own annoying and distressing inner voice. I crane my neck to the side, toward my oblivious Dad, away from Mom, and look behind me.

A sea of gray hair and glinting eyeglasses faces me. No surprise. Most of these elderly folks are strangers to me. I couldn't guess what any of them were thinking, even if they were staring directly at me. But none of them are.

Dense shadows cloak the back pews. I squint to see if RJ is watching me. He sits as still as a hunter's trophy next to his sister. To a stranger, he would appear to be engaged in the proceedings. I know RJ, though. He sometimes puts on a pliable mask of interest. The service might be conducted in Farsi, but RJ can still appear to follow every word. He's doing so now.

Erika leans forward, taking mental notes. She focuses with intensity. She occasionally unnerves me in class with her urgent desire to soak up information. She's not always this consumed. When she is, she aces her next exams.

It's clear to me who's paying attention and who isn't.

I still get the sense I'm being stared at. I don't understand why. RJ flies off on autopilot to some unknown destination. Erika focuses on Father Cleary, not on me. I turn to face front again. I would be happy right now to have RJ's talent to merely appear engrossed. I glance around once more. No one glares at me, the preoccupied and inattentive family member. I feel both relief and disappointment. I'm relieved nobody wants to force feed me a handful of Ritalin. But I'm disappointed I couldn't find who the voice in my head wants me to find.

I keep on looking.

We all head for our vehicles after the service. Dad helps Grandma into the front seat of his little pretend pick-up truck in front of me. Mom climbs into her own compact car behind mine. Dad opted out of the funeral home's limousine offer, partly because of the unsettled family dynamic, and partly because Grandma hates "putting on airs." My decision to drive alone had nothing to do with putting on airs and everything to do with the family situation. I try to put these concerns aside as I strap on my seat belt. A frown tightens into a grimace. I'm looking for... something.

Funny, I feel now like it's an "it" and not a "who."

The idea strikes me as funny because I neither believe nor disbelieve in legends, folklore, the supernatural. Yes, I suppose I put God in the mix. My equal opportunity agnosticism doesn't serve me well right now. I have no inkling what to look for, but I do have a growing sense of why I must find it.

Whatever it is, it doesn't belong here.

"It," huh? Yeah. Sure.

The cars behind me fill with mourners. Nothing extraordinary materializes, of course. I fidget in my seat. This procession might take time to get together. Tom Jamieson struggles, despite help, to situate himself into the passenger's seat of the car behind Mom's. He is only one missed breath short of being mourned himself. So are most of the others.

My car grinds and coughs to life. The heater drives the bleak cold out in a few minutes. The hearse pulls away from the curb, I switch on my headlights, and the funeral procession rolls toward Holy Cross Cemetery six miles away.

Those six miles pass in a blink. The funeral procession turns in to the cemetery entrance, stunning me. *How did that happen?* I remember driving down the dismal mile stretch of Bellaire Road, a poor and neglected, yet still inhabited blight. Weed-packed, vacant lots punctuated side streets with clapboard houses that should be condemned but are not. We then angled onto Puritas Avenue. I sighed with relief when we entered the modest, if not impoverished, neighborhood. But that's all I remember.

I coast up behind Dad's truck and turn off the ignition. I'm disturbed to the core. Behind the wheel of a moving car is not the place to have one's subconscious take over.

I haul myself from my car and join Dad, Mom, and Grandma. Dad's appearance suggests he's the one needing burial. His ashen pallor makes the circles under his eyes darker. His eyes are bloodshot, his features sag, and his jaw line is a bit jowly. Yet, a rare and deep concern furrows his brow as he stares at me.

How bad must I look to get such worry out of Dad?

The pallbearers wheel the casket into the mausoleum. We all gather around. Father Cleary's words soon become a deep human purr again, amounting to, "Blah, blah, blah." I take in my surroundings rather than pay attention.

Burial in a mausoleum...what does that mean?

The word "burial" bothers me. When I think of burying something, I imagine digging a hole, putting something in the hole, and tossing the dirt back on top.

If a thing, in this case, a body, is left above the ground, is it truly buried?

Grandma sniffles a few times and mashes her face into Dad's shoulder. Father Cleary puts his hand on her back. He says something in low tones, too low for me to hear. The service is over.

Grandpop is officially gone.

A substantial hand rests on my shoulder, startling me.

"I'll miss him," Bill Mannion mumbles in the same tone Father Cleary took with Grandma.

"I know, Mr. Mannion. Me too."

"If you don't mind, I'd like a copy of the picture. I'll be happy to pay you."

"I'm sorry, which one?"

"The one you took yesterday of us surviving shipmates. I'd like a copy for each of them, too, if possible." He jerks a pudgy thumb in Tom Jamieson's direction. "Don't take too long, you follow?"

"We're in lock step, Mr. Mannion."

"Good, lad," Mannion thunders. He shakes hands with a knot of departing mourners. They all shuffle toward their cars together. I detect something different about Mannion, something I can't put a name to yet. I share his concern about getting prints of the photo to the others as soon as possible. A course of action forms in my head.

Before I do anything else, I catch up to RJ and Erika at the mausoleum's entrance. "What's your schedule tomorrow night?" I ask him.

"I'm off tomorrow. Then I have emergency room shifts the next five nights."

"I thought I'd be up for the Come On tonight. That would be a mistake. Mind if we hoist a couple tomorrow night instead?"

RJ nods. "That'll work."

I turn to Erika. I want to say something, but words fail me. She rests a gentle hand on my forearm. No words are spoken. None are needed. I'm grateful for her presence, and she knows so. She and RJ cross the parking lot to their car.

Dad and Grandma join me. Dad drapes his left arm around Grandma's shoulders and throws his right arm around my neck. I can't tell if he's hugging us, or if he wants us to drag him back to his truck.

"Your grandmother has a request," he says. "Would you mind cleaning out your grandfather's darkroom tomorrow?"

My gut questions the urgency of the task. One glance at Grandma's face, and I realize this is another sooner-is-better scenario. Dad would never empty the darkroom himself. That's okay. The request helps me with my own plans.

"That'd be fine. Grandma, would you mind if I came a little early? I'd like to make some prints of..."

"Bill Mannion and the boys," she mumbles. "They were boys. They were so young. We were all so young."

Dad and I glance and nod at each other. Grandma should be monitored for a while. We'll tag-team on this duty over the next few days.

"I'll take your grandma home now," he coos more to her than to me.

"Grandma, I'll see you tomorrow."

Dad leads Grandma to his truck. Mom appears at my side, and I give her a hug. She stiffens. I get the feeling, as I always have, that Mom is too brittle for physical displays of affection. She breaks away and heads for her car.

"Sorry, Buddy. I can't stand these places," she mutters. Then she's gone.

I can understand that.

I stare at the mausoleum one last time. Then I amble through the gray landscape under the gray sky, toward my own bucket of bolts. A question comes with me, nags me, follows close on my heels like a puppy begging to be let outside.

If a thing is left above the ground, is it truly buried?

CHAPTER 4

My breakfast dishes make their voyage to the bottom of the sink, where they'll soak in soap and water for a few hours. Dish-washing lies low on my list of priorities today. I never claimed housekeeping as a talent, but I still manage to keep my apartment well-organized. After I move all of Grandpop's stuff in here, the place will be a lot less tidy. The prospect doesn't please me. I hope I can find room for everything.

Diffused sunlight filters weakly through my kitchen window. That's November in Cleveland. I don't bother looking outside.

But I wonder if the dimness might be due to my eyesight more than to cloud cover. I think I've been seeing things lately. When I got home from the funeral yesterday, a figure crossed my rear-view mirror as I backed my car into a parking space. I swiveled hard in my seat. He was gone, or, more accurately, was never there. The street was deserted. The optical illusion shook me. I almost bashed the bumper of one of my neighbors' cars in the process. Parallel parking isn't one of my talents, either. Jumping and twisting behind the wheel doesn't help.

Can I trace yesterday's edgy disposition to the damage I did to myself at the wake the day before? Can unbridled debauchery mess with someone's eyesight? RJ exaggerated on the church steps. I don't drink that much. Five or six beers spread over a week would be a lot. I drank as many in one afternoon at the wake and added a few shots of

Bushmills. Yesterday's hangover packed an unprecedented wallop. I was paranoid the next day. I even believed some otherworldly being had come to pay last respects to Grandpop. The non-pedestrian was as much a ghost as the phantom mourner was.

Alcohol induced paranoia? Impressive. Playing with my eyes, too? Why not?

I still felt so thoroughly poisoned after the funeral that I found myself tempted to pull over about halfway home from the cemetery. I didn't even recognize the neighborhood I was in. I just wanted to sleep the damage off in my car. Luckily, I got home and dragged myself up the apartment staircase, which seemed much taller and steeper than usual. I collapsed on my sofa. An antique wood frame with ornately carved legs, arms, and back, and stuffed seat cushions, my sofa is more decorative than comfortable. But my bedroom seemed so very far away.

I felt much better when I woke up this morning. After shedding the clothes I slept in, I shaved and showered. That was an hour ago. Now I pull my leather jacket on and head out of my apartment.

The door behind me creaks opens. I wheel around. A man about my age exits my neighbor's apartment. His face registers as much surprise as mine, I imagine. I smile. He tucks his chin down into his ski jacket's upturned collar as he mutters a muted, "Morning." The guy hustles down the stairs but misjudges a step, nearly falling. He recovers and scurries outside.

The encounter makes me uncomfortable. I lock my door, wrap the Medalist 620's strap around my fist, and start down the stairs. The chance meeting replays in my head as I walk to my car. The guy's mortification affects me the most. I have an idea where his embarrassment comes from.

The apartment he exited isn't his.

A fiftyish woman named Tania lives in the unit across the hall. Tania covers her petite frame with bright, garish pantsuits. They conjure girlishness, but in a bad way. Her wardrobe can't cover her haggard face, or her brunette bob with the graying roots. The corners of her eyes crinkle deeply. Her perpetual tan points up her age, when I'd bet the effect she hopes for is the opposite. Has she accepted the obvious? Or does she now think she can erase age by coupling with youth?

But how can I judge a March-November romance? What if the tables had been turned? If her boyfriend and I passed each other the morning of Grandpop's funeral, the guy might wonder about my girlfriend and me. He could make a good guess. Kelly gets especially vocal, leaving little doubt about what goes on in my bedroom.

Then again, neither of us ever has much shame when we're together.

No matter. I leave my neighbor's business to my neighbor, where it belongs.

My car eases away from the curb. I head south on Warren Road, smoking my last cigarette. A left turn on Madison Avenue leads to a dingy little beverage store a few blocks away. I pass several more practical opportunities to stop. Both the drug store and the gas station at the intersection I just drove through sell smokes. Habit leads me to Greg's Convenience.

My car nearly bottoms out in the driveway, as always. The old bucket's shocks need replacing. The driveway's sharp angle serves as a reminder. I park and lock my door. I don't want to take chances with Grandpop's camera on the front seat, even in a neighborhood I consider safe.

A cowbell at the end of a tattered leather strap clatters against the glass door as I enter. No one stands behind the counter. I call out, in case the metallic *"CLANK"* wasn't enough warning. "Hey, Gregor!"

My feet stick to the crud-muted, gray-and-white tile floor. Grimy, wooden shelf units frame the main aisle. Boxes and cans, foodstuffs that might be as old as I am, cram the shelves. The aisle leads toward the restrooms and the beer and wine refrigerator. I ignore the aisle. The cigarettes are at the counter.

Someone moves at the back of the store. I twist around and squint. Spotting no one, I assume Greg slipped into the bathroom. He takes me off guard when he hustles out from the storeroom next to the counter.

"Hey, Buddy. Pack of Camel Lights?"

"Two packs, Greg. Thanks. You know you've got a customer in the john?"

Greg peers toward the back of the store. "I would've heard them come in."

"You sure?"

"Yeah. You hallucinating or something?"

Curiosity tempts me to look over my shoulder. I shrug the urge off and hand Greg a ten-dollar bill. "Maybe."

Greg pulls four singles and change from his till. "Sorry about your grandfather. So, they finally killed him, huh?"

"What?"

"The Indians. They finally got to Irish Jimmy."

I grunt at the insensitive joke. "Yeah."

Greg's attention snaps past me. I spin around. A chunky young man, about sixteen or seventeen-years-old, mills around the beer case.

That's no illusion.

"You need a hearing aid, Greg?"

Greg answers with a scowl.

The teen wears a threadbare sweatshirt and tattered jeans. I don't like his demeanor. He shuffles around the beer cooler at the end of the aisle. Fists shoved into his pockets, the kid's eyes flit from the foodstuffs on the shelf to the beer, and finally to Greg. He repeats his reconnoitering cycle, but hovers near the cooler.

An odor wafts through the store from the bathroom. My nose wrinkles. Did the kid eat something that disagreed with him, something that needed emergency expulsion? I almost gag.

"Help you?" Greg seems unfazed by the stench. Once he has the kid's attention, Greg reaches under the counter. He sends a clear message. He keeps something under there, an alarm button, or a lead pipe, or a gun—something no shoplifter wants any part of.

The teen exercises wisdom rare in his age group. He shakes his head and stalks out of the store.

I pocket the change and one of the packs of cigarettes and tap the other pack against my palm. "You should be more careful."

"Guess so. See you in a couple of days."

"Yeah."

"Why don't you just buy a carton instead of coming here every other day?"

"Trying to quit. A whole carton encourages bad behavior."

Greg snorts. "Right. Catch you later."

A trace of the kid's vile odor follows me outside, then dissipates. The lingering stink urges me to check in all directions before I climb back into my vehicle. Was the kid alone? The advice to Greg to be more careful comes back to me. My battered old car, if stolen, might be written off by an insurance claim. The theft would definitely be a low police priority. The possibilities might tempt a youngster looking for an illegal thrill, or a temporary ride. Carjackings are rare in Lakewood. However, bad things happen just about anywhere nowadays.

Not here, and not today. I climb, unmolested, back into my Buick.

In a few moments, I cruise down the ramp to I-90 eastbound, slowing for the split to I-71 south. The ramp banks sharply, and I prefer to remain intact. I check my mirror. The driver behind me rides my rear bumper. He must think tail-gating will get me to drive faster. I continue driving the speed limit because I believe they are posted for some reason other than to tick everyone off. Besides, I won't let his behavior dictate mine.

Am I doing the smart thing? My eyes shift from the road ahead back to my mirror. The car behind me stays glued to my bumper. My stress level rises. The driver remains a dark, faceless shape at the wheel of a thousand-pound, guided weapon. The image disturbs me.

I exit on Fulton Rd. My unwelcome shadow veers into the left lane. I suck in a relieved breath.

The Metroparks Zoo entrance lies ahead. Fulton Road becomes West 47th Street a few hundred yards past the zoo. The scenery changes abruptly there. The Cleveland Metroparks System maintains their public lands to wow tourists and other visitors. The blue collar, residential area beyond the zoo has no Wow Factor. The neighborhood began its decline in the 1960s and never stopped.

I weave my way over narrow, pockmarked streets and brick-paved alleys. This neighborhood saddens me. Residents here are losing the fight against falling property values. Most still have jobs, yet earn little money, and so have little to work with. They continue to fight just the same.

Grandpop lived and died here. If ghosts really did exist, they would live here, too.

I squeeze on to Gifford Avenue. Someone parked their truck too close to the corner. My old

Buick is no prize, but even I might abandon a wreck like that truck. I take care not to brush against it. The truck already defies all known laws of gravity and physics.

A parking space waits in front of Grandma's house. I lock the car door with my right hand while juggling Grandpop's Medalist with my left. I'd kick myself forever for dropping this irreplaceable camera. A deep breath of chilly, damp air settles me, but only for a moment. A sheen of cold sweat still coats my palms. Phantom cotton balls dry my mouth.

Relax, will you?

Another car engine rumbles to life near the decrepit pick-up truck. I can't help hearing the sound. These colonial-style homes, ungainly two-story boxes with windows and peaked roofs, are wedged so close together they almost touch. I feel like a claustrophobic voyeur.

I trudge up the humpbacked driveway, bobbling and almost fumbling the Medalist again. The distinctive rumbling purr of a Jaguar hums closer as I regain control.

Old Chevys and Fords park along these streets, and in the driveways. The sleek, spotless Jaguar doesn't fit here. The Jag's driver shifts his focus from the road to me. A smirk creases his pudgy, middle-aged kisser. He spies the camera. The smirk disappears. Much of his face disappears, too. He brings a beefy hand up to hide his face, and stomps on the gas pedal. Tires squeal. Man and machine dart for escape on Pearl Road.

Residents often complain about the house Mr. Pudgy Face drove away from. Prostitutes live there. I have no intention of snapping pictures of the hookers' clients. Mr. Pudgy Face's business is none of mine.

The stranger's attempt to hide his face—to become anonymous, faceless—makes me shiver. A snippet of the Grandpop nightmare echoes in my head.

"Caught you again, didn't I?"

"Caught who?"

I press the doorbell button at the side door of Grandma's house rather than just walking in. She doesn't need a heart attack today.

Her face brightens as she opens the door. "You look much better, Buddy."

"You look good too, Grandma."

And so she does. Her coal-black blouse and slacks make her skin seem to glow an unnatural white. I try to ignore the pallor. She'll wear black for at least a year, possibly longer. Sadness still hovers around the edges, but she greets me in a lucid, warm tone. Her eyes shine with life. She looks a lot more like my grandma again.

She leads me to the kitchen. "Breakfast?"

"Had some, thanks, Gram."

"Cigarettes and coffee are not a breakfast."

"I made fried eggs, toast, and orange juice an hour ago," I say, risking that heart attack after all. I lay the camera on the kitchen table and take a seat. "I'll take coffee if you have some brewed."

"I have coffee. Black?"

"Thanks."

The coffee's rich aroma dominates the cozy, cheerful kitchen. She sits opposite me and sips her brew. Her eyebrows knit. Something weighs on her mind.

It's the dream.

I reject the foolish delusion. My nightmare about Grandpop's death was just that, a nightmare, a dream. His death the same night was a macabre coincidence. Nothing more. Besides, I had the dream, not Grandma. I told no one, not even Kelly. How could Grandma want to discuss something she knows nothing about? I haven't thought much about the nightmare myself since yesterday. I would bet, if asked, I could scientifically rationalize the dream today.

What if there was more to this? Should a freshly widowed old woman be able to explain something so strange to me?

I decide to steer the conversation in a safe, less hare-brained direction. "What brand is this coffee? This is good—"

"Are you and Kelly going to marry soon?"

Steaming coffee shoots up my nose. I choke, my throat and sinuses cauterized. Grandma thrusts a paper napkin at me. Her mouth opens, her eyes widen. She fusses over me, both appalled and amused. I cough into the napkin, then grab another fistful from a holder in the middle of the table. The burn of hot java overcomes my shock and surprise. I enjoyed my coffee until then, savoring both the flavor and the aroma. My senses of taste and smell are now compromised. I almost wish she had asked me about the dream instead.

"I don't know, Gram," I croak. "We haven't discussed marriage lately."

"Lately?"

"Okay, we've never discussed marriage."

Grandma nods. She leans forward, pursing her lips.

I wait, but not for long. "What?"

"She won't stand with you."

I squint at her like a third-grader walking into a lecture on quantum physics.

Grandma's head tilts, her jaw juts forward. She stares beyond me. "You're a young man, Buddy," she finally says. "Even so, you've already seen a lot. You'll see more."

Well, that sure clears things up!

Grandma rises from the table and heads toward the basement stairs. I follow.

Despite bursting with stuff, the basement is well organized. Grandma navigates a maze of gray, metal shelf units in the murk. The shelves line the walls. Two units stick out toward the center of the room. Cardboard boxes fill all the shelves. The cartons at the top of the unit at the back, nearest Grandpop's darkroom, interest me most. Those boxes hold fifty-years' worth of his professional shots.

Grandma stops at the darkroom's open door. She holds her hand out toward the workbench.

"That's where I found him..." The memory smothers her voice. Her mouth clamps shut, jaws clench. I doubt she will ever go into that room again.

"I'll handle it, Grandma."

She rests her hand on my shoulder, her gaze boring into my eyes. Her words carry a surprising force. "You'll need someone to stand with you." She turns and leaves.

The steps to the kitchen creak, then the steps to the second floor groan. I lived this moment once before. I reach into the darkroom and flick the light switch. The light is wrong.

One of the bulbs is burned out.

The footsteps above me echo louder in my ears. The rhythmic creaks join in a chilling duet with another sound. Leaves. Wind scrapes dead leaves against the sides of the house. They scratch in sync with the movement of demented shadows dancing in the corners. I blink. Grandpop slumps on his workbench. His eyes, half open, fix on a dark shape approaching from the maze of shelves beyond the doorway....

My stomach flops. I brace myself against the door to keep from toppling over.

Light. Need more.

I scrounge around the shelf units until I find a stash of new bulbs. I reach the burned-out bulb without a ladder, which is a relief—no time wasted. The fresh bulb drives the imaginary, demon shadows away.

Shadows again. I should get my eyes checked. Or my head examined. Or both.

Hanging around the darkroom are several

personal photos Grandpop blew up to poster size. Grandma's face graces the wall to my left on one poster. She holds Dad there, as a baby. She's young in the picture, of course, Grandma without the wear of fifty years. This must be a candid shot. She weeps, the wide smile and a single tear on her cheek a marvelous paradox.

I turn. A print of me hangs near the utility sink. I'm a child. Dad and I hug, yelling our heads off amongst a bunch of cheering fans in the bleachers of Municipal Stadium. I almost hear the sounds, and smell the aromas, of mid-summer baseball games.

Grandpop stands just a few feet down the bleachers' concrete steps, snapping away with his Medalist 620, doesn't he?

I carry the Medalist to the sink. My first close examination of the camera makes me wonder how careful Grandpop was with it. This thing stayed around his neck like an extra shirt collar. He never sat down at the dinner table or slept with the Medalist, true. But he snapped pictures of intense conflict with this camera. He took it with him almost everywhere he went for fifty years afterward, including to Cleveland Municipal Stadium. Some might say the camera was safer in the war.

The camera shows no scratches, nicks, or dents.

I close the door, turn the red darkroom safe-light on and switch the overhead lights off. The safe-light paints everything around me burgundy. The room resembles an ante chamber of hell now, an otherworldly cell where my fingers somehow do unfamiliar work with surprising skill, yet without mental direction. I haven't done any darkroom work in several years. My hands seem almost to channel Grandpop, spooling the film from the camera to his film developing canister, a vessel shaped like a cocktail shaker.

My idle mind wanders to the poster of Dad and me. I remember when the shot was taken. A standing-room crowd packed the sun-drenched bleachers for an Old Timers' Game that July afternoon in 1974. The 1954 Indians played the 1954 Giants in a rematch of the World Series the Indians lost in four straight. Fans made a pilgrimage from all over Cleveland. Sure, the regular team had a game afterward, and the surprising Tribe was in contention. But we all knew the Indians of '74 were not a championship team.

We came that day to bask in the Old Timers' revenge. The crowd swelled hoping for payback. No other reason made sense.

Grandpop snapped the picture when the old Clevelanders grabbed an early lead. Dave Pope, overshadowed in his day by a host of Hall of Fame teammates, cracked a home run into the right field grandstands. Dad and I celebrated with the others jammed into the bleachers. Grandpop wasn't working, but the ushers allowed him to bring the camera in with him anyway. He hopped off the rough wooden bench and took the shot.

The lead lasted two innings. The Old Timers lost their fifth straight to those Giants, dating back to the '54 Series.

I hang my dripping negative on the wire to dry. Somehow, an hour and a half passed. Time apparently gets warped down here. I did the work unconsciously, which disturbs me as much as the loss of time. Grandpop sharpened his darkroom technique over years. The process became second nature to him. Not me. Hopefully, I didn't ruin the negative with the one-of-a-kind photo of Grandpop's surviving buddies.

Photo.

The closet door at the far end of the darkroom beckons silently to me. An envelope with a secret lies in the closet. I feel it. The secret sucks in all the surrounding light, feeds on it, grows stronger. The closet's blackness deepens, mesmerizing me, drawing me in...

A grunt escapes my sudden scowl.

Oh, come on!

No skeletons, real or imagined, exist in Grandpop's closet. The fantasy makes me feel like an idiot.

I switch the ceiling lights back on, preparing to print the group photo. Anything else on the negative can wait. I want to empty the closet and the rest of the darkroom afterwards. Carting all the stuff home shouldn't take more than three or four trips. Maybe I'll stop at Pat Catan's, Cleveland's arts and crafts superstore, on one of those trips. Catan's is a little out of my way. Still, they do good frame work. I may as well do this picture thing right, if at all. Then I'll shower and meet RJ at the Come On Inn. We'll down a couple of beers. I won't have trouble limiting myself after the binge at the wake. I can tell RJ about this whole process, and he can laugh at my feeble-mindedness.

I turn the overhead lights off again. The closet doorway blends in with the other black shapes in the murk beyond the safe-light's red glow. The closet holds no power now. I pull a box of photo paper from a cabinet, stifling a laugh at my suddenly overactive imagination. I look forward to finishing this task, and tossing down a few beers afterwards with my oldest, closest friend.

CHAPTER 5

RJ stands in a haze of cigarette smoke, his hand raised, like a mannequin posed by some practical joker. Nestled between his fingertips and thumb lies a dart. He gazes through the cloud at our dartboard and speaks without breaking his pose. "Good thing you know your way around a darkroom. The group prints turned out all right?"

"Yeah. I even had time to drop them off at Pat Catan's to get framed. Nothing to it."

"Digital is the wave of the future. Even less than 'nothing to it' for photographers. That's the word, anyway." RJ's arm jerks forward. His wrist flicks like a striking viper. The compactness, the economy of movement, never ceases to amaze me. The result is numbingly familiar. "Triple twenty. Better close 'em out soon."

I do the math in my head. The results aren't pretty. "Even if I close the twenties, I need three bulls-eyes just to catch you."

"You givin' up?"

"You kidding?"

A grin spreads across RJ's face. He takes a swig of beer and ambles to the dartboard. I take a pull from my own bottle.

RJ and I meet a couple of nights a month here at the Come On Inn, a popular local pub. Crowds pack the patio bar behind the building in the summer. Baseball games on a bed-sheet-sized video screen, and live bands, draw folks to the patio from all over the West Side. From early October on, however, the unpredictable weather shuts the patio down. RJ and I both enjoy the bar room as well, any time of year. This dark, oak-paneled pub feels so much warmer and more inviting than O'Leary's. The Come On's window takes nearly the whole storefront and allows a view of Detroit Avenue traffic—the passers-by as well as the friends about to enter.

O'Leary's feels more like a bunker than a bar.

RJ collects his darts, and steps back behind me. "Your grandma's doing better?"

"Yeah, I think she'll be okay. I'm glad she had me empty Grandpop's darkroom so soon. Not that I want to hurry up and move on..." I shake my head. "It's hard to explain."

"Would be, sure."

"I've got a bunch of boxes and equipment in my apartment now, a lot of stuff to decide what to do with. I'll probably put the equipment up for sale. But what will I get done with the Holidays almost here?"

"You'll get done what you can." RJ narrows his eyes, scratches his head, and changes the subject. "So, what's the story on last Friday? Who would've called Erika at that time of day, and for what?"

"How should I know?"

Before we touched on my visit with Grandma, I was telling RJ about the sound that brought my class to a halt the Friday before Grandpop died. A sudden, weird chirp made me stop mid-lecture. Erika picked her backpack up from the floor, thrashed around inside, and pulled out a tweeting cellular phone. She blushed like a church usher caught with his hand in the collection plate. Then she wilted under the collective stare of the rest of the class. I'll bet if she could have crawled into her own backpack, she would have.

"Didn't she apologize?" RJ asked.

"Yeah, of course. She didn't go into details. I didn't ask. She just told me the call wasn't anything important. Aren't cellular phones kind of expensive?"

"Yeah," he says, "they won't be for long. They'll get cheaper the longer they're on the market, like any other technology."

"Explains why I hear them more often. I mean, they're not totally alien to me. I just never expected to hear one go off in my classroom."

RJ grumbles. "Her cellular is for emergency use. Otherwise, it's just rude and disruptive."

"Okay, what if the call had been an actual emergency? What if, say, your mom was in an accident and Erika's cellular had been turned off? What's the use carrying the phone at all, then?"

My tone, my defensiveness, surprises me. I toss my next two darts, scoring no points, and pull them from the board.

RJ assumes his silly, deadly mannequin pose. His eyebrows scrunch down. "She's a good kid, but I can understand if the other students got pissed. They paid as much for the class as she did. Her time isn't more important than theirs."

"True. But she didn't make her own phone ring." I swallow the last of my beer and collect RJ's empty bottle. "Round two?"

"Yeah, thanks. 'All things in moderation.'"

"That's not the quote. 'In all things, moderation.' Aristotle."

"Yeah? What did I say?"

"Something very different."

He lands a bulls-eye dead center of the board. "Devil's in the details, I guess."

I sigh and head for the bar.

A typical early-November, Friday-night crowd mills around the Come On Inn tonight. A half dozen men and a few women hold an impromptu tournament at the other two dartboards. Couples occupy both booths and three of five tables. A boisterous party crams around the last two tables, which are far too small to accommodate all the revelers.

A wave of chilly air invades the room for a moment. I have no clear view of who walked in ahead of the cold blast. The newcomer's identity somehow matters, though I don't know why.

I plunk our two empties down on the bar. "George, another round when you can, please."

The bartender grins and nods. In one slick, sweeping motion he places a mug of beer and a pinkish concoction, a Cosmopolitan martini, in front of a middle-aged couple. He then glides to the far end of the bar to pour a pitcher of draft for someone else. "Be right with you, Buddy."

All pubs and restaurants share a common ambiance standard, almost a law, using just enough light for guests to see each other, yet not enough to illuminate details. The Come On Inn is no exception. I wonder about the unwritten code. Do pubs keep their lights low because dimness is more pleasing to the eye, more relaxing? Or, do they want to keep things less apparent, better hidden?

I squint at the darkened shapes around me in the smoky murk, trying to "people watch" while I wait. A man settles on a bar stool. He wears a faded navy peacoat and a gray knit cap. George puts a mug of beer in front of him. This could be the newcomer, I suppose. I can only guess at the man's age, maybe seventy-years-old. His stoop-shouldered, wiry frame could be older or younger. The dimness makes it hard to determine his mood, too. I can't gauge his facial expression.

Some things can't be hidden, no matter how low the light. The two middle-aged drinkers slouch over the bar. They focus on their drinks, talking at each other through the sides of their mouths. Their conversation suffers two major flaws. The first problem is volume. Their private chat is not terribly private. They compete with eighty other voices engaged in thirty different discussions, all taking place in the same vicinity. Alcohol makes most folks think they need to be louder than the drunk next to them. Booze intensifies vocal contests.

The conversation's second problem is its content.

The man toys with his beer mug. He pays more attention to what he puts into his mouth than to what comes out. "I'm not giving you a thousand bucks. You'll just give the cash to that loser drug addict son of yours, and he'll just snort it."

The woman retorts with equally heedless brutality. "It's for me, and I deserve it. I'm the one who has to sleep with your worthless ass."

Laundry this dirty, hung in public, astounds me. The other people nearby must hear these folks, too. Sure, life gets messy and couples sometimes lock themselves into horrible situations. The downside makes itself obvious. What's the benefit? Why don't these two seem interested in fixing their dilemma? My stomach turns at these questions.

Seven guys crowd around the other end of the bar, near a wall-mounted TV. They hang on every word as a sports Talking Head barks the truly vital issues of the day. The group stares at the screen in a somber trance. One can always find long faces in Greater Cleveland, but these are beyond grim. I wonder who died.

"I can't believe those kids threw eggs at Belle's house," a man with a thick neck, broad shoulders, and, apparently, a gym membership, groans. "I mean, he's Albert Belle! I just hope they don't dump him for chasing the little punks. He did his part in the Series."

The recent World Series failure explains the glum air. Cleveland's franchise added to its decades-long baseball championship drought last week. These men reflect the sullen mood of an entire city starving for the right to puff its chest.

An older man, his business suit stretched over a flabby middle, glues wary eyes to the TV screen. He takes a conciliatory tone. "Belle should've won Most Valuable Player, and he already got his slap on the wrist for this. Who cares how crazy he is? We'll keep him. We need his lumber in the line-up. Now, if we end up losing Eddie Murray..."

"Yeah! Hitting! Eddie Murray is the man!" The gym rat's response seems over-reactive.

The name of the Indians pitcher who gave up the Series-ending home run pops into my head. My unsolicited opinion pops out of my mouth. "Pitching's how you win or lose the Series. Ask Jim Poole."

Unfriendly faces—at least seven I'm aware of— snap in my direction. Muscle Man's face turns crimson. The veins in his neck threaten to burst through the skin. "The Indians need more production. They only hit .179 for the Series."

"That's what I'm saying. The Braves' pitching proves my point."

The agitated man stiffens. His entire body flexes at once. He edges to within inches of me. "Maybe somebody should break your 'point' off and cram it down your throat."

I take Mr. Muscle's threat seriously and step back. I don't need to get into a fist fight with a beast like him tonight.

George intervenes quickly from behind the bar. "Cliff, cool out or leave. Choose now."

Cliff opts not to apologize, sneering at me instead. He rejoins his friends in their discussion of off-season roster moves that will either take the Tribe to the World Series next year, or sink them to the bottom of the division, depending on who's talking. I should turn this moment into a class assignment. My students would report on the city's connection to its baseball franchise, the lost Series' emotional impact on the long-suffering fan base, the damage done to the civic psyche by decades of futility. If only I could guarantee the assignment would not end in my class's mass suicide.

The solitary old man intrigues me. He sits quietly with his untouched beer, connecting with no one. He seems to prefer anonymity while studying the others, the debating baseball experts and the bickering couple. Have I seen this man before? His unremarkable, partially obscured features make me wonder. In here he looks like anyone, like everyone.

No, I'm sure I never met this guy.

The man suddenly twists and glances over his shoulder at me. He appears older than seventy from this angle. A trick of the lighting, the lack of it, makes me imagine a hint of a smile, as if he recognizes me. That's my imagination. I doubt his eyes work well enough at his age to recognize anyone through the dimness. I only hope he didn't drive himself here.

"Put these on your tab, Bud?"

"Yeah, George, thanks."

"Hey, Billy!" George calls out to the baseball group. "Your beer ain't gettin' any colder!"

"Got it." The flabby businessman detaches himself from the sportscast and takes the mug of beer from the old fellow. The quiet man makes no move to stop him. He merely sits and waits and keeps his cryptic vigil. The moment surprises and confuses me.

I bring our fresh bottles of beer to the dartboards. RJ prepares to throw. The time I spent at the bar troubled me. I'm glad to get back to getting thrashed at darts again. A psychologist might make a study of this. An oft quoted definition of insanity is to repeat an action but suddenly expect a different result. I suppose my repeated attempts to beat RJ at darts defines me as insane.

It's a good thing I come here for him, for us, not for a dart game.

"The Jankowski clan all geared up for Thanksgiving?"

RJ casually flicks his wrist, piling on more points. "Sorta. Erika volunteered to do the cooking. Then my mom and dad decided to stay in West Palm Beach this year. We've got friends coming over. Stop bye if you like."

"Cool."

"She's a good kid."

"Heard you the first time. Twice sounds like a sales pitch."

"C'mon, dude." He collects his darts and tallies his points on the slate scoreboard.

Our conversations wander from the mundane to the momentous, from the personal to the international. Maybe that's why I simply blurt out a question lurking in the depths of my mind. "You don't like Kelly, do you?"

"I'm no one's judge."

"So, you don't like her."

"I'm not the one who has to like her."

"She's gorgeous."

"Yeah, she is. She's intelligent too, and funny, and a whole bunch of other good things. I don't know why I don't connect with her. I just don't."

I chew on this for a moment. Kelly makes people uncomfortable, sharp people who can't pinpoint or describe the reason for their discomfort. This worries me. I find myself defending her to everyone, telling them their discomfort is silly. Tonight, it's my turn with RJ. Despite not understanding his issue with Kelly, I have to allow him his response. Just as I have to accept my mom's dislike of her, I suppose.

Another glance at the scary couple chills me. They still hunch next to each other, as disconnected as if they were a thousand miles apart. Actually, a thousand miles of distance between them might be better. Their relationship is a train wreck limping down the track to divorce.

Does the eccentric old man's solitude stem from his own divorce, his own personal train wreck?

Is this what I want for Kelly and myself? Is this our destiny if we marry? Those around me seem to believe so.

Interesting.... I'm thinking about marriage again, as I did at Grandpop's funeral service. I don't turn thirty-years-old for a few years. The sense that marriage is vitally important in my future overwhelms me. I have no clue where this comes from. But I'm hit hard.

"Bulls-eye!" RJ announces. My last opportunity to score disappears. He collects his darts. The old man at the bar steals my attention, however. He scoots his barstool back and buttons his peacoat.

I stare at the stranger. My frustration mounts. I still believe I should recognize him. He might be one of Grandpop's friends, but I doubt it.

The man turns on his barstool and faces me directly. He smiles. A few seconds ago, I convinced myself his flash of recognition was a mistake, or a trick of the dim barroom light. I don't talk myself into that explanation this time. He obviously sees me well enough. He knows me somehow.

"We gonna do another game?" RJ throws a couple of darts for unneeded practice.

"Yeah. I'll be right back."

I head for the bar. The man rises as I approach. The quick, spry movements from someone his age surprise me. With a wink, he gives me a slight "follow me" jerk of his head and makes his way toward the door. I put RJ and our dart game aside for the moment and follow.

A misty rain falls. The sidewalk, the street, every outdoor surface shimmers. The old man is incredibly nimble; he's already crossed Detroit Avenue despite the slick pavement. He steps onto the curb on the other side of the street. The man faces me in the dimness at the edge of a streetlight. He waits. Traffic weaves between us, keeping me from joining him.

I light a cigarette with stiffening fingers. My curiosity turned to myopic urgency—I trail the stranger before putting on my jacket. I need to pull the guy aside, get a good look at his face, find out where and when we met. Can I do this before hypothermia sets in? I take a long drag on my cigarette and try to settle down.

Why is this guy so familiar to me? Why is he so...different?

The last question heightens my curiosity. The traffic light changes. I step into the street and stride toward the waiting, familiar stranger.

Sounds from my right, splashes, and skidding rubber, grow closer in a hurry. I freeze in the crosswalk. Headlights approach me. They take an erratic path, crossing the double yellow lines. The oncoming car won't stop in time. It can't. I'll be run down in the middle of Detroit Avenue. I can't seem to move...

The runaway car's horn blares. The blast wakes me from my death trance. I scramble, slip to my knees, and scramble again. I stumble and slide my way back to the curb in front of the Come On. The car skates to a stop halfway into the intersection. I mentally measure how close I came to becoming a speed bump. The driver gives me a sheepish shrug.

The stranger hustles around the corner to Warren Road and is gone.

George raises an eyebrow when I re-enter the Come On Inn and limp past the bar. He needs no blast of cold air to alert him. No matter how boisterous the crowd around him, no customer's entrance or exit goes unnoticed. He evaluates my dishevelment, and points at my torn jeans.

"You need me to call the cops?"

"Nah. No point trying to catch the guy now. He didn't do anything anyway, I don't think."

"What guy?"

I point at the empty stool near the middle of the bar. "I just wanted to get the guy's name, find out if we'd met once somewhere. The guy who was sitting there."

George's expression goes blank. "Huh. I don't remember who sat there."

The door opens again. I crane my neck to look over George's shoulder, hoping the newcomer might be the old man. Of course, it's not. Why did I think it might be? George shrugs apologetically and turns to meet his new guest.

I return to the dartboard. My body shakes, but not because of the cold.

RJ frowns at my tousled hair, dampened sweater, and torn jeans. "Somebody take you outside and beat your ass?"

"Something like that. I tried to catch up with a guy I thought I knew."

"Somebody you knew beat your ass? Wonder why."

I pick up my darts and take my place opposite the board. I squint at the target.

RJ wags an admonishing finger. "You've been straining to see the dartboard all night, like that's gonna help you actually score once or twice. Having trouble with your eyes?"

"Yeah. For a couple of days now. No big deal."

"You should get 'em checked. You're sure about the guy? I mean, you're telling me your eyesight is not—"

"I'm talking about a man, not something the size

of a half dollar on something the size of a hubcap ten feet away in a cloud of smoke in a dark bar." I feel instant remorse over my testy retort. Still, RJ's bafflement stokes my frustration. "The old guy! The one who sat right there!" I jab a dart in the direction of the table where the man sat.

RJ holds his hands up in surrender. "Sorry, Buddy. I wasn't paying attention."

I draw a deep breath, drain half my bottle of beer, and let the tension evaporate. "Yeah, sorry. Forget the whole thing, will you?"

"No worries. I just want to ask if"—He shakes his head—"No, I really shouldn't abuse a blind man at the dartboard. By the way, it's seven feet, nine and three quarters inches away. Or should be."

I rise to the challenge, as RJ probably guessed I would. My struggles at the dartboard don't come from my new vision issues. I never beat RJ, good sight or bad. Tonight's incidents stick in my mind, however. Have my eyes been damaged somehow? I didn't get a good look at the guy, but was that due to poor eyesight, or poor lighting? I also never noticed the car that almost ran me down, not until the last moment. The headlights seemed to come from nowhere…

I wipe the scoreboard clean with a bar napkin, breathe in a lungful of heavy pub air, and force my hands to stop shaking. RJ's concern convinces me to bury these qualms for the rest of the evening. That won't be easy. I do my best to shake my head clear.

"Almost doesn't count," I say.

"What?"

"New game."

CHAPTER 6

I celebrate last night's life-sparing luck this morning by returning to my traditional breakfast, a half pot of coffee and three cigarettes. My right knee swelled as I slept. My newest pair of jeans is ruined. But I woke up on the green side of the dirt. Life went on overnight as always, and returning to the familiarity of my routine comforts me.

That's the positive, if inaccurate, light I shine on last night's aftermath.

Unfamiliar issues nagged me all night. My knee injury required a couple of aspirin. A bag of frozen vegetables stood in for the ice pack I don't keep in my freezer. By the time I finish smoking and drinking this morning's breakfast, I'll have shoved the weirdness of last night to the back of my mind. But shredded denim and year-old succotash dampen the comfort of the familiar.

My caffeine-and-nicotine breakfast turns out to be today's only routine activity. Morning stretches into midday. I soon grow uncomfortable not teaching my classes. I forgot, however, what day of the week today is. I teach no classes on Saturdays. I would not be on campus anyway.

Bereavement leave disrupts my routine, and apparently distorts my internal calendar. My excused absence lasts nine more days, including today. The thought alone makes me antsy.

Have I taken too many days off? More time away from the classroom means more time to think. My mind wanders further and wider than usual, into strange places. Questions I can't answer dog me. Am I guilty of some kind of emotional avoidance? What about Grandpop? Will I ever properly mourn him?

Whether I grieve or not, I must finish my project, the survivors' picture. Could the project be part of the mourning process? I hope so. I hope for a cathartic experience. Frankly, I'm not certain if this activity constitutes "mourning a loss" or not. I decide to keep going forward until my course proves itself either right or wrong.

I enter Pat Catan's wishing I had taken a few more aspirin, but for my head, not for my knee. The store swarms with shoppers. The majority are women searching for specific items. A few men accompany them. The men show far less intent. My own disinterest in most of what's here betrays my lack of art education. I'll correct my woeful state of the arts, but not today.

The walk to the framing department at the far end of the store takes me through a dizzying diversity of craft items. Six aisles brim with plastic and silk flowers for budding amateur florists. Knick-knacks, mirrors, and decorative signs from the elegant to the kitsch clutter the aisles to my right. Yarn of every color, shade, and thickness imaginable requires an entire section, and canvasses, brushes, paints, and pastels wait in another huge sector for today's Rembrandts.

Point a gun at my head, and I still couldn't draw a straight line. This environment doesn't help. The sheer number of tools available to those who express themselves through art intimidates this non-artist.

I simply want to pick up my photos, and get back out into the open, relatively uncluttered parking lot.

A middle-aged woman with badly dyed brown hair greets me from behind the framing counter with a toothy smile, and a handshake. "Buddy Cullen! So glad to see you!"

"Thanks, Mrs. Yankovicz—"

"Sally, please."

"Thanks, Sally, but I was here just yesterday."

"And I was glad to see you yesterday, too. I've got your treasures ready for you."

Mrs. Yankovicz's happiness is way too intense. She scrawled my order on a notepad with mechanical efficiency yesterday, until she got a good look at the pictures. She became almost schoolgirl-giddy then.

Mrs. Yankovicz bends over to reach under the counter, breaking our connection. She gives me no time to collect myself when she re-emerges with the framed photos and lays them on the counter.

My curiosity gets the better of me. I only hope I won't pay for it. "I'll bet you've framed a lot of pictures and paintings."

"Over fifteen years, yeah, quite a few."

"Just wondering. Are they all 'treasures,' like the ones I brought?"

Her eyes flash. The corners of her mouth tighten into a half-grin, half-grimace. She leans over the counter and lowers her voice. "No, not to me. I'll do my best to frame some kid's stick figure drawing for his mom if I have to. But I'd count one of these pictures as a real treasure if I had one."

"Why?"

She pokes a finger at one of the framed treasures. "I owe everything to Bill Mannion."

"How so?" My ears prick up. I expect a tale of valor, a heroic Mannion jumping into a raging river, or fending off a gang of muggers.

"He handled my divorce. And boy, did he put the screws to that lousy son of a—"

"These are beautiful frames, Mrs...uh, Sally. You wouldn't have any wrapping paper, would you?"

"Just this plain brown paper."

"I think plain brown would be even better than fancy, frou-frou paper. He'll love it, don't you think?"

Mrs. Yankovicz beams. "Well. You're right. They'll be done in just a minute. Anything for Bill Mannion!"

She mercifully says no more about her divorce proceedings, dividing her attention instead between her gift wrapping, and whatever fantasy plays out in her head. I don't even want to guess what she does to Mannion up there.

I slip her a twenty-dollar tip. Then I make a beeline for the check-out, and dash to the safety of my car. I strap myself in, both relieved and sad.

Dark clouds gathered over the western edge of the city in the short time I spent in the store. I once believed weather forecasters enjoyed an unbeatable gig. Meteorology seemed, to me, the only profession in the world where the best forecasters could be wrong half the time and still be considered the best. I believed so again this morning. Sunlight streamed into my kitchen, defying this morning's forecast.

Defiance clouded over by noon. The skies threaten even more now.

I throw out my plan of visiting the rest of Grandpop's navy buddies after seeing Mannion. I'll have plenty of time over the next week to finish the Hand Out the Group Photo Tour. But I still want to call on Mannion today.

A car pulls away from the curb on St. Clair Avenue, right next to 127 Public Square, my destination. This may be a good omen. Or, is it? The Old Stone Church, the little black house of worship, looms on the corner across the street. I climb out of my car and shudder. But I keep my back turned toward the church as I jog through the crosswalk. Seconds later, I enter the poorly lit lobby of the boxy old Society National Bank Building.

A barely audible rasp comes from the direction of the street. I turn. A steady drizzle, the precursor to sleet, splatters against the glass door. Public Square stretches out beyond the sidewalk. Tower City Center and the Renaissance Hotel sprawl across the southwest quadrant. Everything outside is painted gray—like an aircraft carrier. I imagine

Grandpop's world resembling this at times during the war, thick gray clouds obliterating the color from the sea, transparent spray washing the gray behemoth that served as both home and weapon of war. Good and evil coexisting and mingling, tangling, becoming hard to distinguish from each other...

Black and white, and all the grays they create together.

I climb to the fifth floor, expecting to find Mannion alone in an otherwise deserted office on a Saturday afternoon. Several stressed, almost panic-stricken people buzz around the office lobby, shocking me. A receptionist ushers me into a conference room. She urges me to make myself comfortable and disappears. This all happens in a blink.

I sit in a high-backed leather armchair. The seat somehow forces both comfort and its opposite on me. Seven identical chairs stand arranged around a long oak table. Burgundy wallpaper covers the walls. The color is so rich and deep, the room looks almost brown in the shadows, purple nearest the glow of two floor lamps.

I never sat for any length of time in the conference room of a law firm before. Are other firms this self-consciously masculine? Not that I mind. The deep colors and soft lighting satisfy something in me. Still, the same question I had at the Come On Inn arises here again. Is the atmosphere devised to soothe, or to conceal? Maybe the lawyers and their decorators designed these chambers to intimidate. Any woman seeking a divorce would bring her soon-to-be-ex to this conference room at Smythe and Mannion, and these surroundings would tell him, without question, she meant business. I think I'm glad I'm not Mr. Yankovicz.

Any woman brought here with the tables turned could easily find herself cowed.

I'd bet part of the game involves making people wait here alone. Opponents might be left to cool their heels so their minds can run unchecked, out of control, much like mine runs now. I find myself squirming in the comfy chair. Head games of any kind make me uncomfortable. Perhaps they are necessary in divorce law, at which Mannion obviously excels.

Mannion confuses me. I can't figure out what to make of him, of his relationship with Grandpop. How could two people with such different temperaments be such close friends for so many years?

Mannion's voice rumbles quietly from the hallway. "Give Morgan a call, please. Try your best to get him in here Monday morning. Tuesday at the latest."

When he enters the conference room a second later, his manner is changed. Bill Mannion never enters rooms. He conducts assaults. Today, however, he trudges into the conference room almost meekly.

"How are you, Buddy?" he asks, his handshake firm, yet gentle.

"Fine, Mr. Mannion. Thanks for seeing me on short notice. I realize you're busy. But on a Saturday?"

"Ah, my own fault. I make a mistake, and the rest of the crew has to pay, too. But I can always spare Jimmy Cullen's grandkid a few moments. Come with me."

The infamous Mannion bombast is missing. I follow him through a long hallway accented with fine oil paintings and photographs. He shuffles through the door to his spacious private office. The memory of him standing on a wobbly table reciting his awful poem is still fresh. He invited, even dared, the gathered to jeer at him at the time. He struck me then as incredibly arrogant.

Mannion stands behind a massive mahogany desk. None of his old swagger remains. I note less fire in the eyes, less enthusiasm behind the smile. He moves a touch uncertainly. Some iron is gone from the spine. Mannion wears the profound loss of a close friend like a floor-length, black overcoat.

I hand over one of the brown paper packages. "I've brought you a little something, Mr. Mannion."

"Ah." He hesitates, then takes the package as if the contents confirmed a suspected death. A soldier's parents might react this way to the dreaded telegram from the Department of Defense. Mannion turns the package over and around. Finding no starting point he cares for, he stops fidgeting and tears the paper at a corner. "That's a beautiful frame."

"I had them custom framed for each of you.

Sally Yankovicz did a rush job at Pat Catan's. She sends her best."

Mannion winces but nods his approval as he inspects the photo. "You developed and printed these?"

"Yes, sir. Did the work in Grandpop's darkroom."

Misty eyes meet mine for a moment.

"Thoughtful. Thank you." Mannion takes another look at the picture, his lips crumpling into a wry smile. "We were quite a bunch a lifetime ago. You remind me a lot of your grandfather."

"Hmm. I always thought Grandpop was more, um—"

"Straight-laced? Conservative? Prudish, maybe?"

"Yeah, something along those lines."

Mannion sits behind his desk. He chuckles dryly and motions me toward another leather armchair. "He had the same weakness you have. The war was an advantage for him in a way. It came along, and he changed."

"I'm sorry, I'm not following."

"Jimmy was married for fifty years, yes. But your grandma wasn't the first and only. He was a wild young buck, from high school until his service. His weakness before the war, as yours seems to be, was a woman."

Hmm. Grandma wasn't Grandpop's "Kelly"? Interesting...

I probe to find further connection between Grandpop's youth and mine. "The war changed him? In what way?"

"No. The war didn't change him. Not that experience by itself, I mean."

"I don't understand."

He sinks back in his chair with a soft grunt. "He changed during the war, sure. Nobody lives through something like that without being touched somehow. The war that came after, though, the war he fought for the rest of his life, changed Jimmy Cullen more profoundly."

I settle in as Mannion spins a tale about Grandpop no one else ever before shared with me.

"Jimmy and I were classmates with Al Rakocszy at St. Ignatius High School."

"Catholic schools were always 'all boys,' weren't they?"

Mannion shows no irritation at my intrusion. "They were, yes, but the neighborhoods surely weren't. About evenly split. Lots of pretty girls, too. The Polish neighborhood around Biddulph and Pearl, the Ukranians in Tremont, the Germans all over. Didn't matter to Jimmy where they lived or what their background. Whenever he got an eyeful of dangerous curves wrapped in a skirt, seems Jimmy gave chase."

My face burns crimson.

Mannion chuckles. "Didn't hear any of this about your grandfather before, did you?"

"No."

"He had a fine handsome face and was athletic, too. He enjoyed his popularity with the girls. I mean he *really* enjoyed it. For a while I think he was stringing three different girls along concurrently. I almost wish now I had my practice back then. I might have made a hell of a living off him. Jimmy broke some hearts."

My head spins. I knew what I knew about Grandpop, and that was always enough for me. I never considered the possibility of a past like this. Despite a mixture of surprise, discomfort, and embarrassment, I want to find out more. "He met Grandma later?"

"Yes, after the war. Their bond was a miracle, truly. Most of the girls Jimmy chased before Maureen seemed not quite right. Not that he found fault. He chased the prettier ones, sure. But he didn't discriminate too far beyond the surface. Hell, 'the more the merrier' meant ignoring some things other men might find unacceptable. But I'm getting ahead of myself."

I decide to get Mannion's definition of "unacceptable" later. A more urgent realization dawns on me now. "He almost settled on another girl before the war, didn't he?"

Mannion squirms. "Helen Summers was her name. Al Rakoczy and I privately called her 'Helen of Troy' because she grabbed Jimmy by the...ah, nose, and led him wherever she wanted him to go."

"A real 'looker'?"

Mannion's face flushes. "I would say, 'You have no idea,' to anyone else but you. Helen was much like your girl."

"Kelly."

"Kelly, yes, saints in Heaven. Helen was the

most beautiful young woman any of us ever met. She could have been a pin-up girl then, or a swimsuit model today. A popular one." Mannion leans forward now, his elbows on the desk, his chin resting on folded hands. His expression clouds; the pitch of his voice lowers. "She was impossible to keep eyes off of, yes. And yet, there was something else. Something dark. Something most everyone sensed but no one could identify. Sure, we were teenagers but still, we all felt"—He shakes his head—"Well, all except Jimmy. He seemed totally oblivious."

"What was the 'something'?"

Mannion shakes his head, frustrated and sad. "Boy-o, I still haven't a clue two generations later. Believe me, I would tell you, Jimmy's grandson of all people, if I did."

I digest what Mannion says, and try to keep an open mind, something Grandpop apparently couldn't manage to do.

Mannion equates Helen Summers with Kelly. Him too? Everyone around me can't be wrong about Kelly...Can they?

I need more background to make the connection. "So, Grandpop was saved in a way by the war?"

Mannion's face relaxes, his back straightens. "Yes, the war. Jimmy always had an artistic side to him, you see. Used to doodle. He got in trouble more than once in school for doodling during lectures. Some fine artwork. Well, he and Rakosczy and I went Downtown on December 7th, 1942, to enlist together. We lied about our ages, and got in. I think the recruiter knew, but the navy was still mad as hornets about Pearl Harbor. They weren't too choosy. Anyway, he doodled at every opportunity. When we were in training, some snoopy ensign found Jimmy's sketchbook and kicked it up the ladder. His work impressed someone. So, when we were done training, Jimmy was an official navy photographer, and Al and I were on a forty-millimeter gun crew. We all drew the same vessel, the *Enterprise*."

"You met the rest of your gang on the *Enterprise*, didn't you?"

"Brochetti and Schmidt both came from Cleveland, too. They were East Side boys." Mannion smirks. "I'm surprised the navy allowed a crew as motley as us to sail anywhere, let alone into battle. We all got to be great friends, stayed in touch after we got back home. Tom Jamieson was a little older, from Pittsburgh. Pharmacist's mate. He moved to Cleveland in 1951 and looked us all up."

This stuff is fascinating but not what I need to hear. Something nags at me. I feel the need to keep Mannion on track.

"And after the war?"

Mannion leans back in his chair. "Jimmy sobered a little. I believed the reason was the kamikaze attack off Kyushu, Japan, in May, 1945. Someone once said there are no atheists in foxholes. Well, the *Enterprise* was our foxhole. A giant foxhole with a giant target painted on her. Most everyone on her had a lot to say to God back then.

Jimmy wasn't ready to join a monastery, though. He was ready to take up with Helen of Troy again as soon as we got home. Then he met Maureen at a USO function, before he got to call on Helen. A 'welcome home' dance for us boys."

"Love at first sight."

Mannion's laugh shatters my assumption. "Not at all, no. Don't get me wrong, your grandmother was a pretty lass, but Helen of Troy still led Jimmy by his...ah, you know. Somehow, Jimmy and Maureen's paths kept crossing and they gradually got closer and closer. Helen took up with another man. I suppose a bigger surprise to all of us, Jimmy included, was he wasn't all busted up when Helen dropped him."

"Pays to have a fallback position, I guess."

Mannion bristles. His jaw clenches, his fist slams down on the desk top. "Sonny boy, Maureen Cullen is nobody's second best, and shame on you for even thinking so." He quickly smothers the flash of anger. "Well. Shame on me for presenting it that way. Helen Summers had a way of muddying men's minds, no matter how clear. Still does, I guess."

"I apologize, Mr. Mannion." He nods. I rise to leave. He clears his throat, stopping me. "There's more?"

"I haven't gotten to Jimmy's war after the war."

I sit back down in my chair.

Mannion casts his eyes down at the desk top, at his own reflection on the glassy surface. His face tenses, betraying some inner conflict. He takes a deep breath and begins with a cryptic pronouncement. "This much I have learned. People will believe what they choose to believe. Agreed?"

"I suppose."

"Your grandfather walked away from sketching and painting after his pictures from the Pacific got published. He got hooked on photography. That's how he became such a successful freelancer. But he was through with war."

"Baseball took over."

"Right. Bob Feller was a sailor in the war too, on the *Alabama*. You never saw a fastball like his. We were in awe of him before the war. We still were afterwards. Following Feller's career with the Indians was natural for Jimmy. Of course, his new passion really took off in 1948."

"A few years after he and Grandma married."

"Yes." Mannion pauses. After a long moment, he sets off a bomb. "After the '48 Series he fought his own war of sorts. He believed—truly believed—that the Cleveland Indians were cursed."

I blink. "Cursed."

He swats at the air with a massive paw. "I know, I know. I was afraid he got unhinged in the war. I expected life with Maureen in peacetime would bring him around. Never quite happened. After he told us, he kept his belief mostly to himself. But we…well, we…"

I interrupt him again, shocked that I detected none of this before. "You mean, you all blew him off."

Mannion gives me a level, angry glare. Time slows to a standstill. His anger softens. Sadness and regret cloud his face. "Yes, we did. He swore up and down he had proof. None of us said a word. We would have laughed at him right off, but we loved and respected him. He understood, I think. He never brought the subject up again. Not seriously, I mean. Sure, he would kid about a curse now and again. The team gave him plenty of opportunity for jokes. Forty some years of jokes. And yet, I always felt his kidding was half-hearted."

"Grandpop fought to be heard and believed."

"In a way, yes. We loved the man, but…"

But you all believed he was a little bit nuts.

"I understand, Mr. Mannion."

"I hope you won't hold the doubt against us. Against me."

"No, of course not." I rise and stick out my hand. "Thanks again for your time."

Mannion shakes my hand. He walks with me down the hall. "Thank you, Buddy." He grabs my arm as we near the stairway. "He never showed his proof to me. I understand why. But I wish I had seen it. You follow?"

I nod and leave him in the hallway.

I understand Mannion's unfulfilled wish. As I descend the five flights of stairs to the lobby, I consider all sides of the situation. Grandpop's friends were like him, still young, yet worldly, fresh from some of the most terrifying warfare in history. If I had been any of those men, and a buddy of mine claimed he had proof of a curse, I'd probably believe he cracked in combat. I might have blown my own grandfather off if I had been one of them. If

I did believe him, I can imagine myself keeping quiet so no one would think I was cracked, too.

A new, curious realization strikes me. Mannion believed Grandpop. Not at first, as he told me, but I think I just heard him admit to a conversion of sorts.

People will believe what they choose to believe...

I reach for my cigarettes before I even exit the building. My stress level rises. I end up smoking the cigarette and two more in the short drive from Public Square to Lakewood.

The steady drizzle makes Clifton Road slick. I try to convince myself the driving conditions are what ramp up my urgency. True, the weather, the drop in temperature, concerns me. Should the temperature plummet, the drizzle can turn to sleet, then to a sheet of ice, in a hurry, a common occurrence in Cleveland in November.

The oncoming dusk concerns me, too. The meeting with Mannion pushes me to go through Grandpop's darkroom stuff. I hate to admit this to myself, but I want to get home before darkness sets in, before I bump into something that goes bump in the night. I was never afraid of the dark—at least, not until the other night. This stuff piques my curiosity now. It also increasingly gives me the creeps.

I fumble my pack of cigarettes at West 117th Street. A chorus of angry car horns shoos me through the red light. I manage to light the smoke within a block, but my hands and my head remain disconnected. My head fixates on Grandpop's close friends. They didn't believe. Or they chose, as I think Mannion did, to ignore his claims. I want to find Grandpop's evidence, to go over the proof and judge for myself.

An uneasy sense grows within me, the feeling I might be pursuing something not to be believed by sane people.

I nearly get killed a second time at Bunts Road. A horn blares to my right. I slam on the brakes and come to a fishtailing stop before running another red light. I give the horn-blowing driver an apologetic shrug of the shoulders. He gives me a middle finger. I can't blame the guy.

My brain pushes the offended driver from my consciousness almost immediately. I focus on getting home. The streetlights popped on as I was defying death and vengeful sign language at Bunts Road. I park my car before the last gray of day fades to black.

My legs vault the stairs two at a time. I burst through my own door like a cop on a drug bust. I rummage through both the stuff in the cardboard boxes and the stuff in my head without bothering to take off my dripping leather jacket.

They didn't believe him, didn't believe he had proof.

I riffle through one box, then a second, then a half dozen more. Which one holds what I'm looking for? I'm looking for a specific manila envelope. But dozens of envelopes stand on end in each box. They all look the same.

I'll know which one it is...I'll know...

In less than half an hour, I clutch what I never would have believed existed. A dark anticipation, a sort of electrifying dread, unnerves me. I've seen this envelope before. Green ink on the lower right corner confirms my hunch. Nine-eight-five-nine, just like in my dream. I wonder if I have the same look on my face that Mannion had when I gave him the gift-wrapped group photo, the look that clearly said, "I know what's in here."

The truth is, I don't know what's in this envelope. I stop myself from ripping the package open.

If I open this here and now, I already know what people will believe.

I stagger to the kitchen, return to the living room with my cordless phone, and sit on the hardwood floor. Cordless phones are a marvelous invention, with limitations, much like a cellular phone, I guess. I might lose the handset, the business end, almost anywhere in my apartment and not find it again until someone calls me. On the plus side, I can walk all around my place without being tethered to a wall by a phone cord.

I'm simultaneously connected and disconnected. That's a good thing, right?

A few drops of water slide from my shoulder down my arm. The jacket's leather offers no resistance. The droplets continue down my hand, off my fingertips and on to my phone handset. I wipe the handset dry, pause, and put it down.

People will believe what they choose to believe... Will they choose to believe I'm putting them on? Or worse, that I'm a nut job? Did they really think so of Grandpop? Should I risk bringing the same judgment down on myself?

I surround myself with close friends as Grandpop did, sure, but also with family. My family gives me an advantage. But someone else must witness the opening of this envelope. I want everyone to be assured this isn't some prank if the contents turn out to be hard to swallow. I trust my loved ones. I guess I'm not sure they'll trust me. Not with this...whatever *this* is.

I must be ready to do some research, and I'll need some qualified help. This qualified person should also be my witness. I'll avoid Grandpop's mistakes by combining friendship with journalistic qualifications and integrity.

After a quick look in the White Pages and a rapid punching of numbers, Erika Jankowski answers on the third ring.

CHAPTER 7

The dollar bill crumples in the parking lot collection box's slot. As I did with the first two bills, I stuff the third one through with my car key. There's no point in looking for a parking spot on the street. I need more time than a meter will allow.

The fresh breeze on my face makes me glad to walk the couple of blocks to the Cleveland Public Library's main branch. My knee throbs a bit. The scab that formed overnight rubs against the inside of my pant leg. Still, I take ironic comfort in experiencing anything, even these minor aches. A numbness lasted the whole day yesterday. I felt little except mounting frustration. I can only blame myself.

I stop for a moment at West 3rd Street. I need a cigarette. I need perspective.

I need to stop kicking myself.

My inertia began first thing yesterday. I overslept, flopping out of bed at midday. On Sundays in November, true Clevelanders follow Cleveland Browns football, I told myself. I turned the television on at twelve forty-five to watch the Houston Oilers kick the snot out of the Browns. Then I beat myself up for wasting the whole three hours. I scolded myself throughout the afternoon and into the night for not doing anything, yet I continued to not do anything. A psychic time vacuum sucked up the whole day.

Actually, I did some work yesterday. Rationalizing this meeting with Erika began to take real effort. Mannion's tale grew into a bigger bedtime story with each sensible examination. The notion of possible evidence in the envelope devolved into deeper skepticism. My curiosity shrank. The urge to cancel with Erika grew.

Bill Mannion kept me from calling Erika again.

"People will believe what they choose to believe."

I take a hard drag on my cigarette, striding through Public Square with a spiral notebook and the manila envelope tucked under my arm. Mannion's words weigh on me. They sound like both a reprimand and a challenge. I force myself to lay my sensible skepticism aside. Good journalists view a story from every angle they can find without leaning one way or another. Now I kick myself for suppressing my journalistic integrity, even if temporarily.

I stub out my cigarette on the heel of my shoe, flick the butt toward the gutter, and light another. Chain smoking signals stress in me. Strange. Smoking relieves my stress even though nicotine is a stimulant. The chemical math somehow adds up. I don't understand how.

A man in a business suit and a breathlessly talkative woman in a long coat pass me. She swivels her head in my direction as they pass. Her stare unnerves me. She wrinkles her nose. I guess she's a non-smoker. No problem. I may become a non-smoker myself someday.

My own nose wrinkles as I inhale an odor following in the woman's wake. I'll bet she stepped in a pile of dog dump somewhere. The number of apartment renters and condo owners have recently risen in the city. I assume some keep pets. Did a stray leave the gift? I almost laugh at the woman who can't tolerate cigarette smoke in an open area, yet who has no clue about her own fragrant bouquet.

Why does this unimportant moment cling to me?

I put my cigarette out. My shadow follows me up the bleached steps to the Cleveland Public Library's door. The steps bend and disfigure the silhouette. According to its distorted shadow, my body consists only of right angles.

Distortion dominates the day. The library's Business and Science Annex next door is gone, torn down. A more modern structure will replace the old Annex soon. But an empty space, a gash, distorts Superior Avenue now. Several men wearing suits, trench coats, and hardhats, poke around the construction site. One of the men carries a blueprint.

I push through the revolving door into the lobby. What will Erika and I build here today? We have no blueprint. I hope to find the raw materials in this building. Does the manila envelope contain the tools we need? What are those tools? I assume they are photographs, but I base my assumption on...what? A dream, an illusion, a mental fabrication...

My chuckle lacks mirth.

"A blot of mustard, a crumb of cheese, an underdone bit of potato..." Thank you, Charles

Dickens.

Erika waits inside the door, her backpack slung over one shoulder. She arches an eyebrow. "You've definitely got my curiosity up."

I sound cryptic without meaning to. "Yeah, mine too."

She shakes the awkward moment off, shifting into Good Inquisitive Journalist mode. "Why not the library on campus? I mean, we could find anything we need at Case."

"Including students or faculty who might think this meeting inappropriate, which we don't need."

She nods. "Got ya."

We pass through metal stanchions electronically rigged to detect book thieves. I sigh over this sad commentary. The library owns many rare and valuable books, so I understand the need for security. Unfortunately, the library placed the ugly stanchions beneath the gorgeous marble arch leading to the building's interior. I turn to take a quick look behind me.

Distortion...

We climb a marble stairway to an isolated table in the Literature Department on the second floor. I hold a chair out. Erika blushes. Her reaction touches me. I sit opposite her and lay the envelope on the table.

She gives me a level stare. "You're sure that's the one?"

"Yes."

"What makes you so sure? You said you've got boxes of stuff from your grandfather's basement, and you left dozens more boxes still down there."

"This was in the stuff from the darkroom. I saw him take this envelope into the closet."

"In the dream."

"Yes."

She arches her eyebrow again, unzips her brown suede jacket and unwinds the scarf from her neck. I expect some comment or question about my mental health. She surprises me once more. "Why are you sure this is the one?"

I fidget. "See the mark on the lower right-hand corner? The mark matches the one—"

"On the envelope in the dream, got ya. Okay, well, let's go with it then."

My finger slips under the envelope's flap and rips the end open. Several ten-by-fourteen glossy photos spill out. I shake my head. "Hmm."

"What?"

"Pictures. Big surprise."

"Depends what's on them."

"You're right." I spread the pictures across the table top.

"Your grandfather's work?"

"Yeah."

My face must wear the same puzzlement Erika's does. She inspects each picture for a few seconds. Her eyebrows furrow. Her head cocks first to one side, then the other. Once she's gone over each shot, she reaches for her backpack.

"I wouldn't use your cellular phone in here," I half-joke.

The downward tilt of her head can't hide her

smile. "I shut my phone off when I got here." She finally holds up a magnifying glass as if hoisting an Olympic gold medal. "We might be missing something."

"I'd like to think there's more to this than meets the naked eye."

Or maybe I would not like to think that...

My attention wanders from the pictures in front of me to my student beside me. I suddenly wonder if my investigation plan was a mistake. I never pictured Erika Jankowski in this light before, and I mean "light" both literally and figuratively. Her pale skin almost glows, even in this diffused interior light. Her long, honey-blonde hair shimmers. She wears little, if any, make-up, unconcerned by the faint sprinkling of freckles across the bridge of her nose. I smell no perfume. She dresses in faded jeans and an over-sized cotton sweater. She is unassuming, unpretentious. She is simply Erika, but not the pre-teen Erika who grew up around RJ and me. She comes across to me as a woman for the first time. I wonder how I ignored the change until now.

Probably by focusing on your work, bonehead. The work is in the pictures. Concentrate on them.

I force myself back to the task, hoping I wasn't too obviously distracted. Erika scans the images through her magnifying glass, mercifully oblivious to my daydreaming. I point at one of the pictures. "I can't count how many times I've seen this one."

Erika nods. She recognizes the image as well. "The '48 World Series win. Wow. He just had this knack for capturing the perfect moment."

"No one was better."

The picture exemplifies Grandpop's gift for finding detail amidst chaos. He took the shot from the infield, right after the game ended. Triumphant Indians players maul one another in the foreground. A sea of dejected Boston Braves fans head for the exits behind them. Victory manifests itself through the Clevelanders, who lift winning pitcher Gene Bearden off his feet. Defeat weighs down the slouched backs of departing ticket holders.

Erika fixates on the picture while I scan the others. She shakes her head after a few minutes and clears her throat. "Sorry. I mean, I just need an idea what to look for."

I risk coming off like a lunatic only because I have to. "Something Grandpop said in my dream. 'Caught you *again*, haven't I?' He used the word 'again.' I think we should look for something common to all the pictures."

"Some-*thing*? Or someone?"

"Grandpop wasn't big on stationary or inanimate objects. I guess we should search for a 'someone.'"

"Let's start with more of a close-up then. Okay?"

"Sounds like a solid plan." I grab the only shot that might be considered a close-up, the Old Timers Game photo. "We can eliminate my dad and me as common elements. This is the only shot I'm in. I think it's the only one Dad's in, too."

"Your grandfather's a common element to all four shots, but he's on the wrong end of the camera. Should we eliminate him, too?"

"Yeah, for now, I guess."

"Well, let's search in the margins then."

Grandpop pointed his camera up toward the back of the bleachers, capturing dozens of cheering fans with this shot. Erika begins near the center. A small knot of African-American men cluster there. She inches the magnifying glass in a slow, gradually expanding circle, looping the glass clockwise to the rows of fans behind Dad and me. She then guides the lens toward the photo's upper right-hand corner.

"Hold!" My bark draws a glare from the librarian at her desk.

Erika halts her circle. "See something?"

"I think so," I whisper. "Look at that guy."

"The popcorn vendor?"

"Yeah. Anything strike you as odd about him?"

She squints at the image. The edge cuts the man in half vertically. She points at the expression on the visible half of his face. "He looks pissed."

"And?"

Her eyes flit from one edge of the print to the other. "He's the only one in the stands who does. You think his attitude means something?"

"Could be. The Indians took the lead at this moment. Why would he be pissed? He stands out, so let's look for him in the other shots."

Erika nods. She scans the 1948 photo with her magnifying glass. "At least we're looking for a specific person now, not guessing at..." Her words and her breath catch in her throat. Her jaw drops. Her hand jerks to a dead stop, the magnifying glass locks over the photo. "That can't be right."

I scoot my chair closer to her and gaze down through the glass.

So, you're the one Grandpop caught again.

We find the popcorn vendor in all the pictures within only a few minutes. His presence in each shot breeds a queasy concern in the pit of my stomach.

Erika lays the magnifying glass down. Her facial muscles relax. Her face appears calm, but her foot taps the floor under the table. I try not to guess what she's thinking. Time stretches, becomes yet another distortion. The silence is maddening. My conflict deepens. I want to hear what she thinks more than I fear hearing it, but not by much.

When did I become so ambivalent?

I decide I'm not ambivalent. "No, this can't be right. This isn't possible."

Erika murmurs, her eyes glued to the photos. "'There is more in heaven and earth than is dreamt of in your philosophy, Horatio.'" She looks up, mortified. "Sorry. We're studying *Hamlet* in Drama."

I hesitate to remind her that by the end of the play almost everyone dies a violent, horrible death.

But what if she has a point?

Journalistic integrity forces me to allow for other possibilities, even improbable or ridiculous ones. A hasty plan forms in my head. "Let's divide the research. Which do you know more about, the Cleveland Indians or the occult?"

Erika shrugs. "Well, neither, really."

"Okay. I know a lot about the history of the Indians, so I'll take the occult."

"That's cool with me. But do you mind if I ask why you want the occult?"

"That way, the research won't be tainted by my suppositions."

Erika nods. "Makes sense. The occult?"

"Ghosts, demons, folklore, especially of this region. There must be something to explain this character, even if it's out of the mainstream. Baseball's full of superstitions and legends. Don't be afraid to go down roads that might run parallel. Might be a ghost story buried in the Indians' past."

"What then? I mean, what do we do with whatever we find?"

The question catches me off guard. I think about Mannion's tale of Grandpop, how no one believed his curse claim. I suspect folks wouldn't believe me either, with or without proof. I'm not sure I believe my own eyes yet.

"I'm not sure. Something. First things first. Let's get to digging. Meet back here?"

"I'll be back at two at the latest. I have only one class today at two-thirty. Modern English Lit. Ugh!" Erika grabs her backpack and heads for the hallway. She stops and whispers to the librarian, who writes something on a small piece of paper. Erika takes the note and heads out into the hall.

I make my way toward the librarian's desk as well. The woman's face tightens. She may have something to say about my outburst of a moment ago. Asking where to find books on the occult might not improve her impression of me. I stride toward a bank of computer terminals instead. I'll ask for help only if absolutely necessary.

Once I get to the computer terminal, I pause with my fingers poised above the keypad. I want to make this research both efficient and comprehensive. How do I decide where to start? The simple task puzzles me. My gut tells me to go with a local approach, legends and folklore of the eighteenth and nineteenth centuries, roughly the time span of the white settlers of Cuyahoga County. My research can always expand if I come up empty. I type my search parameters and fill a piece of scrap paper with the Dewey decimal numbers of promising leads. The librarian's glare chases me out to the corridor.

Sunlight floods through a huge, arched window. The light paints the top edges of the marble staircase a stark white. The sharp, dazzling angles jostle the memory of an article I once read about the comedian Jackie Gleason and the mansion he built in Peekskill, New York. Peekskill is well outside our area code, but I might track the piece down anyway. The article described the mansion's bizarre architecture. The place was completely round, with no right angles. Gleason believed ghosts lived in right angles.

I shudder.

Right angles...like my shadow on the library steps.

After taking a breath and shaking off the creepy moment, I climb the stairway. The shaft of sunlight

extends halfway up to the third-floor landing. My
nose crinkles, assaulted by a familiar stink, when I
step out of the light. Dog dirt. Someone else tracked
some up here. As I continue on my way, I make a
mental note to alert the library staff. The odor
follows me, though. I check my own soles to make
sure I'm not the one spreading the joy. Satisfied the
only things on the bottoms of my shoes are the soles
of my shoes, I enter the Social Sciences area.

Eau de Pooch stays in the hall.

Columns of ceiling-high bookshelves extend
from the wall to my right to nearly the middle of the
room. A row of dark, oak tables runs the length of
the wall to my left. The shelves and the tables create
a narrow passageway that funnels me toward the
back. I pass through the claustrophobic floor plan.
The Dewey decimal numbers on my scrap paper
direct me to an aisle at roughly the midpoint of the
passageway. I dart into the aisle, feeling like a lab
rat in search of hidden cheese.

The book at the top of my list sits on a middle
shelf. Its title is a mouthful. *A Postmodern
Dissection of the Legends of the Western Reserve.*
Why is this book so thick? Are there more legends
of the Western Reserve than I thought? Or does the
dissector's writing style make the work so dense? I
hope not. In either case, these shelves house a rich
store of materials. Fantastic documentations of
séances at Franklin Castle and the Gore Orphanage
share space with dry, scientific studies. I collect as
many books as I can handle and turn toward the
tables.

A loud "thump" startles me. I spin around. A book lies on its side in the space made when I took several others.

After I haul my selections to a table, I return to stand the toppled book upright. The adjacent book's cover art, exposed by its fallen neighbor, strikes a chord. A glamorous Eve stands fig-leafed in the Garden of Eden. She contemplates an apple. A snake, with forked tongue flicking from its open mouth, whispers in her ear. The title of the book somehow doesn't matter to me. I snatch Eve and the serpent from the shelf and return to my table. A stack of over twenty books awaits me.

Four and a half hours whiz by. Pure chance makes me check my watch in time. I slap my notebook shut, grab the books I want, and dash back to the Literature Department. I shudder a bit, unnerved.

Erika greets me with gentle reassurance. "No need to panic. I just got here, too."

"I don't think I'd call it panic."

She points at my books. "You had some luck, I guess. I'm not sure if what I've got will help as much. I found more in newspaper archives."

"Notes?"

She hands me a notebook. An astonishing number of pages bear organized, legible, and meticulous summaries and observations on the Indians ball club.

"Impressive." I manage to lift my books and hers together, nine in all. We head for the check-out desk.

"Thanks," Erika says. She slings the backpack over her shoulder. "So, now what?"

"I've got an idea that might sound a little crazy. I'd like to run some stuff by you."

"Okay, but I've got like only five minutes to catch my bus. Can you walk me to the bus stop?"

"I might need more time than that. How about if I drive you to campus?"

Erika's lips curl into a grin. "Less worried about, what did you say…'the look of impropriety'?"

I stifle a laugh. "No, not really. Worth the risk, though."

We cruise eastward on Euclid Avenue through sparse traffic, catching almost every green light. The drive passes quicker than I'd hoped. I rush through my meeting with Mannion, and barely outline a plan and its rationale, when I find myself turning left in front of Severence Hall. We roll up Bellflower Avenue at the edge of the Case Western Reserve University campus. I park next to an open stretch of grass leading to the Guilford House, home of the English Department.

Neither of us reaches for our door handles. Erika said nothing the whole trip. The silence deepens. My patience does not.

"So?"

"What do you need me to do?"

"First, tell me what you think."

"We might want to get into that some other time. If we sit here much longer, people will talk."

I allow myself a tension-breaking laugh. "Come on. I'm going to use my office, spend a little time with what we've got. Or, I might check out what's in our own library. In any case, you can chew my ear on the way to Guilford House."

Erika pulls her backpack out of the car. She joins me on the lawn. "Okay. I have to be honest. What you want to do is risky. Your grandfather did the same thing, sort of, and his plan came back to bite him."

"Yeah. But let's say, hypothetically, we go ahead and tell people anyway. Any ideas who to tell? When we have something solid."

"No, not really. I mean, can you choose a group more carefully than your grandfather did?"

Her question makes me reconsider as we traipse across the university's lawn. My gut tells me yes, I can do better than a few navy buddies. But I hesitate to go that route. Mannion wasn't specific about the others' relationships with Grandpop. How close, in fact, were they? Were they as close as family? What about family? Mannion said nothing about my great-grandparents, or if Grandma knew about photo evidence. Was actual family involved? Would they desert Grandpop? Did they?

I can't answer these questions. My parents have their faults, and Grandma is distracted. But I never got anything less than love and support from any of them.

"Yeah, I think I can pick a better group." I hold the door of Guilford House open for Erika.

She scoots inside. "Okay. How can I help?"

Her question surprises me. I don't have an easy answer, but I do have a warning. "This is risky for you, too. We might both be institutionalized."

"Yeah. But I'm already in this now, and really curious. And I want a front-row seat."

"If you stop by my office after your class, I should have an idea of how you can help by then."

"Good enough." She turns and hikes up the stairs.

The short walk to my office gives my impatience just enough time to grow. My pace quickens. I end up jogging down the hall. My anxiety ramps up even more when I get to the office I share with ancient professor Goldwyn. The office door is locked, of course. Goldwyn's teaching a class. I'm on bereavement leave and, technically, not in.

I fumble with the keys until it occurs to me to put the stack of books down on the floor. Once inside, I move the stack to my desk. I mull over, yet again, Grandpop's failure to convince anyone fifty years ago. My stomach knots up at how Mannion and his friends all believed Grandpop had mentally fallen overboard in the Pacific.

I take in a deep breath and shake off the tension.

My theories won't sound too crazy to folks who are closer to me than Grandpop's friends were to him. But the presentation will be key.

These theories actually began forming as I left Mannion's office Saturday. They bobbed close to the surface during the whole of the Browns' debacle yesterday. I'm now confident I can build a strong case, backed by evidence from several sources.

Then again, does it matter what I think is

believable?

The fragments I have so far convinced Erika. She buys into this enough to search for clues, and to work with me to piece them together. She's rational, so I'm already one up on Grandpop.

The notion of waiting much longer makes me increasingly uneasy. I may be missing an opportunity. Might someone else be able to contribute? How do I know someone else doesn't have a vital piece? It's a long shot, but...

I stop vacillating and reach for the phone. The other end picks up on the second ring.

"Hi, Dad? Do you have a couple of minutes this afternoon?"

CHAPTER 8

No battle plan survives beyond the first shot. I can't explain why I assumed mine might go off without a hitch. Still, I wrestle with growing agitation. I pace from Grandma's picture window to the base of the stairs leading to the second floor.

"Everything okay, Gram?"

"I'll be right down, Buddy," she calls from her bedroom.

I plop down on the third step, on the plush carpet runner. The step creaks a little. The sound soothes me in a way. Old, favorite easy chairs make the same kind of sound. I welcome such comfort. Ironically, part of my tension comes from my presence in this comfortable place.

My restlessness keeps me from staying settled for long. I stop myself from pacing again, though. Grandma hears me treading on the Oriental rug, I'm sure. She couldn't miss my footsteps on the spaces of bare hardwood the rug doesn't cover. I don't want to rush her. I just want her to…well, to rush a bit more.

I set our meeting at O'Leary's for four-thirty. Things initially fell together the way I hoped they would. I got hold of Dad at his apartment, which is no small feat. He's rarely home. Dad dedicates himself almost entirely to his smoky little Downtown dive. He seems to always be at work. We all had to meet at O'Leary's, I decided, because I'd never get him out of there on a business day.

Dad's convenience wasn't the only reason I

chose his bar, but I let him believe what he wanted. Explaining every concern would only take up more time.

"I appreciate meeting there, Buddy," he said when I pitched the meeting. "What's this about?"

"I can't tell you over the phone, Dad."

"That's crap."

"I promise, you'll understand."

"You say so. Bringing that fine girlfriend of yours?"

"Don't be such an old pervert. She'll be there."

I spoke too soon. After hanging up with Dad, Kelly surprised and disappointed me, telling me she couldn't make it to the meeting. I took the letdown without prying.

I called RJ next. He agreed to join us. I can always count on him, and likewise. Our friendship has been that way since the fifth grade.

Mom took coaxing, as I feared she would. She complains about Dad's focus on his bar, but the same kind of tunnel vision afflicts her. She owns and operates her own health and beauty salon south of Hopkins International Airport. Like Dad, she won't trust anyone else with her business for more than a few minutes at a time. Mom offered some hope at first. She told me she had a light schedule the rest of the day. Elliot, her massage therapist partner, had three massages. The only other appointment, she said, was a tanning booth session he could handle himself. Mom seemed ready to leave the salon in Elliot's hands for an hour or two, a major concession.

The chief problem lay in asking Mom to drive Downtown to O'Leary's.

"I won't go to that place again. The wake was bad enough." I could almost hear her teeth grinding.

"Mom, please. That's where Dad has to be—"

"More reason not to come. Why couldn't you all come here?"

"Elliot's not part of this, and O'Leary's is central to everyone else. Erika and I would need to race to Berea all the way from Case, Dad would be late opening the bar, Grandma probably wouldn't get to the salon by bus until tomorrow and might bail out instead."

So much for avoiding explanations and saving time.

A tense silence crackled across the phone line. The silence wouldn't last forever but compelled me to goose her into making a decision today.

"Okay, Mom, I'll beg if you want."

The gentle response she managed stunned me. "Sounds like you need me. I'll come Downtown for *you*."

After getting Mom, Dad, and RJ lined up, I believed everything would move ahead without further problems. First, I planned to spend an hour going over our notes. Erika could hitch a ride with me after her class. Grandma's house lies a block away from a bus stop, so she could take the bus Downtown. That bus gets to Public Square in twenty minutes.

I made those assumptions between my plea to Mom and my call to Grandma. I can't imagine why

I assumed my old grandmother would be comfortable taking the bus, and then walking three blocks alone Downtown from the bus stop to the bar.

She asked me to pick her up. I agreed. What else could I do?

This change sent a ripple through the whole enterprise. I taped a scrawled note for Erika to my office door. The note asked her to hop a bus to O'Leary's—I could no longer wait for her class to end. I stapled a couple of dollars to the inside of the note, for bus fare. Would she stop by my office? I remember only casually asking her to. Now, I also had to hope the note and the fare would still be waiting on the door for her. Thoroughly frustrated, I grabbed all our materials and made tracks for Old Brooklyn.

The plan stood on much more stable ground forty-five minutes ago. *Will everything collapse now?*

The stairway creaks softly as my black-clad grandma descends. Her right hand reaches behind her head, her face scrunched into a grimace. "Buddy, could you give me a hand, please?"

I help her pull her zipper up. "You didn't need to dress up, Grandma. A blouse and a skirt or slacks would be fine for what we're doing."

She shrugs. "What *are* we doing?"

I pat her shoulder. "I don't want to say anything until we're all together. Okay with you, Grandma?"

An impish grin makes her seem almost a bit dotty. "Is this a secret? Your grandfather never kept secrets from me."

I'm not so sure, Grandma...

Her jibe piques my curiosity. I wonder how accurate her assumption about Grandpop might be. I troll as casually as I can. "Did he share stories with you from the job?"

"Oh, yes. He showed me all his pictures, too. I've seen all his work."

All his work? Does she know something helpful?

I lead her out the side door. "I guess you've seen all the good and all the bad, huh?"

"Too much bad, I'm afraid. But the good is always close by, somewhere."

"You're right, Grandma." I sound unconvinced, even to my own ear.

She deadbolts her door, addressing me over her shoulder. "Sometimes the good is hard to see, Buddy. But it's there." She turns to me. Her face lights up. "Did you ever meet Herb Score and his wife, Nancy? They're both such dears. They sent flowers to Jimmy's funeral."

I nod, aware flowers might easily have gone to Score's own funeral instead. Gil McDougald smoked a line drive into the lefty's head in May of 1957. One might say a near decapitation holds little good.

But Score survived. He then became the respected radio voice of the Indians, broadcasting for over forty years after his pitching career ended. Score's story is a fine reminder of good often being hard to find. Who expected anything good to come out of his tragic mishap at the time? I've seen a picture in the Cleveland State University archives of *Score*, with his head swathed in bandages. The photo must have been taken weeks after the impact. His face appeared otherwise unmarred, not like a bruised and bloodied pumpkin.

Picture...this happened at Municipal Stadium. Did Grandpop work that game? I wonder if I have a picture of this somewhere in his stuff. Worth a search for more evidence.

We climb into my car. I make a mental note to rummage through Grandpop's files again later. Grandma buckles her seat belt, and we head into the city.

Erika crosses the street at Frankfort Avenue as we pull into the West 6th Street parking lot. She waits for us at the far corner. I wave awkwardly with the hand already holding our notebooks and the envelope. Grandma holds my other arm. She clutches me tighter on seeing Erika.

"She's a nice girl, Buddy."

"You don't even know her."

"She's not a nice girl?"

"No, I'm not saying that. I'm sure you're right."

We join Erika and make our way together to the Burgess Building. Erika takes Grandma's hand. "Hi, Mrs. Cullen. You're looking well. How are you?"

Grandma's eyes twinkle. "Erika, isn't it? I was just telling Buddy what a nice girl, what a nice young lady you are. He doesn't think so."

I play along, fighting to keep a straight face. "That's not what I said."

"You implied it then, and shame on you, John

Francis Cullen, for sullying the young lady's name."
Grandma says this with a grin.

Erika smiles, too. "Don't you worry, Mrs.
Cullen. He doesn't dare sully my name. I've got a
mean right hook."

"And he's got a glass jaw, dear. You two should
get along fine."

We reach the weathered wooden door where I
grasp the door knob. My mood darkens.

The last time I came here, I told Kelly I felt like
I was descending into a grave. Those words trouble
me now.

Erika and I accompany Grandma to the corner
booth furthest from the door. Grandma sobers as
well. Of course, the last time she was here was for
Grandpop's wake, so I understand the sudden
nothingness in her eyes.

Dad and Mom wait for us. Mom sits poker
straight, statue still, in the booth. Dad stands beside
the table, rocking back and forth on the balls of his
feet. He already set the lighting to the standard pub
dimness, a faint glow over the bar, the corners of
the room left in murky dusk. He bumped the light
up over this booth for now, at my request. But the
place still gives me the impression of a grave or a
crypt, a dark place with dark thoughts and secrets
locked away day and night, forever.

A strange tension mixes with the eeriness. I
wonder if Erika senses the same strain. My parents'
stress is obvious. But something different stretches
my nerves now. The word apprehension comes to
mind, the polar opposite of what the Birthday Boy

feels before opening his presents. Today's not my birthday, or Erika's. I'm surrounded by friends and family, true, but I doubt they'll enjoy the present we're going to share with them.

Dad checks his watch. "Twenty-five minutes," he mumbles.

"RJ said he'd be here. Let's give him another minute or two."

"Buddy, we've been closed for a week—"

"Then a couple more minutes won't matter," Mom cuts in through a forced smile. "This is obviously important."

"So's my business."

"Michael, for the love of God, shut up," she hisses.

Dad clenches his jaws and shakes his head. Silence envelopes us. The only sounds are the humming and occasional hiccuping of the refrigerators behind the bar. The moment sprawls over several excruciating seconds. Dad clears his throat. He jerks his chin in the bar's direction. "Why don't you get me a little something?"

"Your usual?"

"Sure would like one about now."

"Okay. Anyone else want anything? Erika?"

"I'd like a Diet Coke, thanks."

Grandma's eyes light up. "Can you make me a 'Shirley Temple,' Buddy?"

"Of course, Gram. Mom, anything?"

My mother gives me a terse, tight-lipped smile and shake of her head. Dad appraises Erika as if seeing her for the first time. "I'll bet Buddy'd like a hand, if you wouldn't mind."

"Sure, Mr. Cullen."

"'Atta girl."

He stares at us as we split from the group. I move to the back of the bar. Erika garners most of Dad's attention, until I shoot him a glare. He turns to Grandma and strikes up a muted conversation I can't catch from this distance.

Erika waits on the customers' side of the bar. She shakes her head. "Sorry this is so, uh…"

I toss some ice into a tumbler and fill the squat glass with club soda. "Yeah. Hard to find the right word, isn't it?" I twist a lemon peel, run the rind around the rim, and toss the peel into the soda. "*Voila.*"

"Yours?"

"No. Dad's. He's not as big a drinker as he wants folks to believe. Not anymore. Days like my Grandpop's wake used to be the rule until four or five years ago."

"Is that what happened between your parents? Oh, jeez, I didn't mean to pry."

"No big thing. The boozing was only part of what happened." I hand her a frosted beer mug full of Diet Coke. Erika sips the cola through a straw. Curiosity and propriety battle across her face. She obviously has a question but isn't sure if she should ask. I give her leave. "You're a journalist or will be. You will ask questions for a living, so go ahead."

"He kinda looked at me funny. Your Dad."

"Oh. A little creepy for you?"

"A little, yeah." Erika blushes. "Was he, uh,

checking me out?"

I pour ginger ale into a tall glass. "Probably. Don't worry. He's harmless."

At least, I think he is.

She nods as I pour an ounce of grenadine into the ginger ale. She completes the Shirley Temple herself with a maraschino cherry. "I'll trust you on that."

"I think the war messed with Dad's head somehow," I say quietly over the bar. "I was told Michael Cullen went off to Vietnam but came back a different guy. Mom couldn't have been prepared for such a change."

"You think that's what happened to your folks?"

I re-join Erika on the other side. "Well, multiply what I just told you by ten. I never get a straight answer out of either of them, so I satisfy myself with my own math."

We hand out the soft drinks. Footsteps echo in the stairwell. RJ enters.

He must see the annoyance on my face.

"Sorry I'm late," he mutters.

I nod, accepting the excuse-free apology. I half expected Kelly to appear from the stairwell with him. The short time I spent with her on the phone puzzled me. When I called and asked her to join us, she hesitated before telling me she had to work late. I could almost hear her thinking during the pause before begging off.

I have no time to process the moment. Dad wants to get the bar open. I dive in, nervous, wishing I opened a bottle of beer rather than settling for a soda.

"The night Grandpop died, I had a dream."

I hold up the envelope but hesitate, knowing how incredible the rest of this is going to sound.

RJ nods toward the envelope. "What have you got?"

Grandma's face brightens, her spine straightens. "That's Jimmy's. That's his handwriting. He numbered all his files in that silly green ink."

"I found this envelope in the stuff I cleared from the darkroom. Erika and I opened it this morning."

Erika speaks up quickly. "I'll swear to it."

Eyebrows around the table lift at her vehemence and urgency. She shrinks in the spotlight.

Dad clears his throat. "And?"

"Grandpop had this particular envelope in my dream. Same markings at the bottom. I was kind of a witness when he had this in the darkroom. What's in here is...both important and impossible."

"And you want to show us."

"Yeah, Dad."

"Well," he says, his signal to go ahead. I spill the photos onto the table. Dad sips his club soda and grumbles. "A bunch of baseball pictures. Stunner." He draws a withering glare from Mom.

"These two were taken at Municipal Stadium," I say, identifying the shots from the old ball park where I spent so many summer afternoons. "This one is Fulton County Stadium. This must be Fenway Park."

Dad corrects me on the site of the Indians' last World Series triumph. "Boston Braves' Field. The

Red Sox didn't share Fenway with the Braves."

I pick up the one photo of my father and me. "You remember this, Dad?"

"Old Timers game, 1974. You don't forget moments like those."

Dad is right. Twenty-year-old details come back to me as fresh as if experienced moments ago. I especially remember the four African-American men we always sat behind. We looked for them at every game. The 1970's era Indians were awful. Our entertainment often came from those men sitting in front of us. They spent whole games betting on what each batter would do. The jackpot was a single box of popcorn, passed from one to the other, depending on the outcome of each bet. Growing up, I privately came to call them the High Roller Quartet.

The High Rollers took their usual spot for the Old Timers Game, and we sat in ours behind them, July 2, 1974. We jammed ourselves in together with thousands of other fans trying to catch a moment of ironic glory, the revenge of the legend-laden Cleveland team that ended its record setting '54 season with a whimper.

"Who's this, Dave Pope?" The High Rollers' routine was more animated, but otherwise unchanged.

"He'll hit a double. Watch now."

"He's a hundred years old! He ain't gonna make second base!"

"Pope wearin' glasses? Lord! He can't hit nothin' wearin' those!"

Pope swung. Giants' right fielder Don Mueller drifted back. We heard a delayed *CRACK!*—the bleachers were that far away from home plate. Mueller's labored gallop was wasted effort. Pope's fly ball sailed three rows into the stands for a home run. The Quartet members mobbed one another. Grandpop muscled his way down a few of the concrete steps and began snapping away with his Medalist.

That picture now lies in front of us. The Quartet is a touch left of center in a group hug. Dad and I hug right of center, behind the Quartet. Cheering fans surround the six of us.

Beside us on the steps to the concourse is the right half of a gaunt, wiry old man with close cropped silver hair—the popcorn vendor. He stands out from the crowd. I never paid attention to him before, which surprises me. His expression, the strange mix of anger and confidence, strikes me as too odd to gloss over. His cracked leather face, though not hideous, makes me squirm.

I point at the sneering mug. Then I place the 1948 World Series victory photo next to the Quartet's shot and point to a figure obstructing the exiting Boston fans. "Look here."

Someone gasps. I can't tell who. It may well have been me. No one says anything.

I pull out the next image. This shot shows the

Municipal Stadium bleachers from field level, from just inside the center field fence. Another dejected crowd shuffles past a triumphant old man.

"October 2, 1954," Dad says quietly.

"That's pretty specific, Dad."

He points to a big, burly man and a boy sitting next to each other, stunned, near the gleeful old vendor. "This guy's Bill Mannion. I'm the kid next to him. That's the Series game your Grandpop took me to, the fourth game."

My tension grows. I can't quite read anyone around the table. Mom, Grandma, RJ...none of them says a word or moves a muscle. Dad's face betrays inner conflict. I think he's fighting some kind of private battle.

"Want to look at this last picture?" I ask the group. "Dad?"

"Yeah. Let's have it."

Grandpop took this shot in Atlanta a few days before his death. The angle nearly duplicates the '48 photo. This time, the crowd at Fulton County Stadium celebrates wildly. The Atlanta Braves have just beaten the Indians to take the World Series title. In the jubilant crowd's midst is the equally jubilant popcorn vendor.

Still, no one says a word.

I glance at Erika. She casts her eyes down at the table top. My frustration builds quickly, too quickly. I can't believe they are all being so thick. Incredulous words spew from my mouth. "It's the same guy!"

RJ scoffs. "Vendors don't travel from stadium to

stadium."

"But it's him!"

Dad pipes in. "This can't be the same guy. He looks as old as Time in '48. He was probably dead by '54—"

"But there he is! And there in '74, and there in '95!" I stab at each photo in turn. My hand-picked group seems unmoved.

RJ squints at the images. He nods after a moment, satisfied. "Too big a coincidence for the resemblance, so the guys may somehow be related. But they're all about the same age. These pictures cover what, fifty years? No apparent aging from '48 to last week, so these have to be four different guys."

I stare at the image of the vendor, mesmerized by his face, as RJ shoots me down. His voice melds with the sight of the old man's mug...

A light bulb goes off in my head. I open my mouth but hesitate. Should I tell everyone what I just realized, what I hardly believe myself? I think I must be insane. Now I consider parading my insanity in front of everyone else. My eyes squeeze shut tight. How did I miss this until now? How did I ban this memory? I open my eyes and measure my group.

Why not tell them? What have I got to lose at this point?

"This old man was in Lakewood the other night. At the Come On Inn, when RJ and I were shooting darts."

My friend's face is a blank. "I didn't see him."

Dad clears his throat. He works to keep an even tone. "Buddy, I never subscribed to any of that mystical Gaelic leprechaun and banshee crap. When you hear a bump under your bed at night, it's the family cat."

"Except when it's not, Dad. Right now, I'm peeking under the bed, and what I'm seeing *ain't* the family cat."

"Okay," RJ ventures, "what are you seeing under the bed?"

Another breath. *Oh, this is gonna sound SO crazy...*

"I think this guy, this thing, is why the Indians haven't won a Series since '48. He's like the Cubs' goat, or Boston's 'Curse of the Bambino.' He's a jinx, a curse."

They each react, but not in ways I expected. Once again, the response is mixed. RJ's eyebrows shoot upward. What is he thinking? Mom turns her face away from me. She obviously wants to call 9-1-1, but only after shooting me for wasting her time. Grandma shakes her head. And Dad? As with RJ, I don't know what he's thinking. I don't even check Erika for her reaction. Why bother? Her journalism professor just proved himself a lunatic, one about to throw away the key to his own padded cell.

And yet, I can't stop myself from pleading my case.

"Listen, nobody thinks more than I do that this sounds crazy. But it's the same guy. That's obvious."

Mom speaks with her face turned to the wall. "I

don't even see a resemblance."

"This guy? And this one and this one?" I almost yell, poking the phantom in each photo again with my finger. "How can you not see?"

"People will believe what they choose to believe..." I suppose I didn't want to accept Mannion's premise completely. Present company forces me to.

Dad's voice sounds flat, emotionless. "So, how does this work?"

"How the hell do I know, Dad?" I splutter, dismayed. "Maybe he has a thing for the Indians. The '54 team should absolutely never have been swept by those Giants. No way. Here, he seems sure they're going to lose again in the Old Timers Game. Look at how he's celebrating in Atlanta after the Indians lose this year's Series."

"They won in '48."

"And look at how upset he is!"

"So what?" Mom interrupts with a testy edge, tossing the oldest evidence across the table at me. "This guy never ages? No, wait, even better. He exists just to torture a baseball team?"

Yeah, I think so, is what I want to say. But I say nothing.

Erika speaks up quietly but firmly. "We both spent hours at the library doing research. I think some undocumented evidence must exist. Several baseball teams claim curses against them."

Mom addresses me, not Erika. "And what did you find?"

I am at a loss for what to do now. An awkward

silence blankets the barroom, a moment that seems to stretch to tomorrow and beyond.

Footsteps come from the stairwell. All heads turn. Daniel "Dice" Delaney, Dad's business partner, shuffles into the room, his hands jammed in his ragged army fatigue jacket's pockets. The gaunt, stubble-faced man ambles to the office door behind the bar. He gives me a curt nod, his eyes locked with mine.

Dice disappears into the office after his scintillating non-greeting.

Dad jumps on the opportunity to end the fun. "Time for me to open the bar." He collects the photos and hands them to me. He grimaces, avoiding eye contact with me. His face wears an odd, subtle mix of confusion and pain. I put the photos back in the envelope as he heads for the bar, his comfort zone.

RJ excuses himself. "Buddy, I have an ER shift in a few hours. We'll talk tomorrow."

Grandma and Mom rise. Mom stares at me, frowning. "Are you all right?"

"Yeah, Mom."

"I didn't mean to be—I just...I don't know what to say, what to think about this."

"Yeah."

"Take care, honey." She gives me a perfunctory hug before practically running toward the stairwell.

I stare at the floor. Erika breaks a brief but uncomfortable silence, rescuing me. "Can I get a ride home with you? I took the bus today, and I'd rather not—"

"No problem. Mind if we drop my grandmother home first?"

"Of course not," she says with a genuine smile.

I force as light an air as I can manage. "Well, let's go, girls."

Dad stocks beer mugs in the back, bar refrigerator. He pauses to glance at me as I lead Grandma and Erika toward the stairs. I'm heading for my car, heading home.

But I'm also heading deeper into uncharted territory.

CHAPTER 9

Silence wedges itself into our midst. I unlock the passenger's door and hold the front seatback forward. Erika slides behind, to the back seat. She and Grandma get settled while I shuffle to the driver's side and climb in.

I shift into reverse. The clutch acts slow, sluggish. The hesitation isn't enough to concern me, but enough for me to notice. My head now works like my Skylark's transmission, less willing to engage.

Grandma gives me a hand. "Well, so nice to see your mother again, wasn't it?"

Erika and I steal glances at each other. Neither of us basked in any warmth from Mom. The word "nice," uttered by Grandma with deep sincerity, strikes me as hilarious. I burst out laughing. Erika breaks into a more discreet grin.

The moment motivates me to keep the ice broken. "So, what do you girls think? West 25th Street, or the highway?"

"We'll hit traffic either way," Erika says, "but I-71 won't have stop lights."

"Okay. We'll take the highway."

A rare, generous driver lets me sneak into the gridlock on West 6th Street. Erika taps me on the shoulder. "O'Leary's. Interesting place."

"Yeah. Dice Delaney may be my father's business partner, but the place is all Dad's."

"It's kind of a sad place, to be honest."

I nod. Grandma shifts in her seat. I expect her to

comment on her son, the barkeep, but nothing comes out. The line of traffic rolls forward. The road demands my attention.

The traffic mesmerizes me, like a painting's cleverly hidden image that emerges only after staring at the canvas long enough. Slow moving tail lights blend with half remembered snippets of mythology. Cars meld into a single, supernatural beast. We fuse into a giant red snake slithering along the ground, under a darkening sky. Our snake twists left and right through the city street maze. Another giant snake, a white one, approaches us. More of these creatures lurk in the city-maze, slinking in all directions. At least one of them would swallow us at this time of day. No one avoids them all.

Our snake carries us to Ontario Street on its way to I-71 South. We slow to a crawl. Jacobs Field and the Gund Arena take up this whole block. I shake the serpentine fantasy from my head, replacing it with the Chief Wahoo caricature in spite of my best efforts. The Chief's toothy smile draws a frown from me. "Go ahead. Laugh."

"Sorry?"

I crane my neck back toward Erika and tap my temple with my finger. "Chief Wahoo's laughing at us up there."

She gives me a regretful shrug before turning away to gaze out the passenger's window. Her stare remains fixed outward as we crawl down I-71. She has nothing to distract her.

I can't afford distraction right now. If the car

ahead stops without warning, I might put my front bumper in his trunk. Otherwise, Grandma would get more of my attention. She stares, unmoving, at the mechanized serpent inching through the deepening twilight. The occasional blink reassures me she's not catatonic or dead.

I peek at Erika in the rear-view mirror. She reads my mind, turning from the passing cityscape to meet my glance in the mirror. We connect but say nothing.

"You two make a good couple."

Grandma's voice startles me. I turn her way but she stares straight ahead, as if someone else had spoken. Erika focuses out the back window again. A slight smirk curls her lips, keeping me from thinking I imagined the whole thing. I kill the temptation to tell Grandma we are not an item.

I'm afraid of hurting Erika's feelings. Interesting...

The rush-hour jam lurches over the bridge high above the Industrial Flats. Twin, Gothic spires rise above the bridge. St. Michael the Archangel's Church. The spikes jab at the sky just above the bridge. My imagination, more active now than I can remember, and more than I'd like, reinvents the slender, soot-blackened spires as the Archangel's weapons, huge spears rising out of the Tremont neighborhood.

Built to inspire or to impale? What might spearheads that size be designed to skewer? A giant, glowing, red traffic snake? Or maybe a serpent of another kind.

Grandma gives me a quizzical look. I shrug and mumble. "St. Michael's steeples."

"You've never seen them before?"

"Sure, of course."

Just never this way before.

She nods the satisfied nod of the schoolteacher whose slowest student finally grasps the Algebra she's been drilling into him for months. The trouble is, I can't even guess what she thinks I now know.

Erika catches me off guard with a non-sequitur. "So, what's the story on the goat? I was in too big a hurry at the library. I took the notes. I just don't remember the details."

Grandma jumps in before I can answer. "The Wrigley Field Curse. A man named William Saynis—"

"Sianis, Grandma."

"William Sianis tried to get his lucky goat into a game at Wrigley Field in Chicago."

I shake the initial surprise off and add what I remember of the tale. "He owned the Billy Goat Tavern near the ball park. Sianis did, not the goat."

"It happened during the World Series in 1945."

"Game four."

"Game four. They wouldn't let him in with the goat. Sianis cursed the team. They lost that World Series and haven't played in another one since."

And I thought my story sounded weird!

I hate to stick a pin in Grandma's balloon, but I must. "The Cubs last won a Series in 1908, thirty-seven years before the goat."

Grandma chuckles. "Your father would have

brought that up."

I smile. Grandma's right. Dad, the poster child for skepticism, would pour cold water on any myth. My smile fades. I tend to be as big a skeptic as Dad, so I understand his lack of enthusiasm for our evidence. Doubt comes from both sides, I suppose. The concise way Mom, the *über*-skeptic, defined our theory made me sound ridiculous. But I'm now convinced we're right, though the idea is crazy and impossible.

The Cleveland Indians have a curse. Grandpop got pictures of it.

We exit I-71 at Fulton Road. The crumbling stone bridge spanning Brookside Park miraculously supports us once more. We wind our way through the back streets to Grandma's driveway.

Erika jumps out behind me. She scampers to the passenger's side, offering her hand. I expect Grandma to say something like, "No thanks, dear, I'm fine." She has declined my help before. She takes Erika's hand instead, climbing out of the car with unneeded assistance.

Grandma shoots me a grin across the hood of the car. I understand now.

I have a girlfriend already, I mouth to her.

She nods. Her crooked grin stamps her own brand of skepticism on her nod.

"I'll meet you girls inside in a minute," I say, pulling my cigarettes and lighter from my jacket pocket.

Erika holds the side door open for Grandma. They disappear inside.

I lean back against the hood of the car. The engine's warmth lends no real comfort beyond toasting my buns a little. My temples throb, my stomach sinks as if lined with lead, my spirits wane. But my butt is warm.

I push myself off my car hood, negating even this small comfort, and saunter toward the back of the house.

Light floods through the kitchen windows; one casement faces the driveway, the other faces the backyard. I take a drag from my cigarette and amble toward an apple tree that stands alone in the yard, at the edge of the light. Grandma baked this old tree's fruit into countless, great pies. The tree's limbs appear more gnarled and tangled at night than in sunlight. The bare branches and twigs whisper in a language I can't understand, interrogated by a breeze I can't feel.

Could the air-brushed Eve of the library book stand under this tree and torture herself over one of its apples? Might the serpent wrap himself around its trunk, his mouth near the ethereal woman's ear? Many artists depict the Fall of Man in a sun-dappled Garden of Eden. The concept strikes a false note to me. The fabled deed would more likely have been done in the semi-secrecy of deep twilight...like here, now.

I take a last drag, stub out the cigarette, and go inside straight to the trash can. Grandma sits at her kitchen table. She smiles, both relaxed and charmed. Erika pours steaming water into a couple of tea cups, taking care not to spill. Peace and gratitude saturate the scene.

My mind shifts gears. I leave curses behind for now and reflect on Grandma's reaction when I reminded her of Kelly. The love and respect, the close bonds between us in this room, would not be possible with Kelly. I can't deny that. I also doubt Kelly would even consider the possibility of our evidence being real. I think…

I think I'm glad neither Grandma nor Erika can read my mind.

Grandma turns toward me, her eyes meeting mine. She smiles and nods. And I think I may just now have been only half right.

"I was telling Erika about when you were in high school." Grandma puts her hand on Erika's wrist.

The twinkle in Grandma's eyes makes me squirm. My head throbs harder. I can't hide my grimace. "Excellent."

Erika gives me a reassuring wink. She puts her hand over Grandma's before attempting to put out the potential fire. "I've seen pictures in my brother's yearbooks."

"Did you see the picture of him at his senior prom?"

"Yes. He escorted a Prom Queen candidate, right?"

"Jennifer Wallace. They were a cute couple, weren't they?" Grandma's memory stuns me. She met Jenny only once, almost a dozen years ago.

Erika glances my way. "Yes, they were."

"Grandma—"

"I liked her okay. She was a year older than Buddy. She went to college out of state, I think in North Dakota. They were too young, anyway."

"You and Grandpop were about the same age."

"That was different."

I smirk. "Oh, sure."

"It was. Jennifer was nothing like Helen of Troy."

My mouth opens. No words come out. Grandma's knowledge of the Other Woman of Grandpop's Youth shocks me.

Erika's eyes narrow. "Helen of Troy?"

My hasty plan to steer the conversation to safety is to plunge in. Unfortunately, the plan is a bad one because it's incomplete. What should I talk about? I hope a new topic comes to me as I speak. The only other subject on my mind is one I don't want to explore again right now. "Helen of Troy was Helen, uh…"

"Summers. When did Jimmy tell you about her?"

"Grandpop didn't. Bill Mannion filled me in. Anyway, Helen Summers had my grandfather wrapped around her finger. Grandma came along and unwrapped him."

Grandma's eyes widen. Erika casts her eyes downward, biting her lip.

I blush, much as I did when Mannion told me the tale. "That didn't come out quite right."

Grandma and Erika both burst out laughing. I raise my hands in surrender.

Grandma's laughter slows, but her mood stays

light. "Jimmy wanted Buddy to go to St. Ignatius High School. Michael—oh, sorry, Buddy's father—he refused. Jimmy worried about temptation in a co-educational high school, but Michael pointed out that Helen of Troy didn't go to an all-male Catholic school." She gives me a sidelong glance. "I guess men sail toward the siren wherever she sings her song."

I almost begin an irritated defense of Kelly but stop myself. Discussing her in front of Erika seems somehow wrong, rude, tasteless. I bite my tongue, literally. The sharp pain keeps me from breaking some quaint rule of etiquette. However, my core problem still looms. I want to get out of this uncomfortable situation but have no escape plan. I decide to simply wait a while in silent reflection. Maybe I'll come up with a decent excuse to run like hell.

Erika trumps my plan. "Mrs. Cullen, I'd love to hear all about you and your husband. I mean, as much as you'll share with me."

Grandma picks up on Erika's sincerity. "Thank you, dear. I would love to tell you. But there's so much, and it's late."

"May I visit some other time?"

Grandma chuckles. "Why, of course. I'd love to have you." She jerks her head in my direction. "You can bring this one along, if you like."

I stare at them both, trying to figure out what just happened.

Erika pulls on her jacket. "Thanks so much for the tea. Rose hip is my favorite."

I embrace Grandma, happy to spend some time with her, but relieved to be ending this moment.

Grandma whispers into my ear as we hug. "Leave Helen be, Jimmy."

I pull back. "I'm not Grandpop, Gram."

She smiles and shakes the sudden fog from her head. "Oh, of course not. What was I thinking? You children drive home safely."

Erika leads me out the side door. She stops long enough to share a smile and a wave with Grandma. I close the door behind me, trying to leave Grandpop and Helen of Troy…and Kelly…in Grandma's kitchen.

We back out of Grandma's drive. An eerie, muted grumbling fills my car. I turn to Erika. "Was that me, or you?"

"I don't think that was me, but it could've been," she says. "I haven't eaten anything since breakfast."

"Me neither. Let's grab dinner. On me." The specter of impropriety rears its head again. I start fumbling with a rationalization. "That's not a 'come on.' I mean…"

She giggles. "Sounds good. Food, I mean."

We cruise to the shiny, aluminum-clad Memphis Diner a few blocks from Grandma's house. I hold the old diner's door open for Erika. We seat ourselves at a window booth. The aromas of frying beef, roasting meats, hash browns and onions, coffee, and cigarette smoke meld into a greasy cloud of artery-clogging comfort. Erika fondles the laminated menu as if ready to begin gnawing on it.

She leans across the table. "Good thing the Cubs' goat isn't in here now."

"Don't make assumptions. Seriously, service is pretty fast here, and portions are generous. Yeah, I'm pretty hungry myself. What are you getting?"

She hands me the menu. "You know the place. Would you mind ordering for me?"

Our server, a zaftig brunette with "Candace" embroidered on her apron, appears on cue. "What're you kids having?" She's too young to call either of us "kid." We're too young to take offense.

"Two Reuben sandwiches, fries on the side, please."

"Coffee?"

Got whiskey? Can you leave the bottle?

"Ice water's fine for me," Erika says.

"I'll take a Diet Coke."

Candace collects our menus and waddles toward the kitchen. Erika raises an eyebrow. "The Reubens are that good here?"

"Amazing. The rest of the menu's okay, but they found the mother lode of perfect corned beef somewhere. Trust me on this."

Candace returns with our drinks and a basket of assorted rolls individually wrapped in plastic. Erika bows her head before we dive into the bread basket. I file the moment away. A few other questions beg answers first. The little she said in the car and the small talk in Grandma's kitchen made the pill less bitter, true. I steel myself to ask what she thinks about this afternoon's proceedings.

She anticipates my question. "It wasn't a total

bust."

I wince. "No. Not total."

"The other curses, like in Boston and Chicago, seem almost too convenient. What a great excuse for a club owner to use for his bad team for years. For decades."

I wash the last of a Kaiser roll down with a swallow of soda. "For generations. Yeah, except the fans are the ones crying 'curse.' Not the owners so much."

Erika frowns. "I think sportswriters stoke the fire more than anyone else. Almost all of the articles I found were written by guys who wrote like they dig the stuff. I wonder if some of them created the curses themselves, out of frustration." She pauses, shaking her head, baffled. "If any fans should claim a curse as the reason for 'perpetual failure,' Indians fans should. Why haven't they? Until now, I mean."

I mull this over. Candace plops two heaping platters of food in front of us. She trundles off to another table. I wait until she clears out of our area before voicing an observation.

"I think this city has a collective inferiority complex. We expect to lose, so we don't explain the losses away with something supernatural. I think the complex reaches into all facets of life. It's just most obvious with our sports teams."

"Hmm. Could be."

"Think about it. John Elway takes the Super Bowl away from the Browns three times in one decade. Were the collective losses a curse? No. They were a 'fumble,' or a 'drive,' witnessed by many, orchestrated by tangible people."

"Like the popcorn vendor in the pictures."

I stab at my fries with my fork. Uneasiness travels from my soul through my hand, out the utensil's tines, like electricity through a wire. "Okay. Let's suppose he only exists in the pictures and nowhere else."

"You mean nowhere else but the Come On Inn. You followed him out of the bar yourself, right?" Erika takes a bite of her Reuben.

Her observation sinks in. I nod, weighing the possibilities. "I almost caught the guy. The thing. Whatever he is. He was twenty feet away at the most. I waited too long."

"How could you know?"

"I think I did. I mean, I got the idea I'd met the guy once before somewhere. He was familiar to me, but not enough to recognize him right off."

Erika drops her sandwich on her plate. "You think recognizing him could have been a subliminal thing? I mean, you ran across those pictures over and over your whole life, right?"

"Yeah."

"Could be a part of you recognized him from the pictures." She munches on a French fry. Her eyes glaze over. "I'm kinda glad you didn't catch up to him."

"Why?"

She refocuses. "Let's say you got hold of him. Then what?"

"If I believed he was a curse, or whatever, I might not have gone after him at all. But I didn't even suspect that then."

"No, you didn't. But could he know you somehow?"

The question chills me. Mom and Dad and the others might reject the notion of a team curse. RJ might scoff at me spotting the entity with my own eyes at the Come On Inn. But I remember the old man's face, his wink of recognition. Granted, the moment passed in a dim, smoky bar, but I am even more certain now of what I witnessed.

Erika's question grows louder and more fearful in my mind. What if I caught up to him without first finding out what he was capable of and what his intentions were? The lack of a ready answer bothers me. This thing might not be John Elway. He might, incredible to imagine, be something worse. And I saw him.

But will I find him again? If so, what will I do?

CHAPTER 10

My Skyhawk navigates the drive to Erika's place on Clifton Road almost without guidance. The old crate should remember the way well enough. Erika and RJ live in the same house, the house they grew up in.

We pull into the driveway. Two wide, nose-high hedgerows partially hide the entrance from passers-by. I shift into park. My curiosity gets the better of me, spawning a rude question. "Don't you get a little nuts still living with RJ?"

"I don't. Live with him, I mean. I have the second floor to myself, my own kitchenette and everything. With our schedules, we don't even run into each other often. I can't complain. The place is a Godsend. The mortgage was paid off in the '70s."

"So, all you and RJ pay for are property taxes and utilities?"

"Yeah."

"Nice deal. Your dad did pretty well. Not bad for a tool and die maker."

"My folks inherited the house from my Grampa Jankowski."

"Yeah, but it was a good call on your dad's part. Keeping the place, I mean. How does he like early retirement?"

"What's not to like about West Palm Beach?"

I fire off a list. "Heat, humidity, no change of seasons."

"Yeah. That's what my mom says."

"Ouch."

Erika climbs out, reaching behind the passenger's seat for the library books. "Yeah. Dad loves Florida. West Palm's not Vegas, but he's close enough to the horse tracks, dog tracks, off shore casinos on cruise ships, all kinds of ways for him to get himself into trouble. Thank God for my mom." She stops rummaging. "Should we divvy up the research? Which books should I take with me?"

I point at Erika's backpack, already bursting with school books and course materials. "Your slate's full."

"I'll make time."

"You think this is important."

"Yeah. I do."

"Okay." I hustle to the passenger's side. The book with the Garden of Eden cover sits on top of the pile. Its title jumps out at me for the first time— *Fruits from the Garden of Truth and Myth.* I toss the book into the far corner of the rear seat, along with four others I choose at random. "You've got plenty to carry. Let me help you with these. In fact, let me grab your backpack for you."

She blushes, as she did at the library this morning. "I think I can get this."

"Please. You're doing me a favor with this madness." I slip the backpack from her shoulder. The overstuffed pack must weigh as much as she does.

A motion detector trips two security lights under the overhang of the house. A bluish glare floods the driveway. We arrive at the side door in cornea-searing safety. Erika unlocks the deadbolt. She cocks her head, raising her eyebrow at me. "Interesting."

"What?"

"One of the books we left in the car, the one with the Garden of Eden cover. You want to review a book with Judeo-Christian religious aspects? You know, creation and all?"

"I have to. You may harbor a bias."

Erika flicks a light switch inside the doorway. She leads me up a stairwell. "Bias?"

"You took time to say grace before dinner. You put a serious everyday kind of faith in God, don't you?"

"Yeah, I do."

"Wouldn't your belief taint your research?"

"No more so than a lack of belief would."

Words fail me. No glib retort? Not even the seed of a thoughtful answer? We arrive at the top of the stairs, where I close my half-open mouth. I choose not to say more before reconnecting my tongue to my brain.

Erika's hand shoots around a wall to another light switch. She ushers me into a modest living room. Her place is sparsely furnished, but comfortable. A couple of floor lamps bathe the room in a soft glow. A futon, folded into a sofa-like configuration, sits between two end tables, in front of two large windows.

She hangs her jacket and scarf on a coat rack. Without breaking stride, she proceeds to a table next to the kitchenette. "Thanks for carrying all my stuff. Go ahead and pile it on the table. Coffee or tea?"

"Whatever you're having is fine. Don't put yourself out."

"I'll put a pot of coffee on, then."

"Didn't you tell Grandma you like tea? Rose hip, right?"

"I do. But I like coffee, too." She busies herself in the kitchenette.

I rest her backpack on the floor. A heartfelt, but trite, compliment spills from my mouth. "Nice place." I cringe even as I speak.

Erika laughs, lilting and playful. "Just come on in and take a seat at the table, okay? Let's figure out where we're going from here."

The laughter, the invitation to come in, and the focus on research all put me at ease. I relax…until a warning bell sounds in the recesses of my mind. The reason escapes me. I ignore the tiny internal mayday and haul the backpack to the table.

While pulling the books from the backpack, I scrutinize a few of the covers. "Hmm. *Man and Machine: The Industrial Revolution's Impact on North American Myths. Huron Tribal Legends. Whispers from the Great Lakes.* Do you think he's in here somewhere? The vendor, I mean."

"I hope so," she says over the gurgle of the coffee maker. "I wonder if we set the right research parameters. Something your mother said bothers me."

"What about?"

"Does this thing seem like an underachiever? I mean…how did she put it? He exists just to torture a baseball team? How do you like your coffee?"

"Black, thanks. Yeah, I see what you mean."

She places a steaming mug of coffee in front of me and carries her own mug to a place at the other end of the table. "Don't get me wrong. I'm not trying to smother this."

"No, I understand. I wonder if messing with the ball club is a way to attack others."

"How so?"

"I ran into a bunch of guys the other night at the Come On. They were so into baseball they were almost scary. Attacking the team could be a means to another end, somehow harming someone who lives vicariously through the team."

Her eyebrows scrunch down. "Hmm, maybe your mom's on to something. Like, messing with the club is the real goal. Has anything terrible happened to anyone in Boston? I mean, stuff blamed somehow on the Red Sox curse? How about Chicago's goat?"

"Good question. We might want to check into documented tragedies blamed on those curses." I take a sip of coffee, strong but smooth. "This is good. Smells good, too..." I stop short.

Erika leans in toward me. "What?"

"Something came to me that's probably more silly than important."

"How silly?"

"Food, beverages. What does this thing eat? He's a popcorn vendor. I doubt he eats popcorn, but I wonder what sustains him. He doesn't drink beer. At least, he didn't at the bar."

"Does he need to sustain himself?"

"Maybe not. But he lives somewhere, right? Not 'live,' like we do. I mean..." I take a moment to search for the right words. "If he exists, he has to always be someplace at any given time, whether it's someplace we recognize or not."

The wheels turn behind Erika's eyes. "Where does he live? Yeah...Okay, we agree he exists. So..."

My hand darts for my cigarettes. I pull the pack out of my jacket pocket before realizing what I'm doing.

Erika smiles.

Sure, I want a smoke right now, but I won't just light up in someone else's home. I stuff the cigarettes back in my pocket. "Sorry. Reflex."

Erika rattles around the kitchenette for a moment, returning with a small glass ashtray. "I don't smoke, but it's not like I never smelled cigarette smoke before. I'll just open a window."

I gawk at her every step of the way across the room. The warning bell that pinged quietly in my head a few moments ago clangs wildly now. A danger rears up, dismaying me. The peril is almost routine but surprises me anyway.

I need to get out of here.

I jump up, commanding my body to return to the stairwell, to get to my car and leave now. My feet disobey, taking two steps toward Erika instead. What stirs in me isn't right. I can't seem to care enough that I recognize the wrong.

Why don't I care enough?

Erika kneels on the futon, reaching up to unlatch the window. Her sweater follows her arm, crawling up her body to just above her belt loops on her jeans. I get a good eyeful of her contours. The skinny little girl who heckled me from the right field fence when I played high school ball a decade ago is gone. A woman replaces her. A woman shoves the detached image of the student aside, appearing here in the private quiet of her own home, warm-blooded, sweet, magnetic—

What are you doing?

The moment lasts a few seconds, but a poor choice takes only an instant to make. My attention wandered toward her at the library. Re-focusing on our research took considerable effort. I fail tonight. My eyes linger on Erika's body until I realize she hasn't yet opened the window. She freezes in place, as if sculpted or posed. My stare snaps to the reflection of her face in the window.

She stares right back at me.

I can only guess how long she watched me in the mirror-like window, but who cares? My eyes flick down to my loafers. I silently curse my rebellious feet, which now shuffle toward the doorway.

Erika jerks the window open. She sits on the edge of the futon. "Are you okay?"

I try to downplay my inner turmoil, but my face flushes. "Thanks for the coffee. I just can't stay."

She rises but holds her ground, smiling gently. "I got it. Catch you in class next week?"

"Yeah. We'll collate and compare info

afterwards." I pause for a moment on the landing, giving her a nod and an embarrassed smile of my own. Then I race down the stairwell and out to the driveway. I have had enough excitement for one night.

Or, have I?

The security lights blind me once more as I climb into my car. The Skyhawk's engine coughs to life. The old beater lurches backward into the street.

My libido rages like a teenager's. I'm driven by a potent mix of guilt and lust and want to get home fast and call Kelly. I must get Erika out of my head. Kelly—my girlfriend, I remind myself—can do that for me. She and I can share one of those nights that makes me think of nothing else but her. We could spend one of those marathon sessions in bed or somewhere near it if we are too impatient. She'll empty my head of everything but what she's doing to me, and I to her.

My growing need warps time and consciousness. I drive the three miles to my apartment, park my car, and rush inside. Now I can't remember the trip. I might have sprouted wings and flown up the stairs for all I know. My hunger for Kelly builds into obsession.

Obsession...rhymes with possession...

I make a weak, vain effort to collect myself. My whole being bears the full brunt of this obsessive desire. Something else mixes in—something unusual. *Anxiety.*

A growing sense of impending trouble tells me I shouldn't make this call.

I brush the negative feeling off. Kelly's answering machine picks up after several rings. My anxiety goes for naught. I listen to her silky, sexy voice, recorded on her machine, accessible to me any time when the real Kelly is unable to answer...

The real Kelly.

I hang up without leaving a message.

I hoped for something tangible this evening, something visceral. I hoped for something to turn up the flame, a fire to feed my lust, a blaze intense enough to burn the want away. No fire tonight. But what I'll end up with will be worth the effort.

Now I have a mission.

My ad-libbed mission requires some redecorating and housekeeping. The linen closet is in the hall between the kitchen and the bedroom. A few actual linens fight for space there with a rudimentary tool kit, bottles and spray cans of cleansers, and other non-linen stuff. I grab a dark, wool blanket and a heavy-duty stapler, and head into the bedroom. A few dozen staples hold the blanket over the lone bedroom window.

I move some of Grandpop's darkroom equipment from the living room to the bedroom. My trips through the hall become increasingly hurried. After the third trip, I evaluate my bedroom's chaotic state. *Am I actually a little insane?* My bed appears almost superfluous, shoved up into the far corner. Four shallow trays lie on the floor. The photo enlarger stands at the foot of the bed. A wire clip holds a light socket to the headboard, with a red safety light screwed into the socket.

I'll have access to Kelly whenever I want now. Why don't I feel better about this?

I hurry back to the living room, pushing the errant conflict away. My impatience grows. I stuff a film canister into my pocket. An open cardboard box near my coffee table holds jugs of chemicals. I trot back to the bedroom with the chemicals, a package of photo paper tucked under my chin, and the timer in my other pocket.

The negative plops into my hand from the upended canister. I hold the celluloid strip up to the light to find the right shot, the fifth picture taken at Grandpop's wake. The negative slips into a plastic frame, which I clamp on to the enlarger. I turn the ceiling light off. My bedroom takes on an almost sinister appearance in the safety light's glow. I lay the biggest piece of photo paper I can find on the enlarger's base plate, adjusting the lens to make the image as large as possible.

Impatience jeopardizes simple yet precise procedures like this one. I want this picture printed even though the image is already burned into my mind. But I want it done right.

A test print...make a test print first.

I switch the large photo paper with a smaller scrap piece. Then I cover all the scrap with a piece of cardboard, except for a two-inch strip at the top. Kelly appears the instant I flick the enlarger's switch. The sudden bright light makes me squint. Clutter on the left edge of the test print distracts me, but just for an instant. I concentrate on moving the cardboard down the scrap paper an inch or so every second.

Kelly glows on the stark white photo paper. The mystery image on the periphery remains a mystery. Most of the object misses the scrap paper. The dark gray base plate beyond the scrap swallows up too much of the light, obscuring the edges of the shot. I don't bother with the unidentified form. Kelly's the star. I'll crop the clutter out later.

The exposed test print sinks to the bottom of the tray of developer fluid. The proper exposure is revealed, roughly four seconds, and the large photo paper goes back on the base plate.

I set the timer for four seconds and shield my eyes against the enlarger's lamp for the four most excruciating seconds I've ever spent. Rather than waste time cropping the shot, I decide to simply ignore anything but Kelly. I can do that.

The timer rings. I throw the exposed paper into the developer tray. Watching the image appear is much like unwrapping a Christmas gift a week after already scouring the house to find the hidden present. But I now possess the most amazing photograph.

Kelly leans back against the edge of the booth table. I force my eyes to start at her ankles and work their way up her perfectly sculpted calves, up her long thighs sheathed in her clingy black skirt. Her hands push down on the table's edge. She thrusts her pelvis out ever so slightly, toward the camera... toward me. The signal she sends here is not subtle, but effective. I now confirm her blouse was, indeed, unbuttoned one button too many, which for my purposes is just fine. Her auburn locks flow over and beyond her shoulders. Her drowsy lids half-cover her emerald eyes, her lips part in the "come hither" command. Her head tilts down but again, right at me.

Now I turn to the mystery clutter on the left side of the photo.

The clutter is actually a being, a recognizable one. I gasp.

Whispering into Kelly's ear is the phantom popcorn vendor.

CHAPTER 11

I drive like a madman to get to O'Leary's as fast as possible.

A red light on West 9th Street, at the base of the Veteran's Memorial Bridge, catches me by surprise. I stomp on the brake pedal. The book with the fallen Eve cover, and the rumpled paper bag with Grandpop's camera, slide off the passenger's seat. I catch the bag before it hits the dashboard. The book thumps to the floorboard.

A parking space waits right in front of O'Leary's. Maybe my luck is changing. Or, maybe this is the sum total of my good luck today.

My insecurity grows, fertilized and watered by the debacles of the last three hours. I hit the figurative brakes now, vacillating, lighting a cigarette and pacing outside in the cold. After busting butt to get here to talk to Dad, I debate the wisdom of my choice. What can he add? But then, who else should I go to? Should I just drop the whole thing, the way Grandpop did? Do I go in to the bar and risk more ridicule...or not?

My cigarette tastes wrong, stale. Instinct tells me what to do, yet I can't seem to make even the simple decision to pitch a bad butt.

One decision seems stupid. Why do I choose to traipse up and down Frankfort Avenue, smoking in a frigid alley rather than in the warmth of the bar? The chill defeats my upturned collar and stiffens my exposed hands. Yet, here I am. My shivering may or may not be the result of the cold.

Misery, isolation, and indecision dog me.

I considered calling Erika to ask her to come along. Collecting her on the way back Downtown wouldn't have been a problem. I picked up the phone, but I didn't make the call. I still trust her to be objective, clear-headed, honest, and hardworking, to be professional. Do I trust my own professionalism now? Does she? *Can* she?

A couple hustles through the intersection only twenty feet away, up West 6th Street. The pair underscores my own solitude, my isolation. They move fast, unconcerned with anything not in their path. They march forward arm in arm, homing in on whatever their destination might be. Their expressions are set, unwavering.

The picture of that kind of commitment makes me shiver again.

The distraction brings me back on point. The book, the Kelly Cheesecake shot I slid under the book's cover, and the bag with the camera and flashbulbs all make me antsy. Good. The discomfort intensifies my commitment to find the truth. If only I was happier about my commitment.

I stub out my cigarette, toss the butt in the gutter, and yank the door open.

The narrow brick stairwell, so familiar to me, gives me a mournful and fearful impression again tonight. My imagination flies off to a faraway and unpleasant time and place. A bank of tobacco smoke layers the stairwell halfway down, the way mustard gas must have lingered in First World War trenches.

I understand why I'm thinking this way. I feel like I'm about to go into battle.

A few dozen professionals, lawyers and bankers squeezed into ill-fitting business suits, mill around the barroom. Mannion must have skipped his after-work boilermaker tonight. He's absent. Dad's absence bothers me more. Something made his reaction to our evidence seem promising. Or, did I imagine it?

I tramp straight to the bar and flag Dice Delaney down. "Three D, how're things by you?"

Delaney greets me with his customary, cursory glance. He treats me as he does everyone else, with minimal effort to connect. Dice makes me uncomfortable. I'm glad he keeps his distance.

"My dad here?"

His head twitches, barely, toward the door behind the far end of the bar.

"Thanks, D. Nice talking to you." He ignores me as I round the bar and head for the office.

Dad stoops over a huge metal desk in his dank office space. The chamber reminds me of a dungeon with less charm. Prohibition bootleggers built the cavern with an entrance to an escape tunnel. Or, so goes the tale. Dad stores his booze here. Beer kegs line one wall, and liquor crates are stacked from the cement floor to the low, wood-beamed ceiling. The kegs and crates make the brown-bricked vault look like a stockroom. Otherwise, with the single bare light bulb dangling over the desk, this is the perfect place for a Roaring Twenties mobster interrogation.

Dad gazes up at me. "Your grandfather started

me on a hobby when I was a kid. I never did get it. I'm afraid I'm starting to."

He stands up straight. Piles of inventory manifests, order forms, ledgers, and God alone knows what, cover his desk. Dad cleared a pocket out of the mess. A scrapbook lies open in the space, with the 1948 Indians' celebration picture pasted to the page. The familiarity of the image no longer comforts me. The original hangs framed and covered with special protective glass, out of direct sunlight, in Grandma's house. The shielded print looks new, as if taken only days ago. In Dad's scrapbook, time treats the champions brutally, wrinkling, drying, and fading them, and their memory.

A half-full bottle of Bushmills and a glass of ice hide amidst the paper mountains. Dad gives me a level stare. He strides out to the bar, returning with another glass of ice. A healthy dose of whiskey splashes into each glass. He hands one to me.

"I'm not having any, Dad."

"Maybe." Dad plops down on a rickety, wooden folding chair behind the desk. I ease on to its decrepit twin, tossing the print of Kelly on top of his scrapbook. He whistles softly. "Buddy, she is one fine looking—"

Dad stops short, staring at the photo. His jaw drops. He tears his attention from the photo, gaping at me with dwindling shock.

I nod.

Dad sits back, his chair swaying and protesting. "I was roaring drunk for sure by the end of the wake, but not at the start. I knew everybody who came. I never saw this guy."

"Neither did I, Dad. But check this out."

The library book lands with a thump next to the picture. The poses in each, Kelly's and Eve's, the popcorn vendor's and the serpent's, copy each other precisely.

Dad scans one image, then the other, and back. His head nods in recognition, then shakes in disbelief.

I pick up on his skepticism, and hand him the negative. "Fifth frame."

Dad's face loses expression and color when he holds the negative up to the light. "It's the same shot, no argument there. The guy's not on the negative."

"Dad, I swear I'm not good enough in a darkroom to do this."

"I believe you, Bud. What's in the bag?"

"Grandpop's camera."

He takes the Medalist, turns the relic over and over in his hands, and squints through the viewfinder. He even opens the back to inspect the insides.

He won't find anything unusual. I did the same thing myself and found nothing.

Dad lays the camera down. He slips the picture under the book's cover and puts all my materials on the floor next to the desk. "Now I need to show you something."

He jabs his finger at the open scrapbook. The celebrating Indians, the mournful Boston fans, and the vendor share the page with another clipping from the now defunct Cleveland Press. He taps the clipping with his finger. "You're the journalist. Pay attention to the tone of this one."

The story profiles Cuyahoga County's post-war influx of hard-working immigrants. This scrapbook page shows different facets of the city that I never linked before. The Indians were World Champions. The city of Cleveland boomed and prospered.

Dad was a baby in 1948. He didn't cut and paste these specific items here. Did Grandpop try to suggest a tie between a World Series title and civic prosperity? "Okay, I think I get it."

Dad carefully flips a few pages. Dust and decay, the airborne flecks of age, fly toward my nose, settling again on the scrapbook. The clipping and picture on the newly opened page are from the Indians' lost 1954 Series. On the opposite page Grandpop pasted another article. The headline reads, Steel Execs Dismiss Foreign Competition. The connection escapes me. "Baseball and steel?"

Dad downs half his drink. "Your grandfather figured I was old enough to do this with him. Only eight years old. What the hell did I care about the economy? But I knew baseball. I knew, everybody knew, the Tribe built a dynasty like the Yankees. And I guess adults assumed the city would keep riding high because we cranked out so much steel."

I stare at the yellowed press clipping, then back at the picture on the opposite page. The phantom popcorn vendor's toothy smile mocks me. Dad clears his throat. I see something on his face I don't like.

"There's more?"

"Oh, yeah."

Pages turn, dust billows and falls on another article with another picture attached. These are different. They cover a story not involving the Indians. In the picture, a car burns near youths who throw rocks and bottles. The shot wasn't taken recently in Lebanon, or on the West Bank. This picture was taken thirty years ago. The battle was fought not in some foreign country, but right here, in this city.

The photo's redundant caption describes the image. "The Hough Riots. This isn't one of Grandpop's."

"No. July, 1966. A fight over a glass of water turns into a week of rock-throwing, looting, and arson. Four dead. I was in 'Nam, and my home town was looking almost as scary. Hell, more Americans died on Cleveland streets than in 'Nam that week."

I study several box scores pasted on the opposite page. The Indians played at home during the Riots. They dropped four straight games to the Chicago White Sox, not that something so trivial mattered. A cold stone grows bigger and heavier in my gut.

They are connected. The city and the baseball team started crumbling together. Why?

Dad circles the desk to stand behind me. "Done?"

"You tell me. Am I?"

"No."

He turns several pages to another picture, one

that never appeared in the papers, the wider-angle print of Dad and me at the Old Timers Game. I flip the page. "Grandpop didn't put in a corresponding article. No disaster story."

Dad rests his hand on my shoulder. His voice sounds as dry as the scrapbook. "Doesn't need one. He may have had too many to choose from. What do you remember about the '70s?"

"Not much. I was pretty young."

Dad chuckles. He completes his circuit of the desk, dropping back on his dangerous folding chair. "Wish I could just not remember the '70s. You remember what was happening in this picture. I bet you remember what happened afterwards, too."

"The Old Timers blew their early lead and lost the game."

"Right. And?"

A few seconds of silence turn into a few more. Something ugly takes shape in my head.

"And half the stadium emptied before the regular game."

Dad knocks back the rest of his drink and pours himself a fresh one. "The whole city started emptying that decade. Two Cleveland mayors grabbed national headlines in the '70s. One set his hair on fire at a ribbon-cutting ceremony, the guy following him put the city in default. Cleveland turned into the go-to joke for every comic in the country. Everybody started pulling up stakes and leaving."

I flip a page or two, my head and fingers working independently of each other. The room begins feeling dangerous to me, as if the bricks would dislodge themselves and bury us here. Bricks dropping from above...The mental image puts the Hough Riots in mind, of things that are never meant to fly but sometimes do, of beer bottles and chairs and other projectiles launched in anger. "Wasn't there another riot, one at the stadium?"

"Ten-Cent Beer Night, yeah. That was in '74, too."

"There's no picture here."

"Your grandfather was home that night taking care of your grandmother. She was in bed with the flu. If he had been there..."

"He might have gotten hurt. Or, we might have one more picture of this thing. Gee, wonder how the riot started."

"Yeah, well, the geezer has cleared the joint out but good. No more riots at that stadium."

"Guess you haven't been to a Browns game lately, Dad."

Dad furrows his eyebrows until they almost touch. "You live in a cave? Modell made the announcement today he's moving the Browns to Baltimore. There *are* no more Browns. Not after this season."

My brain works hard to process this new civic disaster. Cleveland's image takes another hard hit. One less reason to visit the city means fewer visitors from out-of-town. Significant infusions of cash get yanked from the life support of an economy already close to flat-lining. I can only manage a question Dad can't answer. "You think this thing's involved?"

He shrugs, empty-eyed.

I hold out my glass for a refill, unaware of even having drunk the first round. "I couldn't find anything in literature…I mean, what is this guy?"

Dad snorts. "How the hell should I know?"

A parallel train of thought has me viewing Dad in a curious new light. "Hmm. Interesting."

"What?"

"Your history lesson surprises me. The detail, I mean."

"Why?"

"Something Kelly said the other day. About Mrs. O'Leary's cow on your sign."

"Yeah. Chicago. You think you're the first one to bring that up?"

I shrug. "So, why the inaccuracy?"

"The last owner was a guy named O'Leary. His name, his sign. I never bothered to change it."

"That's all?"

He gulps his drink, smacking his lips. "That's all. Sometimes the answer to a question is just that simple."

A thick silence descends, tainted only by Dad's patrons. The barroom buzz bleeds through the wall as if coming from the next block, not the next room. Neither of us moves. Neither of us dares get closer to the desk. The scrapbook and its contents hold us in our places.

"We should know what this thing is," Dad finally says. "This thing should have a name, and we ought to know it."

I consider our discoveries. I think about the pictures taken over the years, and the guise the curse assumes in them.

"Popcorn," Dad and I say in unison. We laugh out loud, the tension broken.

"Jeez, Dad. You think 'Popcorn' might be a little disrespectful?"

"I do. So what?"

I pull Kelly's picture from the library book. "I'm not quite sure what to do with this."

"What, the picture or the girl?"

"Both."

Dad leans back, his chair squeals. "I wish I could help you with that, Buddy."

Help me, or help yourself?

I shake the rude speculation away. The photo slips back under the cover. Of course, Kelly mesmerized Dad. I want to say she captivates every man she meets, but RJ claims immunity. He either doesn't know why she has no hold on him or chooses not to enlighten me. I can't tell which it is with him anymore.

"So. What are you gonna do?"

Dad's question jars me back to the issue.

"I'm going to take a seat in the pub, have a smoke, finish my drink and go home. I can't come up with a better plan for tonight."

I wander out to the barroom, settle on a stool furthest from the door, and light up. Dad and I just talked about the '70s. Was this pack of smokes made then? Unlike fine wine, dried tobacco does not age well. Three drags is enough. I find the nearest ashtray and grind the cigarette out. The foul flavor already did some damage. Now the Bushmills, a sweet liquid fire on my tongue, tastes almost as wretched. Have I caught a cold or flu bug? No symptoms present themselves, except for my faulty sense of taste. Things I normally enjoy suddenly offend my palate.

I push the unfinished whiskey away. "Hey Dice, can I get a club soda please?"

Delaney puts my soda in front of me. He leans closer and speaks in low, conspiratorial tones. "Your dad's not right."

"How so?"

"Haven't seen him this weird since 'Nam."

"He doesn't seem off to me."

"You don't play poker with him."

Delaney ambles to the other end of the bar, clearing empty beer bottles as he goes. The taciturn scarecrow just spoke a year's supply of words to me. *Strange.* But too many other unnatural experiences need processing right now. I flip a couple of dollars onto the bar. "Thanks, Dice."

He replies with a silent nod.

I climb the steps to the street, glad I didn't touch my second drink. Alcohol in doses as small as tonight's never muddles me. *Good.* With a clear head, I might make sense of the evidence Dad and I shared.

Then again, with a clear head I might conclude we are both nuts.

I climb into my car and light another cigarette without thinking. This smoke is as bad, as stale as the others were. I must be sick. Why else would my taste buds be in open rebellion?

I shift the car into drive. The long route home appeals to me. Drive time often helps when I'm restless. I cruise down West 6th Street toward Superior Avenue and the Veterans Memorial Bridge. Reflecting on Dad and Grandpop disturbs me. The family veterans. Such a big, important part of both their lives is almost unknown to me. Neither of them talked much about their service.

Grandpop's wartime experiences changed him profoundly, according to Mannion. What did Dad endure in Vietnam that changed him?

I glide to a stop at Superior Avenue and glance to my left. A dozen cars approach. The immediate threat keeps me from turning right on the red light. I face forward. A knot of people waits at a bus stop on the far side of the intersection. A solitary figure stands between the bus stop and the building behind it. My fingers clutch the steering wheel. I realize I was wrong.

The immediate threat won't be coming from my left. It'll be coming from right in front of me.

CHAPTER 12

My fingers drum on the steering wheel. This signal takes forever. Traffic trickles through the intersection. Most of the flow heads outbound toward the Veterans Memorial Bridge. I brace myself for what will happen if the light doesn't change soon. I'll run the red light if I have to.

Take a breath...

Popcorn stands alone next to an industry-inspired sculpture in front of the Lausche Building. The sculpture reminds me of a pile of leftover air conditioning duct, dumped out front and painted reddish-orange. The Lausche Building gives me goose bumps. The wedge-shaped structure looms sinister, menacing, like a giant black ax head cleaving through the city to the Cuyahoga River.

In front of the ax head waits Popcorn.

The cross-traffic signal turns yellow. A bus charges into the intersection. *Odd.* These old-style buses went out of service when I was in grade school. The daredevil bus driver wheels left on West Prospect. The clumsy vehicle heels dangerously, about to tip over. Tires squeal.

Hate to be a passenger on that bus.

The bus stops near the artistic heap of duct for a moment, then lumbers forward again. Popcorn staggers down its aisle. He shuffles toward the rear, steadying himself with a hand to a seatback. He sits sideways on the last bench, his face in profile.

My light turns green. I maneuver through the intersection, taking position behind the old motor coach. Popcorn must not see me. The view out the side window entrances him.

What grabs his attention? A parking garage? The colorless backs of office buildings? The city's architects might hide their redheaded stepchild here, if they had one. The entrance to the new Tower City Center is a jewel nestled amongst the bland. The bus doesn't stop there. A dozen people waiting for rides home seem not to mind. They continue staring down the street in my direction.

The traffic light at Ontario Street holds on green. The bus turns left. I follow, careful to keep my distance. I don't know how to be less conspicuous. Popcorn shifts in his seat, turning to face forward.

Good...I'm out of his line of sight now.

We stop for a red light at Euclid Avenue. My fingers tap on the steering wheel again. The ornate Soldiers and Sailors monument stands to my right. A dark hulk, the Old Stone Church, lurks ahead of me in its niche at the north end of the Square.

Strange. The tribute to Cleveland's Civil War veterans comforts me more than the church does. The Monument glows within bright floodlights, an intricate work of art. The church's illuminated black edifice seems ready to be surrounded by villagers brandishing torches and pitchforks. But these are surface impressions. I doubt the sanctuary of the Old Stone Church reeks of drunks' urine the way the inside of the Monument did for decades.

The light changes. Foul, black smoke billows from the back of the bus. I follow through the cloud of diesel fumes. We have looped around the back end of the Square, and now head east on Superior Avenue. The bus makes no stops for commuters. A few turn their heads as we pass, perplexed frustration on their faces.

We roll past East 9th Street, the demon and me, his tail. Downtown's skyscrapers dwindle. They give way to a few apartment high-rises and down-at-the-heels hotels. My surroundings become progressively grimmer past East 13th Street. We crawl through a land of cursed warehouses and shabby, low-rent office buildings.

Popcorn sits still, oblivious, facing forward.

I check the speedometer. We now cruise several miles above the posted limit. Our speed varies, not enough to draw attention, but never dipping down to "legal." Explaining to police that I'm trying to catch a bus wouldn't fly far. I tap my brakes.

The bus and I pass the Gothic St. Peter's church. We stop at a traffic light on East 21st Street. Why? The bus showed no sign of slowing for any reason until now and had the yellow light. Is the driver waiting for me to catch up? I hope not. I doubt it. The driver hasn't shown any sign he knows I'm here, and Popcorn has yet to peek my way.

A larger than life cartoon character, a goofy-looking pseudo-hippie, hangs on the side of a building across the street. The touch of humor lightens the gloomy cityscape. The Daffy Dan's T-Shirts caricature is a Cleveland icon. I consider contracting Dan to make dozens of shirts with the picture of Popcorn whispering sour nothings in

Kelly's ear.

Would anybody understand? Would they care?

The light changes, and the low-speed chase continues across the bridge over I-90. If I had any sense, I would take the highway west back home.

I guess I haven't got any sense.

The buildings and lots get seedier and weedier past East 30th Street. A few stray trees dress the area about as effectively as covering a naked sumo wrestler with spray paint. This area could be so much better if only it hadn't given up on itself.

Funny. Why blame inanimate buildings for their decline rather than the people inhabiting them?

We approach a railroad trestle spanning Superior. The trestle's scary-looking, crumbling, concrete columns make three narrow portals. The bus shoots through the right-hand portal. A lesser, or more careful, driver might have slowed to squeeze through. My Skyhawk is much smaller than the behemoth ahead of me. I tap the brakes anyway.

The bus turns right on East 55th Street without signaling. Great. All Popcorn has to do now is turn his head to his right. I'm in luck. He continues facing forward. Is he talking with the driver? I can't tell in the inadequate wash from the streetlights and from this distance.

Talking with the driver from the back of the bus? He'd sit closer to the front, wouldn't he? Why doesn't he check back my way?

The bus approaches a traffic signal a mile and a half down bleak East 55th. A cluster of old African American men to my right distracts me. They mill around the sidewalk in front of the Fellowship Baptist Church, taking turns shaking hands and patting one another on the shoulder. The group disperses. All but one of them heads around the corner to their cars, I assume. But the straggler stares transfixed at the oncoming bus. He steps toward the curb.

But the rotund, white-crowned man doesn't want a ride. He shakes a hammy fist at the passing bus, his whole body quaking as if electrified. Popcorn jumps up from the back bench and presses his face to the window. I can't tell what's happening. I don't like the tension between the two of them.

The bus lurches into a sudden left at the light. I glance at the man on the sidewalk. He wears old, faded, but not shabby, clothes, poor but dignified. He stares back at me. His expression changes abruptly from fierce defiance to…recognition? But I have never seen him before.

Another stranger who somehow knows me. Terrific.

I trail the bus on a narrow street not unlike Grandma's. I don't bother with the street signs. The markers almost don't matter to me. They should. I'm not an East Sider and still need to find my way back home. Knowing which street I'm on might help. Instead, I glance at the strange man in my rear-view mirror once more.

He stands on the corner, gaping at me.

The bus makes another sudden left turn at a traffic signal about two blocks ahead. I gun the engine. A citation doesn't matter to me anymore than the street signs do. As I race to the light, I decide to cut my stupid behavior in half and take a quick peek at the street signs. I'm on Lexington Avenue, crossing East 65th Street. The bus turns the next corner.

League Park. Well, how about that!

I ease off the gas, drifting to a stop across the street from the old ballpark's ticket gate, one of the few parts of the structure still standing. The grandstands and most of the brick walls are long gone. So are the outfield fence, the clubhouse, the dugouts...there's little left but the grass and a makeshift infield. This proud place hosted the World Series' first grand slam and only unassisted triple play, as well as Babe Ruth's 500th home run. All that survives now is this forlorn, neglected building. Most folks today might mistake the ticket gate for an undersized, abandoned train depot.

The old bus idles beside the site. We have apparently reached the end of the line.

Has Popcorn been here all this time? What about Municipal Stadium, where all the real disasters took place?

The bus's hydraulic door *fooshes* open. Popcorn makes his way to the front and descends the steps to the pavement.

I fumble around the passenger's seat for a moment, pulling the Medalist and a flashbulb from the paper bag. Then I roll my window down. Once I snap the flashbulb in place, I bring the camera up to my eye.

Popcorn turns slowly to face me.

I push the button. The flash floods the street corner, the ticket booth, the back of the bus and the phantom in bluish lightning. My eyes adjust more quickly than at O'Leary's. I'm both glad and sorry for that. What I see tells me a lot. Popcorn's deliberate turn tells me he has been aware I was here. He expected me to take the picture. He doesn't fear me, doesnt worry about me catching up to him tonight.

His crooked, serpentine smile tells me he's led me into a trap.

Movement, a kind of shuffling at the far edge of the park, catches my attention. I squint across the open field into the darkness—but that's what seems to be moving, the darkness itself. Shapes move within the shadows, shapes made of even darker shadow. Darkness shaped like men. Shadow men rise near the back yards of houses surrounding the park. I almost laugh. They rise as if interrupted while doing push-ups. The shadows begin forming a column of lines four abreast.

The gathering shades hold my fascination until more of them appear much closer to me. Shadows stir behind the ticket booth's façade. They amble around the interior, passing back and forth behind the window casements. The transparent figures quickly begin spilling out through the missing and broken window panes. They squeeze through the door's cracks. Then they start their own column on the sidewalk.

I've seen enough.

I slam the gearshift into "reverse" and stomp on

the gas pedal. Tires squeal. My car lurches backward. I lunge forward. The seatbelt strains to keep me from the windshield. I don't check the rearview mirror. I hope no one's crossing the street. The Skyhawk screeches backwards through the intersection and about fifty feet past. I shift into "drive." Gears grind in protest. I ignore them, wheel left, and gun the engine. The front wheels jump up on the sidewalk and right off again.

No pedestrians, thank God.

I check my mirrors. The shadows are coming. The columns follow fifty feet behind me, trotting in step. They're keeping pace. Gaining. I close my window and speed up...forty-five miles per hour, forty-nine. I ignore Lexington's dimness. Anyone wandering the street will have to stay out of my way.

Shadow men run beside my car, just beyond my windows.

What the hell!

I wheel hard right at East 55th. The old man still stands on the corner, yelling at me and jabbing his finger upward at the streetlight. A single word fights its way through my closed windows.

"Light!"

Light...I need to stay in the light!

My mind races. Superior Avenue is a block or so away. Mistake, too dark. Carnegie Avenue is a better bet. I rule Euclid Avenue out, too. But Carnegie is behind me...

I make a snap decision. A sudden tight U-turn reverses my direction. I barrel between the pursuing shadows.

Adrenaline shoots through my system. My senses speed up, everything around me seems to freeze. I drive more than ten miles over the limit but the gap between the old man at Lexington and me closes at an excruciating crawl. The man's expression takes an eternity to change. His surprise turns to confusion, then concern...and comprehension.

He understands my plan.

The realization gives me no comfort. If he can figure out what I'm doing, so can these creatures. A glance in my mirror confirms my fear. The shadows charge toward me.

Why am I running from shadows?

My head processes the weird, paranoid question as I blast past the old man. These shadows are doing things shadows shouldn't be able to do. What else are they capable of? I don't want to find out. This bothers me. I should investigate this unknown and write about my discoveries. An investigative reporter investigates—a journalist writes. What kind of teacher am I if I don't apply my own lessons?

A live one!

The signal at Chester Avenue turns yellow. I tap my brakes on instinct. The street lamp nearest the intersection goes out as I slow. Streetlights turn off randomly like this to conserve energy. The clever but odd practice strikes me as really inconvenient right now.

A shadow catches up to my passenger window. The thing's face has no features, and I see through it to the convenience store behind. I lunge, locking the passenger door.

Idiot. This is a SHADOW!

I flick the dome light switch. Nothing happens.

I'll trade or scrap this old beater before I change that bulb...

The shadow's arm passes through the closed window, reaching across the passenger's seat. The temperature drops twenty degrees. The sour, unmistakable stench of rotting, dead animal assaults my nostrils. My stomach quivers and flops.

I gun the engine again.

Light! Find light!

The car pitches forward. My shoulder blades dig into the seat. The shadow swats at me, unaffected by the sudden acceleration. Bile rises in my throat.

Plan B—steer toward the next lamp post. We swerve into a pool of light. The shadow shrinks back, like a hand from an open flame. The stink evaporates in a puff of gray smoke. The vile apparition falls away from my car, rejoining its ranks.

I've shaken the uninvited hitchhiker off the side of my car, but not off my tail. The fractured darkness keeps pace fifty yards behind. The man-shaped wraiths flit from the edge of one pool of streetlight to the next. The darkness keeps coming after me.

Carnegie!

I yank the wheel right. The car almost rolls over. The left tires squeal, the right tires threaten to leave the pavement. The Skyhawk stays upright, speeding forward. My gut turns to stone. Cold sweat coats my palms and forehead. I peer ahead down Carnegie Avenue, assessing the light.

Not exactly bright here, either.

Breaking the law goes against my grain, but I hesitate only long enough to peek into my mirrors. The phantasms have gained on me.

The gas pedal makes a loud slapping sound hitting the floor.

The crumbling cityscape whizzes by. Fragments of theories and ideas pop into my head. They dissipate just as quickly. Questions dodge their answers. A goal, the one conscious goal I didn't have until just a second ago, hits me with clarity and force.

Get to the Jake.

The faster I drive, the more urgent the goal becomes. Jacobs Field and Gund Arena are almost always well lit. *These things couldn't survive near the Jake. Could they?*

The reality is, I don't know. But if I don't get to the ballpark, what I do or don't know might not matter.

The view in the mirror makes me shake all over. The streetlights between the shadows and me go out as the columns approach. They light up again as the phantoms pass them. The shadow men are somehow creating a wave of blackness, surfing the dark crest to my rear bumper!

I suck in a ragged breath, taking another glance in the mirror. Only the streetlights turn off. Billboards and the odd office light remain lit.

Jacobs Field still seems my best bet.

I bump my speed up to over sixty miles an hour. Any faster and the potholes on Carnegie Avenue will blow out my tires or snap an axle. The last rut almost cost me a couple of teeth.

I fly past East 22nd Street just as the signal turns red. The entire intersection loses power. Shadows run only two car lengths behind me. The Jake seems an awfully long way off.

At this speed, I'll be in the vicinity in less than a minute. A minute can be a lifetime, especially on this stretch of Carnegie. Downtown's new clubs don't reach this far south. They are all on Prospect and Euclid Avenues a block or two north. Poorly lit buildings brood here. I pass more deserted office buildings and the Gray's Armory, a demented cousin of the Old Stone Church.

East 9th Street approaches, the edge of the area I need. Light washes over me. The Jake is indeed well enough lit to keep the shadows back. I apply enough brake to slow to the speed limit without throwing the car into a skid and make a right turn. The ballpark stands across the street to my left. I keep as close to the park's ambient light as I can. A check behind allows me to breathe again. The light stopped the shadows cold.

The blackness of the Erie Street Cemetery, one of the oldest in the city, and rumored to be haunted, yawns to my right. I consider crossing the double yellow lines. Should I risk oncoming traffic to get away from the cemetery and closer to the ballpark's light? No. I'm stunned I haven't already been jailed.

Nothing moves amongst the ancient headstones beyond the cemetery's stone arches anyway. I'm safe now.

Right.

East 9th glows, better lit than I'd hoped. I'll think about what just happened in a minute or two. My fingers need convincing to loosen their death grip on the steering wheel first. A car vacates a parking spot in front of one of the new restaurants the sports complex spawned. I pull over to take a longer look behind me.

Everything appears normal at first glance. But a line of intense darkness straddles East 9th at Carnegie. The line doesn't move. Stillness is the shadows' camouflage. They blend into their surroundings, drawing no attention to themselves, making themselves invisible…that is, invisible except to someone who knows what to look for.

I shiver despite myself and pull back on to East 9th. The heat blasting out the dashboard vents causes the sweat on my forehead, I tell myself. The weak lie never takes hold.

I speed toward Prospect Avenue. This section of East 9th seems darker, less populated, and so, less illuminated. A left turn on Prospect leads me to a corridor of bustling restaurants and pubs, and more importantly, light. The activity on Prospect calms me somehow. My eyes snap to the rear-view mirror. Nothing but traffic moves behind me. That's fine. But it occurs to me I could spend the rest of my life looking over my shoulder this way.

I'm not going to do that.

I've driven Downtown streets so often my car practically leads me home while I consider what just happened and what to do about it. Pounding down a couple of strong drinks tops the list of what I'd like to do. O'Leary's comes to mind as the most likely spot. All I stock in my apartment is beer. That will do for tonight. A beer or two in a familiar and brilliantly lit place...

A dogleg left puts me back on Superior Avenue, and the Veterans Memorial Bridge. I can't help peeking into the mirror. Still nothing. I-90 presented an option on two separate occasions. I was too focused on getting to the ballpark to even consider the highway. Did the shadows herd me to Jacobs Field?

Doesn't matter.

A realization dawns on me. I have to map the rest of my way home. I didn't consider the whole trip. The West Shoreway seems my best option. The entrance ramp at West 25th Street lies just at the far end of the bridge. Detroit Avenue has too many bleak and dim stretches, too many traffic signals that might not cooperate. I want to get home, find as many hundred-watt bulbs as quickly as I can, and burn them all night long.

I have the green light at the foot of the bridge, and angle slightly right. What a crazy intersection! To the left is West 25th. The road straight ahead leads to Detroit Avenue. Ninety degrees right lies the way to the Flats. A hard right gets me to the Superior Avenue viaduct. Any new visitors to Cleveland should avoid this intersection at all costs unless they want to get lost in a hurry—

The streetlights on every corner of the intersection go out simultaneously. I look up to the dead lamps, then back to the street. Twin balls of light from nowhere barrel toward me. I work the stick shift and stomp on the gas. The Skyhawk's balky clutch hesitates, the gears spin and grind, but the car doesn't move. I cringe. The sound of a giant, crumpling beer can engulfs me. Glass explodes into my face.

Everything goes completely black.

CHAPTER 13

I wish the neighbors would stop using their leaf blower at this ridiculous hour. I can't sleep...

Wait. I live in an apartment. My neighbor is Tania. She doesn't own a leaf blower.

I can't sleep, but I can't seem to open my eyes either, until I force them open. Small blobs of light float around on a black canvas in front of me. I swipe thick, gooey sweat from my forehead. My hand comes away covered in sticky brownish-red.

"Don't do that!" A commanding voice booms at me over the noise. My hand stops mid-swipe as firemen work to pry me from my car. The noise isn't a leaf blower.

Power saw. Oh! This guy's got the Jaws of Life. Never seen 'em in action before. Cool...

I blink.

Two faces take up space on either side of me. They came during my blink, I guess. The bodies attached to the faces wear Emergency Medical Service uniforms. The EMS technicians drift back and forth from my head to my feet as I lie on the ground.

Hmm. I'm out of the car.

"I can't get this thing on."

"We'll need to straighten it."

Their words make no sense to me. I prop myself up on one elbow. My right side hurts like fury. The paramedics bend over my left leg, which seems to have an extra knee where my thigh ought to be. The extra knee bends at an horrific and unnatural angle.

189

Uh-oh. <u>That's</u> not good…

Someone pushes on my chest, pinning me to the ground. A faint but unpleasant sound, a muffled crackling, drifts up from my thigh. I understand now why I'm being held down. The "thing" they couldn't get on was a splint. The "it" needing to be straightened to get the splint on was my corkscrewed leg. I writhe, twisting toward the paramedic holding my shattered leg's ankle. Excruciating pain shoots up my thigh and over from my right side simultaneously. My eyes squeeze shut…

"I don't smell alcohol."

One of the paramedics, a thick-set, broad-shouldered guy, a linebacker without a helmet, holds an I.V. above my head.

Who put me on this gurney, and when?

"Have you been drinking, sir?" The Linebacker's partner prods my chest with an ice-cold stethoscope.

Voices, nearby but out of my sight, bark like confused bloodhounds.

"Where's the other driver?"

"Good question. Jeez!"

"Run the plates. Might be stolen."

"Somebody walked away from this?"

"How the hell should I know?"

"Sir, can you tell me what happened?" A police officer, one of the Barking Bloodhounds, hovers over my gurney, walking beside the stretcher on the way to a waiting ambulance. He scribbles something in a notepad.

I'm getting a ticket now?

"Shadow." My voice is raspy. My mouth moves with numb sluggishness.

"What?"

"Cold shadow. Stinks."

The Bloodhound elbows the Linebacker. "Booze?"

The paramedic jerks his head toward me. The cop inspects my face. He nods, tucking his pen into his shirt pocket. I want to touch my face, but I am too tired to raise my hands. I would rather sleep now anyway. My eyes close, but I'm already dreaming an unpleasant dream...

The gurney shakes without warning. The big paramedic stumbles, almost falling on me. He grabs a metal bar above his head.

Oh. We're in the ambulance.

"Shocks," I slur. "You need new shocks."

The paramedic chuckles. "Yeah. But you need a whole new car."

"Wanted to trade up anyway."

The paramedic snorts and laughs again. I don't see his partner. He must be driving. Better than me, I hope, though he seems to hit every pothole. My body twitches, reacting to every hole, bump, pebble, the odd dog or pedestrian, or any other thing in his path...

"Shadows."

The paramedic shines a bright pen light into my eyes. "Cold smelly shadows, right? I heard you tell the cop. What about 'em?"

"Your driver running 'em all over?"

The big man frowns. "You took a pretty good crack upside the head, I guess."

I guess I did.

The ambulance makes a left turn faster than I'd like. The driver knows what he's doing, I tell myself. Still, in the back of my mind I hope the vehicle doesn't tip the way the old bus almost did—

The old bus!

I try to sit up, to escape. Someone buckled me to this stretcher. I twist my body and jerk my hand up to try to break the strap. Pain in my leg makes me stop. Did someone just whack my knee with an aluminum baseball bat? A strange sound assaults my ears. I realize after a moment the sound is my own howl.

An over-sized paw pushes my chest back to the gurney. "I wouldn't do that. We're almost to the ER."

I surrender, but not willingly. My mangled leg will keep me from getting far. I don't care. I want to run, or limp, or belly crawl to safety.

The ambulance door opens, Mr. Linebacker clambers out. I'm jealous of him. I can't climb or walk, I can only watch him do it. Popcorn will probably show up in a few seconds, wearing the same EMS uniform. He'll have me. What will he do with me?

But someone else helps the big paramedic pull the gurney out. A neck brace keeps me from turning my head to see. These are the only two guys wearing the EMS blue as far as I can tell. The other paramedic, Linebacker's helper, tall, sandy-haired and young, must be the driver.

The paramedics push me toward the hospital entrance. I relax, closing my eyes again.

"Buddy." A stethoscope dangles under the familiar face looming above me.

"Hey, RJ, how's things by you?"

He shakes his head, frowning. "What happened?"

"Out cruising." My tongue is heavy and dry, and unresponsive.

"Guess so."

Scattered fragments of an accident come back to me. I remember the wreck taking place in the chaotic intersection at West 25th and Detroit, and the West Shoreway, and the viaduct...RJ's presence baffles me. He's at the wrong hospital.

He must recognize my bafflement. "You're at Metro General."

"Lutheran was a block away."

"Yeah, but our ER is equipped for this kind of thing. Lutheran's isn't."

"That bad?"

"You won't be running a marathon any time soon. And I'd stay away from mirrors for a couple of weeks. Don't sweat it. We've got an excellent plastics guy. You'll take a while to heal up, so until then..."

"Frankenstein?"

"A little bit, yeah."

RJ forces a grin through a mask of concern, patting me on the shoulder. His clipboard taps against the palm of his hand. He strides away to give the scoop to a doctor in a long white coat. They both look my way. Their low murmurs carry across the room. The doctor glances at RJ's clipboard. He says something. More mumbling, whispering. Secrets. I want to know, but I don't want to know.

My friend and caretaker returns. "We're gonna take you to ICU as a precaution."

"Head injury."

"Yeah. We want to check for any internal injuries, too, make sure nothing clots near your broken femur and turns into a pulmonary embolism."

"Heart attack?"

"Sort of. We want to keep an eye out for a while. Don't worry."

"Easy for you."

An orderly or nurse, I can't tell the difference, wheels me to a space in the Intensive Care Unit. The room is bright. My entire body aches, but I'm sure if I close my eyes the pain will go away.

I give it a try.

Enough light bathes the ICU to produce a ghostly gray through my closed eyelids, a calm, gray nothingness. I'm grateful. The ICU appears to be safe, or at least safer. I relax. Tension flushes out of my jaws and shoulders.

I stir for a moment when a nurse jabs a needle into my arm. "Morphine drip," she says. "You'll thank me later."

I close my eyes. The new, gray world I inhabit on this side of my eyelids gives me a sense of peace, while the place I just left teeters on pandemonium. The loudspeaker crackles the terse words "code blue." A nurse orders her staff to bring a crash cart, "Stat!" Urgency swirls in the waking world, a strange hybrid of confidence and panic. The medical staff's years of experience can't completely erase the desperation of their work.

Part of me wonders if the crash cart is for me. I can't muster up anything more than a passing curiosity.

Morphine drip. Morphine's addictive. Will I want *to thank the nurse later?*

My gray world brightens. Someone turned on more lights...I'm not alone. I open my eyes. My surroundings make more sense. A burly man in dark blue scrubs helps RJ kick at the bed's wheels, I suppose to unlock them. I note RJ's red-eyed, stubble-faced exhaustion. "You look like hell."

Both RJ and his burly blue buddy laugh out loud. My friend doesn't laugh long. "Let's get some pictures of your leg."

"Pictures. X-rays."

"Yeah." The orderly leads the bed through the hallway. RJ pushes from behind. He leans down close to my ear. "You weren't drinking, were you?"

"Went back to O'Leary's. Only had one."

"Didn't think so. Nobody smelled any alcohol. Why'd you go back to O'Leary's?"

I'm feeling lots of real physical pain despite the morphine. But my mind is still clear enough to realize I don't know who I can trust. I never imagined I would ever mistrust RJ. Of course, the morphine gives me pause.

Is this drug-induced paranoia? And if not?
"Doesn't matter why."

The orderly bumps a square metal pad on the wall with his butt. The doors to the Radiology Department swing open. I am quickly rolled on to a metal table the staff must keep stored in a meat locker. The radiologist shrugs in apology. In a few moments I'm rolled onto my gurney again and wheeled back to my space in ICU.

RJ turns to leave. He smirks with both concern and amusement. "Get some rest tonight. I'll call your dad. See you tomorrow."

I understand his amusement after a while. He must have known I would get no rest at all overnight. Assorted nurses wake me several times, waiting, I'd bet, until I'm at the edge of sleep. They check my eyes with a penlight, ask me to move my tongue, and ask me to smile. I find the process bizarre, especially the smiling. I answer questions, too, telling them who I am and where I am. After the seventh tongue-lolling, eye-rolling, smiling interrogation, I realize they are checking for brain damage.

I'm too drugged to care and drift away on a bank of high-grade pharmaceuticals...

Daylight fights its way through a thin sheen of grime on the window. My father stands in the hallway outside the ICU. He plants his feet wide apart, as if bracing himself against a load being heaved on his shoulders. A doctor holds an x-ray under one arm. He speaks to Dad in a low monotone. I can't hear what's said. Dad hangs his head for a moment. I guess the doctor told him something he didn't like. Dad holds a paper grocery bag that weighs his hand low down his side. The doctor says something over his shoulder. Someone else is present but hidden beyond the doorway.

The doctor ambles into the room. Dad follows. He appears pale and ill. He greets me with a strained, dry voice. "Buddy, this is Dr. Hurth."

The doctor corrects Dad's pronunciation. "The 'h' at the end is silent." He does not wait for a smart remark from me, to Dad's obvious relief. "I've just been talking with your father and your girlfriend."

She's not my girlfriend. She's my student.

Dad jumps in. "She stepped out for a smoke. She'll be in to visit with you in a minute." His tone is flat, not grave, but not reassuring, either.

"Kelly's here?"

Dr. Hurth clears his throat, the universal signal for getting down to business. "This is our situation." He holds the x-ray up to a fluorescent ceiling light. I stare at the film, mute, dumbfounded. The doctor drones on, oblivious to my reaction. "You've got a pretty bad 'green twig' snap, starting a half inch or so above the knee here, going about four inches up the femur. With so much of the femur damaged a knee replacement this soon is risky."

I cringe. *Knee replacement?* "What's the danger?"

"If things went wrong, I'd need to amputate."

Dad lowers his head. He shifts his weight from foot to foot, the paper bag bumping against his thigh.

The gravity of the situation fights against the morphine for space in my brain. "What are my options?"

"We can try to patch up the bone, hold the femur together with a metal plate and screws. If it heals, and if necessary, we can talk about a knee replacement."

"If?"

"I can't put the bone shards together like a jigsaw puzzle. Doing so would require separating them from their blood vessels. The damaged section would end up as dead bone. I'll eyeball the femur and mush the pieces together instead, as best I can, to get the plate on."

"Doesn't sound too hopeful."

Dr. Hurth beams, supremely confident. "Actually, the 'ifs' are legal coverage. I think it's the best way to go. I'm eighty-five percent sure the procedure will work out okay."

"Why a knee replacement?"

Dad blanches, failing to hide his discomfort. I appreciate the effort. The x-ray is a mess, and I haven't seen the rest of me in a mirror yet. Still, his reaction seems extreme.

Dr. Hurth tucks the x-ray back under his arm and explains. "You'll never get full range of motion in the damaged knee no matter what. It's a mechanical impossibility. How much you'll be able to do on that leg is a question I can't answer, but you will be limited. There's also a high probability you'll suffer arthritis in that knee, more likely sooner than later. Short term prognosis, you'll walk, eventually without a cane. Long-term, without a knee replacement, you may end up needing another person's help."

Now I understand Dad's squirming. A twinge in a different area brings up another concern. "My right side…"

"Oh, the side's nothing," the intact and healthy doctor tosses off. "Cracked ribs, probably caused by your seat belt. Didn't the air bag deploy?"

"Didn't have one. Old car." Dr. Hurth clucks his tongue and shakes his head. I hate to ask, but I need the answer. "The long-term prognosis…not so 'long term'?"

"No. I don't believe so."

Dad avoids my gaze. I'll get no help from him on this. "So, what's the question? When can you screw the plate in?" My own words paint a picture in my head that makes me gnash my teeth.

"Day after tomorrow. We'll be done before lunch."

Dr. Hurth wheels and marches from the room without another word.

Dad shuffles closer to the bed. He seems embarrassed, his voice tentative. "How do you feel?"

"How do I look?"

"A little beat up."

"Yeah."

He pulls Grandpop's camera from the paper bag. "Found this in the wreck, on the floor under the dash."

I turn the camera over in my hands, expecting a

few nicks, some scratches, a dent or crack or something. I examine the sides, the back, the bottom, the lens.

Nothing.

My father's face is a blank mask. "There's a used flash bulb here. Take some more pictures?"

"Nothing interesting."

"Hope not. I'll bet you forgot the camera was empty, didn't you?"

My groan tells Dad he would have won that bet.

He juts his jaw and frowns, taking no pleasure in the knowledge. His voice lowers. "Anything you want to tell me?"

"What do you want to hear, Dad?"

"The truth."

"No, I don't think you want to hear that. Not really."

Judging by his wince, I'd guess I struck a nerve. I didn't think I would. He struggles for a moment before speaking more deliberately, and with more true emotion, than usual.

"I don't pretend to know everything. There's a lot I don't get, I admit. Like, I didn't understand why your grandfather tried so hard to get me interested in photography when I got home from 'Nam."

"He did?"

"Yeah, and no. I mean, I guess he was trying to hook me on photography in general. Maybe he wanted me interested in his work specifically. Maybe I just didn't get it."

"When did all this happen?"

The wheels spin. Dad's mind works back

through something painful. The process plays out on his face. His eyes narrow. After a moment, he nods, his jaw set. "He and I talked over dinner about two months after I got back to the world. I was telling him about Mai Ley."

"The massacre? You were at Mai Ley?"

He nods again and brings his gaze up to meet mine. "Yeah. I used the word 'evil' when I told him about what happened 'cause that's how I felt at the time. Then I started thinking, that's just the way people have always been. Human nature's a mix of good and bad, no need to get too judgmental. We can't help what nature puts in us. Anyway, I only started to think that way later. But when I talked with him, I called it evil. He smiled at me like he knew what I was talking about, said he wanted to teach me how to use this thing." Dad stared down at the Medalist, regret shading his words. "I went another way. Tended bar for O'Leary, bought the place a few years later. Did some pretty stupid crap. I never really listened to my dad."

He opens his mouth. He seems to want to want to say more. I wish he would. I'm no longer sure of our conversation in his office. Are we weighing all the evidence, complete or not, and coming up with the same conclusions?

But Dad says nothing.

Someone edges into the doorway behind him. Dad rests his hand on my shoulder. "I'll stop in tomorrow." He takes the camera and the bag and leaves, pausing for a moment at the door.

Kelly approaches, gawking at the mess I am. A

wave of cigarette smoke corrupts her Chantilly. She only glances at my face. I have still not seen a mirror, and this moment gives me a chill. She stands beside my bed, her eyes drifting from my face to the lump my mangled leg makes of the bed cover. Her gaze wanders back up to my chest, the only part of me that doesn't show overt damage. Her lips move, trying to form words. None come out. The silence grows, becoming more awkward by the second.

Something besides the obvious is wrong.

I clear my throat and try to lighten the mood. "Gargoyles aren't all that ugly. To be honest I think they're kind of—"

"I can't do this."

The interruption surprises me. A big red banner runs up my mind's flagpole. I want to diffuse the situation, but I don't know what, exactly, the situation is. I probe with as much care as I can muster. "You don't need to do anything. RJ says they have a good plastic surgeon. I won't scar too much."

"I'm not ready to be a nurse." She refuses to make eye contact with me, gluing her eyes to my chest.

My head swims. *She can't mean what I think I am hearing from her.*

"You won't need to be a nurse."

Her answer is resolute, her voice flat and hard. "You don't know that. The doctor said…" Her voice trails off, leaving a silence thick as tar hanging in the space between us. The silence deepens with each heartbeat, every second lasts an hour. After what seems a millennium she sniffles, checks her watch and turns her back on me. "I'm sorry, Buddy. I just can't. Good luck."

With that, Kelly walks out.

A doorbell-like sound dings from the nurses' station. Someone's moan of pain reaches my ears, not quite muffled by the mumbles of other people in conversation. Papers shuffle. Laughter bursts out, brief and embarrassed. The sounds of the ICU clarify and intensify but seem disconnected from reality. Nothing around me moves. Time comes to a complete stop. I tell myself I just experienced an hallucination brought on by the highest-grade pharmaceuticals, but I cannot escape the truth of the moment.

Kelly just dumped me.

My brain hurts. I try to make sense of my sudden and shocking loss. Kelly stood in the hall with Dad and Dr. Hurth. I assume she heard the whole prognosis. Some challenges will present themselves, today and in the future, as the doctor told me. So, she's not up to helping me meet those challenges, to be a nurse, in her own words. Is she too young to take on such responsibility? Too scared, too self-centered? I can't bring myself to accept any of these excuses, her pessimism, or her fear of the mere possibilities.

A memory, a conversation pops up inside me. Grandma's usually comforting voice unnerves me now.

"She won't stand with you."

I am wrong. Everybody is right about Kelly, and I am wrong.

Two nurses come in. They chatter about this and that as they move me from ICU to a room. I miss most of what they say. The room transfer flies by without my awareness of most of the process. Kelly's visit crowds everything else out. The moment repeats itself again and again and again.

They deposit me in a bland room, alone with thoughts that dog me into the evening. Something about Kelly's behavior strikes me as not right. I wish I knew if Dad said something to her on his way out. If so, what did he say? I wonder if anything he said contributed to her bailing out on me. On one hand, I wish Dad had stayed, though I doubt his presence would have helped. He was in a hurry to get out. He hates hospitals with a passion...

She checked her watch.

The wall clock opposite me confirms a growing suspicion. Six o'clock. My new ex-girlfriend visited during her lunch break instead of spending a significant amount of time with me after work. She left herself the barest minimum of time, so she could claim an excuse for leaving, if she needed one.

Something about this is important. I don't know what, or why. My eyelids droop...

My eyes blink open. I remember why I'm here and panic—I forgot to ask for the light to be left on. My shattered ribs prevent me reaching the reading lamp above my head. The pain yanks a grunt from me.

An outline fills the doorway. The figure is not a shadow. My panic intensifies.

Popcorn is here for me...No, he wasn't so big. But couldn't he be anything he wants?

The shape steps into the room. I fumble around but can't find the button to the nurses' station. My breath catches in my throat. The shape approaches my bed.

"Let me get that for you."

CHAPTER 14

The reading lamp pops on. Light bathes the broad, aged face hovering above my bedside. A battered, unbuttoned, brown topcoat reveals a faded, blue cardigan, and black shirt with a clerical collar.

I remember him...

The old preacher smiles. "Gabriel Newhouse. You're John Cullen. John Francis Cullen."

"Buddy's fine." My memory clicks the moment I introduce myself. "East 55th and Lexington?"

"In front of the Fellowship Baptist Church, yeah. Surprised you made it this far, the way you drive."

I laugh despite myself, which brings excruciating pain in my side.

Reverend Newhouse holds up his hands and frowns. "Sorry about that."

"Not a problem."

My mind reels. This visit surprises me in many ways. Questions arise, so many of them. My visitor grins, waiting patiently. Despite failing to organize my head, I decide to fire away. "How'd you find me?"

"I had a hunch you'd end up in a hospital. Called around 'til I found which one."

"Makes sense. Why?"

The reverend dodges my question with one of his own. "Why were you way over in my neck of the woods?"

I try to evade, caught off guard. Not everyone needs to think I am a lunatic. "Journalism. I had a story to follow up on."

"On what? Emergency rooms? Near death experiences?"

"No, not exactly."

A thick-fingered hand sweeps over me, head to foot. The reverend stifles a chuckle. "Looks like you got a little more than you bargained for then."

"Could say so, yeah."

"Can I get you anything?"

"I'm dying for a smoke. No offense, Reverend. I'm aware those things kill."

"Son, only God decides when each of us dies. What's up to us is what we do with our bodies 'til such time as we're called home."

"I didn't choose this. This wasn't up to me."

"No. And you ain't dead yet, either. You've got more choices to make."

In my head, memories bump into the reverend's observations. The collisions create new questions. Nervousness creeps in as I remember his reaction to me in front of the church, his expression. He recognized me, a stranger. "We've never met. Am I right?"

He pulls an armchair closer to the bed, his face breaking into a wry smile. "Not you and me, no. I've forgotten a face or two. All part of getting to be an old man. But last night I saw Irish Jimmy Cullen, young and scared. Just like in the Pacific."

"You fought on the *Enterprise* with Grandpop?"

The smile dims a touch. "Yeah, sure did. The Navy put us Negroes—that's what we were before we were African-Americans—put us in, uh, less prestigious posts." He chuckles at his own understatement. "I was a baker's assistant, below decks a lot of the time. Almost invisible, 'cept to your grandfather and a few others. Irish Jimmy was good people. 'Scuse me." He pulls a handkerchief from his pocket and blows his nose.

"Sorry I missed you at the funeral."

"Ah, I was getting over a case of bronchitis. Mrs. Newhouse had me locked up at home." His hearty laugh ends in a cough.

I smile, realizing, and not caring, that a few hours ago I wondered when I might smile again, if ever. This gentle old man reminds me in many ways of Grandpop. But Reverend Newhouse is not Grandpop. He's a stranger.

"Excuse me, Reverend, no offense. Why are you here?"

He leans forward. His jaw sets, his smile disappears. He becomes deadly serious for the first time. "I saw something last night."

"A shade of Irish Jimmy, you said."

"Yeah, and something else. Came to bring you something." He pulls a small black book from his topcoat, holds the book over my face, closes his eyes and bows his head. "Almighty Lord. Give this young man the healing he needs to meet the challenges ahead of him. Light his path. Keep him strong. Amen."

His prayer sounds both hopeful and fearful, a disquieting combination to my ear. "Thank you, Reverend. Thanks for coming all the way out here to visit me."

He slips the book into the nightstand drawer. "God bless you, son." A question creases his brow. "Your grandmother still with us?"

"Yes."

The old minister nods. "I should pay a call. Haven't seen Maureen in an age. I'm sure I'll see you again, John Francis. Buddy. But I'll leave you to rest now. You'll need some."

He leaves. I wonder about the short visit, but my brain is too morphine-addled for a deep or accurate analysis.

I return instead to Kelly's defection, her lack of loyalty, her cowardice. Our split is so abrupt. How did this happen? We never ounce argued, never even had any misunderstandings I can remember. We weren't together long enough. The past five months now reside in a thick fog of pain killers. I find no escape, not from the fog, nor from the pain. The kindly reverend's face fades, replaced by a vision of the most beautiful woman I will never lay eyes on again.

No, I'll probably run into her on occasion. Won't that be fun?

What happened? What did I do? How can I fix this? My head churns with questions that have no ready answers. They consume me nonetheless.

I pass a restless night; sleep is fitful. I assume I slept. Muted sunlight peeks through my hospital room window. Huge chunks of time are missing from the end of the reverend's visit to the present moment. Throughout the night, I turned my semi-awake brain toward Kelly regardless of myself.

209

Even when I re-hashed the reverend's visit, I ended up remembering his prayer, his hope that I could meet the challenges ahead. But I conclude my biggest challenge will be to get Kelly back. I keep returning to that fertile field, but to no effect.

A nurse bustles into the room, checks my pulse and sticks a thermometer into my mouth. "No breakfast today," she says. "They'll be working on your leg in a few hours."

I can't muster much enthusiasm. "Okay," I mumble around the thermometer.

"Don't you worry. You'll be just fine."

A small gaggle of hospital personnel swirls around my bed for a while, shaving my mess of a leg, sticking me with needles, and doing Lord knows what else. They explain what they are doing to me as they do it, but I only half listen. I don't care much at the moment.

A short trip down the hall to an elevator includes a brief visit from RJ, who wears street clothes. He's either off today, or on his way to, or from, an ER shift. He pats me on the shoulder and says something. His words bump against a wall of apathy and anesthetics.

My eyes flutter closed a few minutes after I hit the operating table, and flutter open again. "That was quick."

Dr. Hurth circles my bed. "That was about three and a half hours." He says this with a broad smile. I strain to prop myself up on my elbows, prevented again by my bashed ribs.

The doctor frowns. "Not much to see. I

accomplished what I said I could. Not a bad job, if I do say so myself."

"Thank you, Doctor." My gratitude is sincere, but I say nothing more. He can pat his own back enough for both of us.

"Tomorrow or the day after, we'll get you up on crutches, teach you how to use them if you never have before. The rib fractures are hairline, so they'll be painful but not dangerous. You'll get used to it."

Get used to pain? Guess I'll have to.

The surgeon shakes my hand with a limp-fish grasp. He exits without further instruction, encouragement, or warning. If questions arise, I assume I should ask a nurse.

Nurse, how do I heal what's wrong with my girlfriend and me?

The clock next to the television advances to ten forty-five, but the hands stick there.

The device fascinates me. Have clocks like these always existed? I don't believe I've ever seen this type before. The face is a simple, round, plain one, like those found in classrooms and offices the world over. But this one is somehow different. This one holds time in place. The second hand circles over and over, but the hour and minute hands hold their positions.

Kelly approaches from the doorway. She's decked out in the same clingy black skirt and barely-buttoned blouse she wore at Grandpop's wake. She saunters up to my bed. A cloud of Chantilly billows around her. Her hand, gentle but firm, grasps mine. Electric desire pulses through me as she purrs in my ear. "Come with me."

I swing out of the bed and stand up. My hand shoots out for support. She drapes my arm over her shoulders. I wobble and stumble a bit. "Where are you taking me?"

"Does it mater?"

"No." *I'll follow you wherever you want me to go.*

We leave the room. A short, dim hallway takes us past the deserted nurses' station. A narrow brick stairway, long and steep, leads up to the street. My weak leg improves with every step. By the time we reach the top, I no longer need to lean on her. She keeps her arm low across my back anyway, her hand reaching across to my hip. The warmth of her touch keeps my senses stirring. We reach the top together, exiting into a murky alley.

I twist around. The O'Leary's sign hangs above us. Someone splattered the sign and the surrounding sooty brick wall with tomatoes and bright crimson paint. The sight frustrates me for some reason.

She turns me back toward her. Emerald eyes gaze into mine, fixing me in place. Kelly's beauty sucks the breath from me. "Know the best way to get rid of frustration, Buddy Cullen?"

She smiles her sly smile.

A small group gathers around us, strangers, young and old men. We face the odd crew, our backs to the building. The newcomers jostle me. They shove me and one another, trying to get to Kelly. She delights in the strangers' attention even as she presses against me. Her excitement builds.

The group multiplies. I become claustrophobic, bounced around and buffeted by the swelling throng.

A few women join the ranks. Everyone's behavior turns bizarre and disturbing. Two scrawny, stubble-faced, older men in need of showers take turns drinking from a bottle in a paper bag. They whisper in each other's ears between drinks. The unwashed pair laugh at a fat, middle-aged man, who slips his hand into the hip pocket of one of the mob. A trio of teen-aged girls screw their faces into lemon-sucking scowls. They accuse three other innocent men of the fat man's deed, pointing at each blameless target.

A fierce, angry young man pushes away from Kelly. The man bulls his way through the crowd and picks up a baseball bat from the gutter. A hulking figure, an older man, approaches from West 6th Street. The young man trots up to him and beats his unsuspecting victim with the Louisville Slugger. The young man swings without remorse in a growing frenzy.

His prey tries to fend off the blitz. He staggers across the street to a loading dock. Unable to escape and finding no shelter, the victim finally crumples beneath his attacker's blows.

Glistening, dripping blackness covers the bat. The hoodlum drops the lumber back in the gutter and resumes his place in the crowd.

Few besides me heed these actions. No one, including me, does anything to stop the killer, or the fat thief. No one defends the innocent men from their false accusers.

It's not my business. What could I do, anyway? I'm just one man...

Something stirs in the doorway behind us. Kelly snaps a backward glance at the door. Her body tenses up against mine. She detaches herself from me and joins the crowd. They all disappear, drifting around the corner into the Warehouse District.

I turn around. O'Leary's door swings open. Light rises from the bottom of the stairwell, as if someone carries a lantern up the steps. The growing glow fascinates and disturbs me. A voice comes from within the light. I can't distinguish the words. I should be able to, but...

"Hey. You okay?"

A moment passes before I can shake the nightmare from my head. The clock lost its power to stall time, evidently. Its hands now indicate three minutes past noon. A familiar form stands near the door. I can't work up the energy even to nod my head. "Yeah. Dandy."

Erika stays where she is, her backpack slung over her shoulder. "You were dreaming something bad, I guess. The wreck?"

"A different wreck, but a pretty bad one, yeah."

She steps closer to the bed, pulling the backpack off her shoulder. "Sounds like something I read about the other day. Some kind of psychological issue the soldiers from Desert Storm are suffering from."

"Post Traumatic Stress Disorder."

"Yeah, sounds right. I'm not sure what's

involved."

"I think my issue's more than that. More than the accident, I mean. When I dropped you home the other night—"

"It's okay."

"No, it's not."

My woozy brain tries to untangle the messes in my head from the messes in my heart. The attempt falls short. I blurt out the personal events of the past day and a half instead. I babble about the second meeting at O'Leary's with Dad, the surveillance at League Park, the frantic race back to Jacobs Field.

The break-up with Kelly is detailed without restraint. I try my best to stick to the facts. But I no longer care about appearances. Do I sound insane? Does Kelly's behavior make her look bad? Yes, to both? *Oh well, too bad.*

Erika listens to me ramble about the dream I just woke from, too. Her stare unsettles me.

"You either don't believe me or you think I'm nuts, right? Or both."

"Or neither. First," she says, edging closer to my bedside, "don't beat yourself up about the other night. Nothing happened. Nothing was gonna happen that wasn't supposed to. We'll talk later. But the other night is not at the top of the priority list. You're a little stoned right now, and we'll need to focus on one thing at a time if we can."

Her words calm and intrigue me. She pulls a notebook from her backpack and hauls an armchair from the corner of the room. "I dug up some stuff at the Western Reserve Historical Society. Might mean something, might not."

My curiosity rises. "Research?"

"Yeah. How relevant is this stuff? Well..." She opens her notebook to a page where she sketched the familiar Indians team logo, the hook-nosed cartoon Indian with the toothy grin and the single feather sticking up from his head. "This guy's been disputed for a long time."

I nod. "Native American groups have protested the team name and mascot for decades. I didn't get to tribal beliefs and practices, their legends and religions. You find something? An occult angle? A connection to the team, a spell by a ticked off shaman or something?"

Erika squirms. "The Indians had a Native American player named Louis Sockalexis, around the turn of the century. The team wasn't even called the Indians yet."

"The Cleveland Spiders, in the National League, right?"

"Right. Word went around that Sockalexis once threw a baseball across the Penobscot River. Six hundred feet."

I grunt despite myself. "Like Washington throwing a silver dollar all the way across the Potomac."

Erika's eyes widen. "Maybe. But one of his throws from the outfield measured over four hundred feet on the fly, in front of a whole ballpark full of fans. Witnesses."

"Jeez."

"His other stats are awesome, too," she says and

rattles off her findings without pause. "He stole six bases in one game. In his first sixty games his rookie year, he hit .338 and stole sixteen bases. His rookie season was his best, his one moment. Messed up his leg running from a brothel, and only played two more years. Didn't play well, either."

This moment evokes a sense of marvel in me. Erika gushes about a man whose deeds are long forgotten. I wish I could have sat in the stands and followed his exploits on the field. His elemental sorrow also reaches across a century to touch me. I mourn the unhappy life he led, dousing his athletic gifts in alcohol, dying young and lonely on a reservation in Maine. He was not the first or only athlete to fall this way. But a pitiful few outside of the curious, like Erika and me, ever run into the name Louis Sockalexis, even by accident. This truth grieves me.

I refocus on the issue at hand. "I can buy the Native American angle. A native being angry enough to somehow curse the invading white men through one of their own sports? Sure."

Erika's brow furrows and she shakes her head.

I wet my lips. "You don't think it's Sockalexis?"

She flips a couple of notebook pages. "No. But while tracking Louis down, I ran into another couple of possibilities. Neither of them played ball, but I checked to see if there might be a connection."

"Native Americans?"

"Two. Joc-O-Sot and Chief Thunderwater. I didn't really mean to make them sound like some carnival attraction—"

"I didn't take it that way."

"If you had, you would have been close. Joc-O-Sot was royalty, a chief of the Fox tribe. Wounded in the Black Hawk War. He hooked up later with a traveling theater troupe doing nonsense 'history' plays about American Indians."

"History about as accurate as minstrel shows."

"Yeah. He wanted to die in Iowa, his native land. He died in Cleveland instead, in 1844. He's buried in Erie Street Cemetery."

Hmm. I might have been right to keep clear of the cemetery.

"And Chief Thunderwater?"

"He was an Iroquois from New York, born twenty years after Joc-O-Sot died. They're buried next to each other. Thunderwater was supposed to be the inspiration for the Indians' logo. Here's the cool part." Erika scoots closer to the bed. I feel like a kid listening to a spooky bed time story minutes before being told to go directly to sleep. "Joc-O-Sot supposedly haunts the Erie Street Cemetery to this day. His original tombstone fractured into chunks. No one admitted to vandalizing the stone. Legend has it he got so mad at being buried in Cleveland that his angry spirit crushed the stone marker. So, they say, anyway. Word is he also haunts the ball park."

"Which one? Jacobs Field? Municipal Stadium, League Park?"

"If he's responsible for the whole city's various disasters, why couldn't he follow the team from one park to the next?"

The question makes sense. It raises other questions, though. "But the Indians won the Series in 1920, then again in '48."

She nods grudging agreement. "True, but they lost one of the best and most popular players of the era in 1920. Ray Chapman. Got beaned in a game at the Polo Grounds in New York and died a couple of days later. The Chapman killing could suggest a curse. The vendor followed the Indians to Boston and Atlanta. I wonder if he was at the Polo Grounds, too."

The mental image of Chapman's skull getting caved in reminds me of the gore-splattered bat in my dream. I shudder. "What about 1948? They won the Series, and nobody on the team died."

She shrugs. "Yeah, the hole in my Joc-O-Sot theory. As curses go, an insulted Native American spirit should not be trumped by a pissed-off bartender's goat."

I chuckle then groan. Erika keeps serious. She seems reluctant to go on, so I coax more out of her. "You don't think Popcorn..."

"Popcorn?"

"Yeah, my dad and I hung the tag on him." She smiles and giggles now. I go on. "You don't think Popcorn is Joc-O-Sot?"

She sobers again. "No. In fact, I'm sure he's not. I hope you don't mind." She pulls an oversized photo from her backpack, holding it facing her, hiding the image from me. "I met with your grandmother this morning. She's just so sweet...She's coming to visit you later, by the way.

Anyway, she showed me around the house. I saw this picture hanging in the hallway."

"Which picture?"

Erika raises an eyebrow. "This was the first time anyone ever showed me this picture. I'm surprised you didn't catch this."

Erika hands me the photo. With one glance, I mentally kick myself. How could I have missed this when she and I first started tying Grandpop's baseball pictures together? Dad, Mom, Grandma, no one else familiar with this image said anything during our evidence-sharing debacle. How could they miss it, too?

The photo Erika hands me is of the diving kamikaze. The grimace on the pilot's face belongs to Popcorn.

Questions brew up in my head and begin simmering there, questions about what Popcorn is, and new ones stemming from what we've guessed so far. "Okay. Would you mind terribly taking a couple of notes?"

She produces a pen from her jacket pocket and turns a page in her notebook. "Fire away."

"Questions about Popcorn. One…Is he a curse on the Indians? If so, is the whole city just collateral damage, or is it the other way around? Two…"

She stops her furious scribbling and holds up her hand. "Whoa, slow down."

I was unaware I was babbling. My newfound excitement gets reined in, but just barely. I try to slow my speech without losing my bearings. "Sorry. Two…Has he been waiting here all along, or did he follow my grandfather to the Pacific and back?"

Pen scratches paper. Erika fires off my own next question, as if reading my mind. "Three...If he followed your grandfather, either to or back home from the war, *why*?"

The implication disturbs me. "Good question. Following Grandpop half way around the world suggests a more personal agenda."

Erika's eyes narrow. "True. But you heard about the Browns skipping town, right? That's gonna rip some hearts out. What if he had something to do with that, too? I mean, if he did, there's equally strong evidence supporting the city-wide curse theory." She frowns at her notebook, tapping her pen on the open page. "We've got evidence pointing in two different directions."

The excitement that stirred a half hour ago continues to build. I feel invigorated, but frustrated. I trust Erika but itch to do some investigative work on my own. My thumb presses down on the nurses' call button.

Erika's body tenses, ready to spring to some sort of action. "Are you okay?"

"I just want to find out how soon I can get on crutches."

"Are you ready?"

"Doesn't matter. I have to get back on my feet."

CHAPTER 15

The short trip down the hall tells me the next two months will be hellish. A physical therapist brought me crutches earlier this morning, the lightweight aluminum tube type, and adjusted them to fit my height. The reconfigured crutches still dig into my armpits. They irritate my sides. The cracked ribs on my right side are even worse than simply irritated.

A nurse walks next to me. The name tag on her ample bosom reads "Mabel," but she insists I call her Miss Mabel. In her mid-sixties by my own conservative estimate, Miss Mabel's skill must come from a lifetime of experience. Her commitment amazes me. She shares a strong empathy with her patients. Surviving the onslaught of emotions from battered patients and their worried loved ones would be impressive enough. But Miss Mabel goes well beyond mere survival. She also performs her medical duties without fail or flaw. The way she soldiers on, and still manages to put so much love into her work, impresses me most.

"Hurts don't it, Baby?"

Her gentleness tempts me to downplay the pain, to stifle what now sounds to me like a petty complaint... in other words, to lie. "Not too bad."

A familiar laugh stops us at the nurses' station. I tangle my crutches trying to turn, nearly falling in the process. Miss Mabel clucks her tongue and grabs my arm. She props me up. "Careful now, don't put any weight on that leg just yet."

I don't need to be warned twice, not after the surgeon showed me my most recent x-rays yesterday after Erika left. What once resembled a natural human femur now appears less straight, less smooth, less natural. Adding to the unnatural look is a foot-long metal plate, fastened to the bone with a dozen inch-long screws. Almost as disturbing as the x-ray was Dr. Hurth's reminder. Once the bone heals, he threatened, he will open the leg again to unscrew and remove the plate.

The inside of my leg could be something out of the library construction site. I wouldn't feel safe testing one of the new building's upper floors before construction is completed, and I don't feel the need to test my leg before it's ready.

RJ trots up to us and lays his hand on my shoulder. "You better listen to Miss Mabel. You better stop lying about the pain, too. She can't do her job right if she's not told what's what."

Miss Mabel smiles. "Dr. Jankowski. Always good to have you."

"Always my pleasure, Miss Mabel."

The old nurse coos encouragement to me. "You're doing just fine. How's it feel?"

"Okay. Actually, the leg's fine. But these crutches make my armpits hurt like hell."

My companions chuckle. RJ attempts some semblance of seriousness. He clears his throat. "A-hem. That's sorta more like it."

Occasional moans spill from an open door near mine. The three of us turn, in a kind of group reflex. We peek in as we pass. An Indian woman in a bright blue sari hunches at the foot of the bed. Sorrow and worry etch her face. She clenches her hands in front of her chest but doesn't move. She makes no sound, either. The moans come from the bed, its suffering occupant hidden from us.

Miss Mabel's calm impresses me. Her steadiness and RJ's seem to mimic each other. They both face forward again. I want to go into the stranger's room and say something, to offer comfort of some sort, to offer hope. An even stronger urge pulls me toward my own room, separated from the pain of others. My own self-interest wins out, and I re-focus on what I'm doing. I wore diapers the last time walking took my actual concentration.

The elevator down the hall *dings* in unison with a buzz for assistance at the nurses' station. The sounds stand out. The electronic flurry conflicts with the steady, constant activity around us.

A couple in their early forties gets off the elevator along with someone behind them. I can't make the third person out well from here. A hope flickers that Kelly might visit again, that she might come back.

The couple approaches. The woman stares at me. But no one follows them.

I hate my painkillers.

My thoughts must be visible. The curiosity in the woman's eyes deepens as the distance between us shrinks. Her companion walks beside her, holding her hand, oblivious to her interest in me.

Is she showing interest in me? Or am I out of my mind?

As if on cue, the woman's eyes dart toward RJ for a moment, then back to me. My discomfort grows under the strange woman's scrutiny. In another place like the Come On Inn, I might be flattered. The woman isn't a timeless beauty, but she's far from unattractive. The bar comes to mind now because a dark, smoky night spot is where this kind of silent connection belongs. I don't believe I've misread the signals. I might only have missed her lack of subtlety if she was across the street in a crowd.

The couple draws nearer. I almost wish they were across the street. A fog of cheap cologne surrounds them, an overwhelming bouquet of sweet rose. The couple passes. Am I still under the woman's gaze? I can't tell from behind. The essence stays with me, as if woven into my pajamas. Another even less pleasant scent mingles with the cloying rose. Maybe the woman chose a three-dollar gallon of cologne over a hot shower.

I cough a little and frown at myself. I don't know what the woman's circumstances are. She stinks like someone interrupted her during a dumpster dive, but she's obviously not homeless. She wears clothes that are too expensive, too good for the street. Could she have some sort of glandular problem? Or, maybe her choice isn't about her. Maybe she bathed in perfume to mask her companion's allergy to soap.

Maybe my compassion needs feeding and exercise.

The nurses' buzzer goes off again, demanding a

response, grating on my nerves. Miss Mabel gives the vacant station a doleful glare. "That new girl's gonna get herself fired quick. Dr. Jankowski, I ain't supposed to do this, but..."

"Other folks need you, Miss Mabel. I got him."

Miss Mabel peeks over the nurses' station counter and shifts into another gear, waddling on feet that can't help but be sore. She trundles down the hall and disappears around a corner.

RJ lets me lean on his arm. He guides me to my bed, not as expertly as Miss Mabel, but well enough. My leg throbs. I swing the splintered limb up onto the mattress. The throbbing subsides once I'm situated on the bed, and I begin to wonder about this visit from RJ. I choose not to push. "Thanks for the help."

"They're letting you go tomorrow. Those stairs to your apartment are gonna be a pain."

"Tomorrow? Already?"

He grunts. "You'll understand when you get the bill. You got the best care we could give you, but a three month stay at the Ritz would be a bargain compared to two weeks here."

"Terrific."

My discomfort grows, partly because finding a comfortable, or at least less painful, position seems unlikely, and partly from a vibe RJ puts out. He shifts his weight from foot to foot, his only "tell" as far as I know. We play darts, but I'm not masochistic enough to play poker with him. Still, this would be the moment to call his hand. "What's up?"

He pauses and clears his throat. "We had somebody in the ER last night."

My ears prick up. I shoot off one-word questions I fear the answers to. "Mom? Dad? Grandma?"

"No."

Relief mixes with dread. "Who then?"

Not Popcorn. Serious injury to him would be too much to ask.

"I didn't recognize the guy until we pulled his ID. Big, older guy. You talked with him at your grandfather's funeral. Bill—"

"Mannion."

"Yeah. He's dead."

"How?"

Queasy distress slithers into my stomach. I didn't need to ask because I witnessed Mannion's death. I now imagine myself in his place, hulking down Frankfort Avenue for a late pop at O'Leary's after a hard day of helping couples split up. A brutal crack thumps the back of my head. My legs buckle, I stumble in a daze past the door. Rough, dirty hands pull me across the street to a loading dock where the blows begin raining down without pause, raining down forever...

RJ's voice pulls me back to my hospital bed. "Somebody caved his head in with a baseball bat." He blinks and furrows his brow. "You don't seem surprised."

I don't hesitate. Much as I want to share my prophetic nightmare, I no longer trust I can. "Should I be surprised? The man practiced divorce law."

"Yeah."

The moment sounds a sad note. My grandfather's oldest, best friend suffered a brutal, fatal attack, and I no longer trust my oldest, best friend as I used to. I doubt I can talk with RJ about any of this, so I choose to stay on safe ground. "The police say anything?"

"Nah, not much. But I think you're on to something. If he was mugged, the muggers did a pretty crappy job. They left an awful lot of money in his wallet. No, this was personal."

His observation feeds my queasiness. RJ has no idea how right he is, but he's wrong in a way, too. The same thing that eats like an acid at the fabric of this entire city now singles out people who were close to Grandpop, including me. I keep calm as I tick off a mental list of others Popcorn might consider a loose end. Who else might he come after? RJ and Mom are safe, I'm sure. They showed neither interest nor belief in anything Erika and I presented. But for the rest…

"You okay?"

My effort at nonchalance apparently made me appear ill. I use his mis-diagnosis the best way I can. "A little tired I guess. That's all."

RJ heads for the door. "You need anything, don't hesitate to hit the buzzer. Miss Mabel's the best."

"Sure is." I give him a jaunty wave, another lie of sorts, which he smiles at before disappearing out the door. My nerves jangle. I have little choice but to wait for my release tomorrow. The next twelve hours will be exceptionally long ones for me.

The television, society's Idiot Eye, stares blank-screened at me from its perch on the opposite wall. A diverting program might help me fill in time until my release. Some mindless "tube" might shift focus from my mangled leg, my dismantled relationship with Kelly, and deep concerns for my hometown and my loved ones living here. I reach over to the top of the nightstand for the TV remote. The kamikaze picture lies underneath, untouched. I don't want to deal with Popcorn today. The problem will still be with me, with us, tomorrow. For now, I just want to shut my head off.

The truth soon dawns on me, however, that I'll find no escape via the television. Inanities clog the airwaves. Finding programs of no real substance is easy enough. Too easy. But the mental anesthetic I seek doesn't come with them.

I stop on each available channel for no more than a moment, but the last program amazes and mesmerizes me. A shouting match on this network takes place in front of a studio audience. A middle-aged man with a beer gut launches a verbal attack on two loud, corpulent women. The women respond with a vicious and foul-mouthed defense. The noise swirls around a self-satisfied, smarmy, but silent host, the instigator of this low-rent *Circus Maximus*. The combatants know each other. They are a family. Split. Splintered. Divided and, though they have yet to figure it out, conquered. No one walks away from this a winner, no medal or trophy awarded to anyone. The viewer can only tally a psychic body count, and a pretty high one at that. The audience loves this. They hoot and holler for more.

Divide and conquer…

The screen goes blank when I press the remote button. Merciful silence fills the room again. I must ask the nursing staff if one of them might get me soap and water. I feel a sudden need to bathe.

A silhouette darts into the doorway and steps inside—the strange woman from the hall. She closes the door behind her. The closed door plugs the room's biggest vent. The sickly-sweet odor of a ton of roses races to every corner. The stench of rot comes in, too. The woman keeps her distance, leaning her butt against the door. She wears a mysterious expression. Her narrowed eyes, feral and hunted, lock on me. A predatory grin curls her wide, full lips. The intruder reaches for the light switch on the wall next to her.

I grab the nurses' buzzer. "What do you want?"

She answers with a flick of her finger, extinguishing the overhead fluorescent light. We plunge into early evening's dismal twilight.

I press the button. My hand shakes. Can I somehow make the buzzer outside grate with more urgency?

"You n-n-need to leave."

My stuttered command produces an unwelcome reaction. The woman's grin grows to a smile, one that brings no joy to her face. Her hands move behind her, slipping between her hips and the door. The pose is sexual in a deviant way; she could well be bound from behind and gives me the impression she might enjoy handcuffs a bit too much. A half-chuckle, half-moan oozes from her lips.

The total effect gives me the creeps. My thumb clamps down on what I now consider the Panic Button. The buzzer chirps in the hallway. No one answers.

The woman moves...yet she doesn't move. Her body leans against the door, but its shape changes. She grows wider. A shadow creates the illusion. The shadow detaches itself from her, taking on a life of its own.

The shadow approaches my bed. The odors intensify with each step, both the reeking of too many roses and the stench of corruption. Decay. Death.

I mentally correct myself. A bath would not improve the woman's scent, not unless she bathed in formaldehyde.

The shadow reaches my bedside. Its stink overwhelms me. The woman remains at the door, still visible through the dark figure hovering beside me. Her chuckle degenerates into a low laughter, a demented, turned-on enjoyment airing itself. I squeeze my eyes shut.

I can make this nightmare go away—

Something presses down on the side of my mattress. A body? I open my eyes. A scream catches in my throat.

This shadow has substance and weight.

But I can still see through it!

The cold touch of a corpse's hand caresses my

chest. The cadaverous stroke glides up to my face, brushing my cheek. I cringe. The touch slithers back to my chest, then lower, down my belly, and lower still. The reek makes me retch. Bile builds at the back of my throat.

A new realization pops like a firecracker in my head. *If I stay frozen this way I'll be lost. Forever.*

Clammy pressure pushes against my chest and then all over my torso—the shadow thing is mounting me. My vocal cords thaw and spring into action. An icy putrescence brushes against my open, screaming mouth before clamping down. I struggle against the death kiss being forced on me.

The woman across the room writhes in a pole-dance parody. She licks her lips like a drunk offered a full glass of single malt scotch. She moves her hands from behind her. They travel up to her breasts, then down her torso. Her smile widens, her moans grow louder, more urgent.

The woman suddenly bumps forward, the door bursting open behind her.

Miss Mabel bustles into the room. "What in blazes is going on in here?"

She flicks the light switch. The fluorescent tubes bathe the room again in bluish-white light. The pressure of the non-existent body bounds off me like a nervous prom date.

Miss Mabel misses this. She leans back out the door, shouting for assistance, then hustles with surprising speed and agility to the stranger. The intruder edged toward the foot of my bed after the door hit her from behind. Miss Mabel grabs her elbow now. The old nurse's words drip sugar, but her face is stern. "Here you are Miz Richards. We been looking high and low for you."

The creepy Miz Richards's companion rushes into the room. Two orderlies follow at his heels. He takes her other elbow, and he and Miss Mabel steer her toward the door. The man tosses a non-apology over his shoulder as they leave.

"Sorry about that. She hasn't been the same since the accident."

They all exit together. I wonder if the wayward Miz Richards had an accident, or if a catastrophe landed a loved one here, someone whose pain unhinged her. The distinction drops on my list of important issues. The urgent and repeated wiping of my mouth with the back of my hand tops the agenda instead. My effort fails to rub away the essence of week-old roadkill. The lingering horror can't keep me from judging the man's parting words to be more excuse than apology. But his intention doesn't matter.

This was no accident.

True evil violated my mouth in more ways than I care to count. Miss Mabel will kick my butt if she walks in and catches me doing this, but I can't help myself. My legs swing off the bed. The crutches lean against the wall next to me. I wedge the little hospital-issue toothbrush and toothpaste between my fingers before grasping the crutch handles.

Despite my inexperience with the clumsy props, I bound into the bathroom. Desire, an almost pathological need to scrub myself clean, overcomes fear of injury. The bathroom is dark. I doubt I ever switched a light on with as much urgency. Nothing moves. The bathroom is vacant. Tension drains from me until I glimpse my face in the mirror.

The reflection reminds me I haven't looked into a mirror since the crash. Medical embroidery limits my scrubbing. Half a dozen separate, short scars mar my left cheek. Puncture wounds from the shattered windshield? A stitch or two holds each of them closed. A much longer scar stretches just above my brow, from a third of the way across my forehead to my temple, curving down at the end toward the corner of my eye. The skin appears torn, ripped open from impact the way a boxer gets cut by smooth leather gloves, a sharp jab tearing rather than a sharp object cutting. The disfigured areas and their tiny threads beg for me to pick at them.

I didn't imagine I was quite this ugly.

My stomach roils. I squeeze some paste on the brush and begin. Brushing my teeth soon frustrates me, however. I wish the bristles were made of steel wool or something else much stiffer than this soft nylon, or plastic, or rubber, whatever this thing is made of. The toothpaste tube also claims a refreshing peppermint flavor. But the horror of what I just experienced blocks the paste's attempt to eradicate, or even just to cover, the rancidness in my mouth...

I dive head first for the toilet. The unpleasant but natural vomit leaves my mouth feeling less clean, but still better than the man-made, breath-freshening toothpaste. The irony will not keep me from brushing again as soon as my stomach settles, however.

Another reflection dances across the bathroom mirror. I twist toward the doorway while still crouched over the toilet bowl. My reaction causes me to fall over my crutches. I land in a heap, yowling in pain.

"What are you doing? I'm pretty sure you're not supposed to move around without help." Erika stoops down to pull me up by my armpits. The process is slow. She assists me with care.

"They're letting me go tomorrow. I won't have any help then."

Her gentle retort disarms me. "That's tomorrow."

She guides me back to the bed. I hop on my good leg while she retrieves my crutches. Her head tilts, she grimaces. "You hurt yourself, didn't you?"

I won't lie to her, so I say nothing.

Erika reads my silence well enough. "I'll get a nurse."

"No."

"If you're hurt, you need attention."

"If I'm hurt they might not let me go tomorrow."

"What's one more day?"

The kamikaze photo catches my eye from the nightstand as I heave myself back up on the bed. Erika's question, more of an admonition, rings in my ears. I should risk Miss Mabel's wrath and ask her or a doctor to check my leg for newly inflicted damage. I may have cost myself some healing time. Or, I may have cost myself the decent use of the leg altogether.

What's one more day? Maybe nothing. Maybe everything.

My eyes search Erika's. She doesn't shrink from them, encouraging and emboldening me. "So far, you haven't run screaming. I appreciate that. But your courage might carry a price. I think the people around me are...I think you're in danger. I think we're all in danger."

CHAPTER 16

Dad paces a few steps, does a couple of shallow knee bends, and rolls up on the balls of his feet. Then he repeats the unconscious ritual. I glance back at him while pulling on a pair of gray sweat pants. The fit over my cast is tight. My attempt to dress is slow and awkward, but all mine. Dad offered to help. I shooed him away. I might as well get used to dressing myself.

He wants to do something useful. I can tell. So, I toss him a bone. "Hey Dad, can you collect my stuff?"

"What stuff?"

"The stuff in the nightstand."

Dad accepts the minor assignment with gratitude. He opens the nightstand drawer and grunts. "Whose is this?"

I forgot about Reverend Newhouse's visit. "A chaplain came by and left a Bible for me."

My own less than honest answer makes me uncomfortable. The bigger issue, however, is my sudden shame for not cracking the gift open yet.

Dad shrugs. He pulls a balled-up plastic grocery bag from his fatigue jacket, and drops the Bible in. Then he and his bag head for the bathroom. I don't need to ask what he's doing. I hope no one stops by to check on me, only to find my dear old father burglarizing the joint. Sarcasm won't help, but I can't let the moment go. "You want a hospital gown for your wardrobe, too?"

"Hey...toothpaste, soap, whatever. We're

entitled. We'll be paying enough."

"Yeah, I've heard. What do you mean, 'we'?"

"You'll need help."

"I have insurance through the university."

"Won't cover a hundred percent. Not even close."

Dad's generosity now trumps his larceny. I'm at a loss for words, except for those that are too pat for the moment. "Thank you."

I want to walk out of here, even if on crutches. But a silly hospital rule requires a staff member to haul me out in a wheelchair. Miss Mabel joins us at the nurses' station. She stays with us on the elevator down to the main floor and out the exit. Dad leaves us at the emergency room doors and trots out to the parking lot.

Dad's pick-up truck approaches. Miss Mabel helps me out of the wheelchair. She smiles a satisfied smile at me. "You're a fine young man. I don't ever want you in here again."

Sadness, relief, apprehension, and joy all tug at one another. "I'll do my best. Thank you, Miss Mabel."

"Mind what I said, now." The old nurse helps me into the passenger's seat, waves her hand, and disappears back into the hospital.

Dad stomps on the gas pedal harder than usual. We hurtle through the parking lot. He almost tips his truck with the right turn on West 25th Street. The special red, hexagonal sign at the end of the lot must read, "All Stop, Except Michael Cullen." I wouldn't know, since we whiz past the sign so fast.

Two blocks later, I manage to buckle my seat belt. Another sarcastic crack escapes me. "Good thing we're this near a hospital."

Dad shakes off my jab. "I didn't expect to wait so long to get you out."

"Sorry. Hospital bureaucracy, I guess."

"Oh, I'm not blaming you." He wheels left on Lorain Road in the face of angry, oncoming traffic, again nearly putting his vehicle on its side. I don't mask my angry, terrified glower. He races on, ignoring both my glare and most traffic laws. "Dice is at O'Leary's by himself."

"He's handled the bar solo before."

"Yeah."

Dad's reaction mystifies me. He guns the engine, makes a hard right on West Boulevard and scoots onto I-90 West on a yellow signal.

I remind him where he's heading. "You might want to slow down to seventy or eighty miles an hour. Getting pulled over in Lakewood will make you even later and a lot poorer."

A police cruiser idles under the Bunts Road overpass. Dad eases off the gas pedal. I chuckle to myself.

That would _really_ frost him, getting pulled over a half mile from our exit!

Michael Cullen's Death Defying Carnival Ride comes to a merciful stop in front of my apartment building. Dad jumps out and hustles around to my door. Mom's car is nowhere in sight. He plans on leaving me alone to my own limited devices, I guess. Another car catches my attention as I struggle out of the truck, a red convertible parked halfway to the next intersection. The familiar Chrysler rag-top makes me smile as Dad and I make our way to the building.

RJ's here.

The stairs pose less of a problem for me than for Dad. I lean on the crutches with my left hand, on the banister with my right, and put weight only on my good leg, climbing up one step at a time. Dad follows behind me, checking his watch. His anxiety grows with each step. I want to hurry more, but don't dare.

RJ opens the door when we are still four steps from the landing. "You won't be sneaking up on anybody."

"Wasn't trying to."

"Good thing." He extends his hand. I am about to grab hold when Dad thrusts the plastic bag of hospital loot at him.

"Sorry guys, I have to run. Buddy, I'll be by tomorrow."

"Thanks, Dad." My gratitude is genuine.

Dad replies with a tense-bodied mix of anticipation and guilt. "You're in better hands than mine, Buddy." He whirls and bounds back down the stairs and out the door.

RJ peeks into the plastic bag. "Soap? Shampoo?"

"My room didn't have a mini bar for him to raid."

"He's got a full-size bar of his own."

I nod and enter my apartment. My mouth drops

open at the sight of another unexpected guest.

"Hope you don't mind. I thought I could help somehow."

I assume Erika volunteered her time without any shoving from RJ or Dad. My little dive in the hospital bathroom spooked her, no doubt. But the memory of my embarrassing behavior at her place clings to me, twisting this sensitive and caring act of kindness into a surprise.

But I can't let any kind of insecurity carry too much weight now.

RJ plops the bag down on the coffee table. "Didn't expect you back quite so soon."

"My dad's a maniac behind the wheel."

"Yeah, well we just got here a little while ago. I need to clear a path so you can actually reach your bed."

I forgot about the clutter from Grandpop's darkroom equipment. RJ disappears to address the shambles in my bedroom. Erika helps me to the wood frame sofa. The seat cushions are even less comfortable than they used to be. Then again, I doubt anything will be comfortable to me for a while.

I ease down on the torturous sofa. Erika offers her hand in support. I wave her off instinctively, apologizing even as I situate myself. "Sorry. I'm afraid I'm not a good patient."

"Don't try to soft-pedal it," RJ booms from the bedroom. "You're a crappy patient."

"Were his ears always as big as his mouth?" I ask Erika.

RJ steals her thunder. "Yes!"

Erika smirks. She points at the plastic bag on the table. I give her a rueful shrug. "I scored a new Bible out of the whole deal."

"You seem kind of flip, if you don't mind my saying."

"Haven't had much use for one so far." My comment apparently makes little impression on her. Her eyes focus on the wall, her mind engaged in some other area. I give her a moment before interrupting. "What are you thinking?"

"The Bible. Miracles, supernatural stuff. I mean, we both spent a whole day at the library. I spent another two while you were in the hospital."

"And?"

"We poked around bunches of areas... historical, legendary, apocryphal, mystical, and paranormal. Okay, I get your concern about religious bias, but we ignored a whole book full of possibilities."

Erika makes a good point. I claim not to buy into God, not entirely. But I find no problem with looking for Popcorn in pop culture?

"Hand me that bag, please."

I pull the Bible out. The book opens to a page marked by a picture, a print three inches by five. I'd be happy never to see another photograph for the rest of my life. How did Dad miss this at the hospital?

Or, did he?

The photo sparks my curiosity. Terror and chaos dominate the image. Oily smoke billows from a gaping chasm in the deck of a large ship, an aircraft carrier. Men, sailors, are suspended forever in time. Some are captured running toward, and others away from, the huge hole. The angle of the shot tells me the photographer stood at an elevated distance, possibly from the bridge.

Erika sidles up to look over my shoulder. "What have you got?"

"I'd bet money this is the *Enterprise*." I jab my finger at the smoking hole that used to be the ship's flight deck elevator. "And if I'm right, our kamikaze made this mess."

"The Bible was from the reverend? Is this his picture, too?"

"Um." My eyebrows knit as the wheels behind them turn. "Something's wrong with this."

"What?"

Ideas, memories, possibilities, all tumble around in my head like a litter of over-caffeinated puppies. Who is this preacher? A friend of Grandpop's, one I never happened to meet before. Not before the night of the wreck. I remember him standing in the dimness of East 55th Street in front of the Fellowship Baptist Church, his shock when I sped past him the way Dad might, the reverend pointing up at the streetlight...

He saw them! He saw the shadows!

My jack-hammering heart pumps my blood harder and harder. I become light-headed. I place the picture back in the Bible. The picture...

"I believe Reverend Newhouse took this picture with Grandpop's camera, and now he can see the shadows. He can even see Popcorn. I don't know how or why. I'm not even sure if I'm on the right track."

"Easiest way to find out is in the phone book."

"There's a White Pages somewhere on the kitchen counter by the phone."

"Got ya."

Erika disappears into the hall and around the corner into the kitchen. I want to kick myself with my good leg. My behavior the other night equaled Dad's when he was checking her out at O'Leary's. Yet, I still can't take my eyes off her until she's walked all the way out of the room.

When did she stop just being RJ's kid sister?

A knock on the door startles me. I take a breath, trying to slow my racing mind. Dad won't be coming back, not tonight. Grandma gets around only as well as the Regional Transit Authority does. The bus trip from Old Brooklyn to Lakewood is a long and difficult haul.

Another knock. Neither Erika nor RJ seem to hear. I eliminate Popcorn as a visitor, putting my fear to rest. Why would he bother knocking? I pull myself up from the sofa and grab my crutches.

Mom. Of course.

The crutches actually hinder me once I cross to the other end of the living room. As if stoned, I take a few too many moments to figure out I can work the doorknob by emptying one hand. I lean one of the crutches against the wall and cuss my decision-dulling pain meds.

I almost drop the remaining crutch when I open

the door.

"I saw someone through the window. I didn't think they'd let you out so soon."

Either Kelly's body is made for tight-fitting clothes, or it's the other way around. I can't decide which. But even her business clothes—I assume she stopped in on her way home from work—form-fit her the way they would a professional model. She dressed to be noticed today, as she always does.

But her Chantilly...does perfume have an expiration date?

My eyes dart from one corner of the landing to another, then down the stairs and back. Nothing moves, no shadows, none I can detect.

Is this stairway that well-lit? Does it matter? Where there's light, there's shadow.

"Buddy?" Her voice brings me back. "Don't you want to let me in?"

"I didn't expect you."

Kelly lowers her head. "I'm sorry about the way I behaved. I was just...you know."

I freeze in the doorway like a soldier illuminated by a flare in No Man's Land, unable to move even to save myself.

But do I need to save myself? From what?

"No," I manage, "I don't know. I guess I don't really know you, do I?"

Kelly gazes into my face. She makes a move to enter my apartment. Her eyes dart from mine to something over my shoulder.

I turn my head. Erika approaches with the White Pages in one hand, and the phone in the other.

If the metaphor of steam shooting out of a person's ears was actually possible, Kelly would be stripping the paint off my door frame. She glares at me. "Oh. I get it."

The growing clutter in my head clears. "Probably not."

"She one of your students?"

Erika steps toward us. Her calm demeanor and even tone underline her courage. "Yeah, I am. I'm helping with Professor Cullen's research."

"Research. Interesting word."

"Do I look like I can do anything more than read and write?" My question lowers the flame under Kelly. She merely simmers now.

RJ saunters in from the bedroom, disarming Kelly completely. "Everything okay in here? Oh, hi, Kelly. Sorry I missed you at the hospital. All your visits must have come and gone on my break."

Kelly does her best to ignore RJ's vicious shot. She hands me the crutch I leaned against the wall, leads me out to the landing and closes the door behind us. "Buddy, I need a minute in private."

"Okay. What's on your mind?" My manner is cold, even to me.

Kelly bows her head again and cozies up to me. She speaks in a near whisper. "I hurt you at the hospital. I'm so, so sorry. I just had a lot going on." She pauses, biting her lower lip.

"Go on."

"I have to tell you. I…my timing sucks, but I have to come clean. I cheated on you."

The revelation surprises me only a little, but still

hits me like a crowbar to the gut. "Hey, great. Thanks for sharing." I reach for the doorknob. She puts a soft, firm hand over mine. Her warmth speeds my heartrate up even more.

"No, you don't understand. I had an affair, a meaningless, stupid fling. It was wrong. And now it's over. I don't want anyone but you, not ever again."

The initial pain dulls with surprising speed. Her indiscretion leaves only a dent. And I have fewer problems with her confession than I suppose I should. I want to believe her.

But morphine dampened a memory at the hospital. The morphine's leaving my system now, and the memory of her provocative pose with Popcorn comes back to me. I doubt she is even aware he was in her ear. No one else caught him in his corruptive whisperings, including me. Is she an unsuspecting pawn? Or did she sell her soul? Neither scenario works for me. I want to forget the whole thing but can't. I have a print of the incident to remind me. Even if the photo is lost or destroyed, the image will stay in my head.

Can't un-ring a bell.

I try to be gentle but end up unable to make a clean break. "I'll have to think about it."

"Think about it," she says, "and give me a call."

Kelly takes her leave. I shuffle back into my apartment and close the door again.

Erika sits on the sofa, alone. She scoots over, making room for me. "She's in your head, isn't she?"

I sit next to her. "Yeah, she is. I don't know why, to tell you the truth."

RJ returns to the living room with three bottles of beer. I wave him off. "Pain killers, chief. Help yourself, though."

"One won't hurt you. Trust me. I'm a professional."

Erika shakes her head, declining as well, but changes her mind and grasps a cold one. We all clink our bottles together.

"Cheers," RJ toasts, "and welcome home. Mostly intact."

"Thanks." A memory creeps into my head as I take a swig. "Hey, RJ, you remember the weird lady at the hospital?"

"The stalker that got bounced from your room?"

"Yeah."

Erika tries to catch up to us. "Who?"

"That's a whole story," I groan. "Did you notice anything about her in the hallway when we passed her?"

RJ furrows his brow. "Not that she was as nuts as she turned out to be, or anything like that. I remember she had a man with her."

"Husband?"

"Maybe. Who knows? It's the 'nineties."

"You catch any odor?"

His eyes narrow. "She wore a rose perfume. Smelled like something Mrs. Jacoby wore."

Erika snickers. "The old fourth grade teacher at Hawthorne?"

I nod. "No other scent, RJ? Maybe on the man?"

RJ shrugs. "None that I recall. Nothing unusual."

"How about on the landing here, tonight. Either of you guys get a whiff of anything?"

RJ shakes his head.

Erika shakes her head, too. "No. What should we have smelled?"

"I thought I caught a nose full of dead rat."

RJ nods. "Sometimes a good bash upside the head will make you imagine odors that aren't really there. Sometimes meds will do the same thing. You smelled something like that at the hospital, didn't you?"

"Yeah."

"Well, there you go. It'll wear off. Now, if I'm gonna be serious about this beer, even this garbage you keep in your 'fridge, then I need to make some room. Excuse me." RJ heads for the bathroom.

"Gracious of you, friend. Shoot straight."

"Yeah, yeah," he says before closing the bathroom door.

Erika's amusement straightens into serious concentration. "Dead rat?"

"Dead something. RJ might be right about the concussion and the drugs, but I don't think so. I caught a good nose full of something similar before my accident. I need a second opinion." I thumb through the "N" section of the White Pages. Many Newhouses call Cleveland home, but only one Newhouse, Rev. G.

The phone rings at the other end. Four, five, six rings. My tension rises with every ring. I wonder what to say. How will I frame my insane question in a way that sounds less insane? I begin to feel like a desperate telemarketer.

Erika opens the reverend's Bible to the bookmarked page. She reads with myopic intensity, leaning forward, as if she's in class soaking in information. She made a good point about the Bible. Is this the right place to look, the right direction to take? Nothing else led anywhere. I definitely have the uneasy sense the clock is ticking. With luck I can find a shortcut over the phone...but not if no one picks up.

I jamb my thumb down on the "off" button, frustrated. "No one home."

"What next?" Erika asks, her eyes still scanning the open Bible.

RJ saunters into the living room. "What do you mean, 'what next?' "

Erika offers me a blushing, silent apology as I punch in the number for O'Leary's. I don't worry about RJ's opinion of my stability at this moment. "She means, who do we call now for help."

"Help with what?"

"Help with this thing and what to do about it."

RJ plops down on an overstuffed easy chair, the only other chair in the room, a hand-me-down from Mom. "What do you mean, 'do'? You're in no condition to 'do' much more than heal."

I try to articulate my growing dread as I wait for Dad or Dice to answer. "Something has been hurting this city, hurting us, for a long time. A little at a time, under the radar."

RJ snorts, reaches over, and takes my half-full bottle of beer from the coffee table. "Jesus, I guess I was wrong about this stuff."

"Stop it." Erika's command stuns RJ, freezing his hand in mid swipe. His eyes could not grow wider if she pulled an oak tree out of her left ear. She continues, unwavering. "Okay, I get that different people might interpret evidence in different ways. So what if this stuff doesn't jump up and scream, 'Hey, this is definitely what I am?' Disagreement doesn't mean the evidence doesn't exist. The evidence exists, and it's right here in front of us."

RJ's face roils with outrage first, then concentration—I want to think Erika's words sink in at this point—then disbelief. His flat refusal to believe melts to softened skepticism. "Okay. So. What now?"

"Dad's not picking up."

"They might be busy." RJ's suggestion sounds reasonable enough.

But...

"It doesn't feel right."

Erika taps my arm. She holds the Bible out to me. The color drains from her face, her mouth tightens. I discover the reverend does indeed know what we are dealing with. My blood chills as I read the passage from the book of Mark, Chapter Five:

"He shouted at the top of his voice, 'What do you want with me, Jesus, Son of the Most High God? Swear to God that you won't torture me!' For Jesus had said to him, 'Come out of this man, you evil spirit!'

"Then Jesus asked him, 'What is your name?'

"'My name is Legion,' he replied, 'for we are many.' "

Erika's hand on my forearm snaps me out of a trance of sorts. I remember an icy finger tracing my spine, nothing more. But that's enough. I must have spent a long time staring at the passage. The ringing on the other end of the phone turned to the "beep" warning me my phone is off the hook.

Concern plasters itself on RJ's brow. "Buddy?"

I grab my crutches and rise from the sofa. "We've got to move."

CHAPTER 17

We dash through the oncoming dusk toward Downtown. RJ frowns into his rear-view mirror. I sprawl behind him, still and silent, unable to escape his grimace. Erika ignores him. She squares her shoulders and stares straight ahead from the passenger's seat. RJ's glower demands an explanation from me. I keep my mouth shut. Erika and I shot our bolt just to get him to drive us to O'Leary's. My gut tells me something is wrong. But nothing I say will convince RJ to trust my gut.

He shakes his head. "I can't believe I'm doing this."

We seem to slow to a crawl, tooling past the fine houses of Lake Avenue at five miles per hour under the limit. My impatience grows. A peek at the speedometer shocks me. True to form, RJ risks jail time for excessive and dangerous speed.

Some responsibility lies with me if he's ticketed. I chose the route. Rush hour traffic clogs I-90 this time of day. The Shoreway would lead us to within three blocks of O'Leary's doorway. I gambled on Lake Avenue's traffic lights slowing us less than jams on the highway and around Jacobs Field.

Erika twists backwards to face me. "Did he say anything to you on the stairs before he left?"

"Dad? No."

RJ snaps. "Then why did you co-opt me into endangering your recovery?"

"What worried me was as much what he didn't say as what he said. Dad always plays his hand close to the vest. I can't think of a better explanation."

RJ grimaces. "Great." He glances at Erika, who glares back at him. RJ backs down. He returns his attention to the road, but makes a grudging concession. "I agree, your dad was squirrelly. He had someplace else he needed to be. Yeah, he puts more importance on the bar than you or I might. He was the same way the other night when you called us all together. O'Leary's is his livelihood. Can you blame him?"

We barrel past an old apartment complex and fly through the intersection at West 117th Street. I chew on RJ's opinion. Dad was anxious to get us out so he could open his bar, sure. But did he have the same concern today?

"I get your point," I say, "but Dad's urgency was different when he dropped me off. Kind of like the other day, but different."

RJ opens his mouth. He turns to his sister again, no doubt looking for support before speaking.

But Erika gives him none. "Between the two of you, Buddy's the one who knows his dad better, RJ."

"Thank you," I say. I appreciate her support. Still, her statement isn't saying much. As Mannion said at Grandpop's funeral, the Irish are a mysterious lot…mysterious, I might add, even to their own.

RJ ignores the yellow light at West Boulevard. We dart onto the Shoreway. The long afternoon shadows of Edgewater Park's trees meld into the approaching evening. The sun sets behind us. The blue above deepens and darkens. My nerves stretch more with each passing moment. I just now realize I've been tapping my foot on the back of RJ's seat and force myself to stop. He hasn't said anything, but he must be annoyed. I would be.

A plume of thick, black-and-gray smoke rises from Downtown. Fear and apprehension fill the car. Erika takes in a sharp breath. "Oh, no."

"Public Square," RJ mutters. "Traffic's gonna be a problem."

My heart pounds as my blood turns to ice.

Public Square or the edge of the Warehouse District? O'Leary's!

We weave from one lane to the next, never slowing. RJ plays daredevil for us. He veers across two lanes of traffic to get to the West 6th Street off ramp. A quick peek backward brings relief. A dozen other motorists are nail-spitting mad, but we left no wrecks in our wake.

Multiple sirens scream nearby, before we even merge onto West 6th Street. A line of cars stretches up to St. Clair Avenue. We're stopped at the end. Sooty smoke descends from above the rooftops of the buildings lining West 6th. The smoke clouds our view of the century-old façades. Flashing lights slice through the haze from the intersection ahead.

I tap Erika on the shoulder. We come to the same conclusion; she reaches for the door handle.

RJ twists in his seat. "What do you think you're doing?"

Erika jumps out of the car and grabs my

crutches. I put my hand on RJ's shoulder, trying to calm him without compromising. "The police will block St. Clair. A cold beer says they're re-routing traffic now. Driving will take too much time."

"Buddy..." RJ stops short. He sits in glum silence as Erika helps me to my feet.

I owe my old friend more than just the sight of our backs as we walk away from him. "I can't just sit here and do nothing but watch."

"Everyone else who isn't a fireman or a policeman is sitting and watching!"

"You're right. I don't know what I'm gonna do. But I can't do anything at all from the back of your car."

"Sometimes doing nothing is the right thing."

I concede the point with a nod. "True. But sometimes it's not. How can you be sure this is one of those times? That's my father out there."

"You don't know that!"

"Yeah. I do."

I can't waste any more time. Traffic isn't moving and won't again any time soon. Erika and I cross West 6th Street. We hurry together up the slight rise to St. Clair Avenue.

Great. With these crutches, I run into inclines much more often than I did without them. Awesome. Magic crutches.

Chaos rules at the intersection. Two policemen stand in the heart of the junction. They coordinate traffic, as I suspected, stopping vehicles in all directions, except for fire trucks and ambulances converging on the scene. My spirits sink. A bank of black, gray, and brown belches from the far end of the next block. Firemen swarm around their vehicles. A dozen men haul hoses, axes, and other equipment around the tight corner to narrow Frankfort Avenue.

The Burgess Building. O'Leary's.

The tips of my crutches don't even touch the crosswalk when one of the traffic cops bellows in our direction. "Sir, you can't cross here now!"

I pull back up to the sidewalk. Erika takes my arm, leading me down St. Clair toward the next corner. "We might be able to circle up West 9th, around the back way. If you're up to trying."

"Let's go."

A door opens at the back of the Burgess Building. The open doorway coughs out a thin breath of smoke. I wince. "The fire's spread."

Before I can alert the policeman, a figure emerges from the doorway. Dad. He brushes his fatigue jacket off and starts strolling away from us. The pesky West 6th policeman somehow caught the whole thing. "You! Sir!"

Dad stops in his tracks. His shoulders sag, his head bows. His posture suggests to any witness, law enforcement included, that he may have something to hide. I only hope he doesn't.

The policeman halts traffic. Once he's sure he won't get mowed down by an impatient rush hour commuter, the cop waves Dad over. The cop toggles his collar-clip radio with his other hand. We stand close enough for me to hear some of his conversation. "I got smoke coming out my end of the building," he says. "We need more help here, too!"

Dad trots to our side of the street. We stand between him and the traffic cop, who eyes him as he approaches. Erika raises her hand to greet Dad. He misses the gesture as two firemen scamper into the door he just exited, distracting him. Dad twists to gape at the firemen. His feet tangle with each other, and he tumbles to the pavement a few yards ahead of us.

Okay, Dad's no actor. So, why the act?

The policeman takes only a few steps toward us. He can't leave his post. We reach Dad as he holds up a hand toward the cop. "I'm all right," he calls out, sitting up.

Erika sticks out her hand. Dad takes his time accepting it. When he does, she blinks in surprise.

Dad mutters instructions in a low voice. "My truck's in the lot behind the bar. St. Clair side. Get to your grandmother's. She's not picking up the phone."

Erika palms the keys Dad just slipped her. Dad pretends to dust himself off and check for injuries. He rubs his thighs and knees, flexes his arms. I hope the cop stands far enough away to miss how contrived and awful Dad's performance is.

Get to Grandma's?

"Hey, Dad."

"Yeah?"

"Seeing something besides the cat under the bed?"

"Found out last week Dice took out a big

insurance policy on the bar a month ago."

"Can he?"

"No. Forged ownership papers, I'd bet."

"Where is he?"

"Boiler room."

I can guess what happened here. Neither of us needs to ask what condition Dice is in. I doubt Dad was involved. The weasely Dice most likely caused his own death by botching his insurance scam. I hope the arson investigators agree. "Thank God you got out, Dad."

"Thank God for Prohibition." He grunts, smirking and shaking his head, appreciating the irony. "Ever wonder what's behind the wooden door in my office? Ah sure, you know. Bootleggers' escape tunnel. Runs the length of the building." Dad pats us each on the back and raises his voice. "Thanks young man, young lady! Appreciate the help!" Then, with a slight, fake limp, he shuffles toward the waiting policeman.

Grandma's not answering her phone...

Cars wait idling in every direction. Erika and I jaywalk through the traffic jam, almost laughing as we do. I hobble across St. Clair on crutches, no less. If the traffic cops see us, and I don't know how they couldn't, how frustrated are they that their hands are too full to issue citations?

Why am I taking such a perverse pleasure in this?

Erika spots Dad's truck a third of the way into the lot. She settles me into the passenger's seat, stows my crutches behind me, and hustles around to the driver's side. The engine rumbles to life. We race to the Frankfort Avenue entrance and jerk to a stop. Either aggressiveness at the wheel is a latent Jankowski trait, or they both took driving lessons from Dad.

"Highway or West 25th?"

I don't hesitate. "My gut says West 25th."

The words rush back down my throat as Erika stomps on the gas pedal. We make a wild right out of the lot and a hard left at West 9th. Both my head and stomach reel. She yanks the wheel into another sharp right on Superior Avenue. Her foot never touches the brake.

Something slides and thumps behind us with each flying turn. My groping hand finds a rumpled paper bag. Erika asks without turning my way. "What's that?"

"My Grandpop's camera."

"What's your grandfather's camera doing here?"

"Dad brought it to the hospital. I guess he forgot it in here afterwards."

Erika slows down on the Veterans Memorial Bridge. Not by choice. Traffic waits to turn left at West 25th Street, at the end of the bridge. The line is short, six or seven vehicles. But the vehicle right in front of us is a semi truck.

Terrific.

Her fingers drum on the steering wheel. Her shoulders hunch, tense. Once again, I'm struck by her compassion and concern for Grandma. I do my best to reassure her. "We'll get to her in time. She'll be fine." I knot up inside. My reassurance is as much for myself as for Erika.

Our lane gets the green arrow. The semi lumbers into a laborious left turn. Erika flattens the gas pedal. She crosses over the double yellow lines to pass the semi.

Three cars turn onto the bridge from West 25th. They head straight for us. Two of the cars careen left of us. The third passes on our right. Tires squeal. Erika squeezes Dad's truck onto West 25th ahead of the semi, but not quite out of the oncoming lane. Horns blare all around us.

I say a silent prayer of thanks, though if I was driving I would have done what Erika did. We put some distance between the intersection we just terrorized and ourselves…where I was almost killed a few nights ago. My whole body shakes.

Common reaction, showing fear only when past the danger.

My senses awaken as Erika mirrors my panicked race of the other night. Thoughts grab at both the present and the past. In my head, I can't escape the crash.

Night. Like now. Night's almost here, sky's almost black. Street lamps, store fronts, traffic lights all around. No shadows, no unnatural ones. None I can detect. Where are they now?

Another illegal lane change into horrified oncoming traffic near the West Side Market snaps me back into adrenaline-fueled numbness. Is Erika's eyesight sharper than human eyesight should be? Or has she figured out where the police lie in wait for crazed motorists like her? I suspect the latter. She slows to speed limit near the bridge over Train Avenue. A police cruiser idles in the lot of a nearby auto body shop.

Once we cross the bridge, Erika unleashes her right foot again. She weaves in and out of the right lane. We motor past the RTA bus depot and over the bridge above I-90. She sighs and taps the brakes. Another clot of traffic plugs the Clark Avenue intersection. Trendy Tremont lies east on Clark. A lot of people are heading for their renovated homes, for a drink at one of the new bars, or for dinner at Lola or another restaurant. We're burning time here.

Commuters mill around the bus stop at the corner. If not for them, I'd bet Erika would use the sidewalk.

A green light saves a score of unsuspecting pedestrians. We make only fair time up to Metro General Hospital. The place gives me the same shiver I felt when we passed my accident site.

Flashing lights approach from the opposite direction. An insistent, pulsating beep grows louder. The oncoming ambulance halts traffic everywhere while pulling into the emergency room drive. We stop. Erika raps her palms on the steering wheel. Then we move again for a quarter mile, heeding the speed limit on the bridge over I-71.

West 25th Street changes names to Pearl Road on the bridge. The span ends at Riverside Cemetery. The imposing Romanesque gatehouse looms still and dark behind gates closed for the night.

An omen?

I keep my misgivings to myself.

We fly through the Denison Avenue intersection, then past the YMCA. Young Men's Christian Association. The nearly deserted parking lot crumbles behind a chain-link fence. The squat, inelegant building's desolation saddens me somehow. I make no effort to consider why.

We approach yet another bridge. The open, multi-lane bridge mirrors the style of spans found on interstates. Police love the deception. The bridge is a notorious speed trap. Lights flash behind us. I crane my neck. A police cruiser pulls a speeder over several cars behind us. Erika slows to the speed limit. Getting stopped will take more time we can't spare.

We slow and stop again at Broadview Road, about a mile from Grandma's house. I want to believe the pause won't be a problem. But an ominous sight ahead of us puts a lump in my throat.

A tower of thick smoke rises into the sky on Grandma's side of the street.

Traffic clogs Pearl Road in both directions. Erika can't even cross into the oncoming lane, as she already has a dozen times. We crawl forward a few feet at a time. My foot taps the floorboard. "Just like the Warehouse District."

You're heading into a fire, folks! Are you blind? You can't cross here now!

Erika turns to me, her eyebrows raised. "Same problem. Same fix?"

I scan the surrounding area. We're only one car length from Memphis Avenue. "Yes! Turn right here!"

We rush down Memphis and make a screeching left on West 47th Street, hurrying to Grandma's house the back way. Erika fights to exercise some restraint. She loses, blowing past a stop sign. The uneven pavement, a pucker here, a pothole there, bounces off the bottom of the truck. We make a sharp left turn on Ardmore Avenue. Another stop sign blurs by, unheeded. Vehicles parked along the curb squeeze the already cramped street. Driving this fast is more target practice than anything else.

"Turn right up here."

"What about the alley up ahead?"

"Too close to the house. It'll be blocked."

"Oh. Yeah."

She turns right on West 45th Street. More parked cars constrict the narrow, red-brick road.

The red brick road. A touch of old time blue collar charm. The way to Oz, or the back alley to Kansas?

"Jeez!"

Erika cuts around a parked car. Too fast. She loses control for a moment. We clip an old, dirty, steel trash can near the curb. The can clatters across the bricks ahead of us, coming to rest on the dent we made in it. No time to waste; can't stop. A tire-squealing left on Gifford Avenue takes us away from the wounded trash can.

We don't get far. A fire truck and ambulance block Gifford at West 42nd Street. Erika throws the gear shift into reverse, and parks in an empty space at the curb. She checks to see if she blocked the homeowner's driveway.

She doesn't need to bother. This homeowner may well be out here already. People, neighbors, congregate at the corner of West 42nd. I check them out, but only to keep my eyes busy. I don't want to look ahead. I don't want confirmation. I need none.

I already know whose house lights up the night sky.

CHAPTER 18

Erika tenses up behind the wheel. A horrified murmur escapes her lips. "Oh, my God." She collects herself, jumps out of the truck and helps me from my seat.

I hand her the paper bag with the camera. Why do I want to bring the relic along? I don't know. Maybe I'll chuck the bloody thing on the fire.

We make our way across West 42nd Street. A female firefighter patrols the intersection. She manages to be imposing despite her lack of size. She comes off a bit like an adolescent playing "dress up" in boots and rain gear two sizes too adult for her. But the way she thrusts her palm at us stops us on the corner. "Can't get any closer, folks." Her incredulous tone says she thinks we're idiots for even wanting to try.

"That's my grandmother's house." I point with a crutch

The firefighter's face drops. "Oh. Sorry. Still, the area's not safe."

The fire crew hoses down the houses to either side of Grandma's. These tinder-dry, century-old colonials sit close together. One burning house could turn the whole neighborhood into a giant, smoking hole. I understand the firefighter's concern for my personal safety, too. If danger rears up, I can't clear out with any kind of speed, not with these crutches.

Erika's shoulders droop. Tears well up in her eyes. She grabs my arm and pulls me in as close as my crutches allow.

The firefighter averts her eyes from Erika and addresses me. "Sir, was your grandmother home?"

"I don't know. You haven't found a bod—you haven't found anyone?"

"Someone went in to look. The structure won't hold much longer."

I grasp the urgency. "Bedroom's upstairs in front. She doesn't spend much time in the living room. Kitchen's at the side door. Don't even bother with the basement."

You're so sure about the basement, Buddy?

Oh, yeah, I'm sure.

"Thanks, sir. Please wait here. No closer." The firefighter trots back into the turmoil, barking information into her radio.

Flames lick at the window frames and the front door, devouring the house from the inside out with a dull, hungry, empty-bellied rumble. The old house's dry bones crackle in the insatiable fire-beast's mouth. Running rubber boots pound the pavement with rapid, hollow *ploops*. An ax adds staccato whacks from somewhere within the cacophony of the urgent, desperate work.

Erika's hands tighten around my arm. "You think she's in the house?"

I'm tempted to downplay my fears. I choose another course. Be brave. But be honest. "I'd be surprised if she stepped out so soon after the funeral, but she might have something going. At church, maybe."

"Possible but not likely."

"Yeah."

If she's in there they might still get her out.

My hope never gets through my head to my mouth. A crackling groan grows louder. The firefighter shouts into her radio. "Roof's giving way! Get out!"

Four firefighters burst through the front door three seconds later. One of them trips, tumbling to the lawn and down the steep slope. The popping and snapping multiplies, growing into one continuous roar until the roof caves in and crashes all the way to the first floor. Triumphant arms of fire pump skyward, their fingers pointing toward the stars.

The spectators across the street gasp. Erika and I both hear the communal horror and turn our heads toward the gathered.

I recognize many of Grandma's neighbors, some of whom attended Grandpop's funeral. They'll be at Grandma's service too, I suppose. My stomach knots up. Erika weeps openly now. She sobs at my side as she turns back to Grandma's funeral pyre. I can't, *won't* look.

The commotion swirls unabated. The tumult of disaster grates on my nerves, the spitting and sizzling of the burning house, and the clatter of the people trying to keep the inferno from spreading.

Futile. Like trying to extinguish hell. Hellfire. Grandma was so good. She shouldn't have had to go out this way, roasting in Hellfire.

A clammy deadness permeates my skin and seeps through to my core. Many folks felt Grandma was no more than a sweet, kind old lady. Erika's view goes deeper. She and Grandma connected right away. Now my brain runs into a problem. What did Grandma really mean to me? What did I feel about her? An emotion begins bobbing up and down in my throat. Remorse. A casual stranger might have been closer to her than I was, her own blood. Grandpop knew her best, but he's gone. How alone she must have been this past week since his death. She might as well have been a familiar stranger's face filed away at the back of my memory, like one of the folks across the street.

A figure at the far edge of the knot of spectators stops me in place. I speak as evenly as I can, trying to be heard only by Erika, as if enlisting her aid in snaring a feral cat. "Don't move. Try to get a peek at the back of the crowd without being obvious."

Erika sniffles. I don't turn her way. Movement draws the eye, so I want to keep my own movement to a minimum. I want to make myself small.

I can make myself small. Made myself small for my dresser, didn't I?

After a few seconds, Erika answers. "I don't recognize anyone."

I glance over my shoulder. How could she miss…The sudden realization pops into my head. He's invisible to her, hidden in plain sight. He was hidden to me, too, until Grandpop's wake. I took a snapshot of him, and now I run into him everywhere.

I fight against my excitement to keep my voice down. "We're going to do some acting now. Gotta be better than my dad's acting, okay? Take a look at the fire, then drop your head, like you're depressed."

"Won't be too hard."

"Okay, soon as you do, squeeze my arm. I'll act like you. Then we're going back to the truck."

"Buddy, what's going on?" Quiet alarm edges into her voice.

"When we get to the truck, come over to my side and help me in."

My stress level rises until the gentle squeeze on my arm. I hang my head and turn back toward the truck. Erika leads me anxiously.

"Slow down," I whisper.

"Buddy, I—"

We step into the middle of West 42nd Street. I continue filling her in on a plan that, I admit to myself, might or might not work. "Once you get me in, take the camera out of the bag and shoot a picture of the back of the neighborhood weenie roast."

"There's no flash."

"There's no film either, but I'm hoping it won't matter."

We slow our pace. The truck seems to be parked a mile away. Every second passes like an hour until we get to the passenger's side. Erika opens the door and slides my crutches behind the seat. I peek at the onlookers.

Good. We're not too late.

I climb into the truck. "Okay Erika, take the shot."

The rumpled paper bag protests as Erika pulls the Medalist out. I watch the group through the windshield. No one leaves. Then I hear a raspy "click" behind me, and an interrupted query. "Okay, now what am I supposed to…Oh my God!"

"You see him, don't you?"

Erika ducks down, her face just outside my open window. "Popcorn! I see him!"

"Sh!"

The demon's sneering face swivels toward us. He turns and walks up West 42nd Street.

"Get in! We're gonna follow him."

Erika runs around the front of the truck but stops in the glare of approaching car lights. A rusted old Ford pulls up behind us. Reverend Newhouse slides out of the vehicle. He hurries up to Erika as his passenger's door opens. "What happened? I met Maureen for the perch fry at the Memphis Diner…"

Grandma pulls herself out of his car. Her eyes fix on her decimated home, her body stoops in shock and sorrow. A mournful "Ahhh!" escapes her.

I call out to the reverend. "No time now! Take care of Grandma! Erika, let's go!"

The truck rumbles to life before Erika's butt hits the seat. Popcorn scurries off toward Ardmore Avenue. I take a last, grateful look at Grandma and the reverend. Grandma squares her shoulders. Anger and determination replace her initial shock; I do know her well enough to recognize those signs. Reverend Newhouse, however, tightens his mouth and creases his brow.

He's guessed what we're doing. What are we doing?

I shove my own misgivings aside. I want this

thing. "Tend to Grandma," I repeat to him through my open window.

Erika takes my cue. She blasts us off, away from the curb and onto West 42nd. We screech to a halt at Ardmore. The intersection is deserted.

I bash my fist on the dashboard. "He's gone. Damn!"

"No. There!" Erika doesn't bother pointing him out. She pounds her foot on the gas pedal instead. We execute the wildest left turn I've ever experienced. I squint down the street as my stomach unwraps itself from my spinal cord. A lone figure flits from the edge of one pool of street light to the next, from one shadow to another. The battered navy peacoat, shoulders slightly hunched—it's Popcorn all right.

The fugitive doesn't try to masquerade as something other than what he seems. His legs run like normal legs do, but much faster, covering far more ground than they should be able to cover. Of course. He isn't normal. We clip along at forty miles an hour, fifteen above the limit. Popcorn rounds the corner of West 47th Street ten miles per hour faster than us.

Erika shakes her head. She marvels at his speed despite herself. "He's quick."

We tear around the corner. Down the hill, Popcorn already reaches Memphis Avenue, a quarter mile away. Erika ignores speed limits and stop signs alike. I ignore the loud bang of protesting metal when she bottoms Dad's truck on the pockmarked road. We get to Memphis Avenue as the traffic light turns yellow. Headlights appear behind us.

Terrific. Cops from the fire scene?

"You see the lights?"

Erika glances into the rear-view mirror. "Yeah." She guns the engine.

We barrel forward, whether the lights are from a police car or not. I'm not totally unconcerned. What if our tail is a cop? If we get pulled over, what explanation could we possibly give that wouldn't result in a time-consuming field sobriety test? We could, I suppose, tell the officer we are chasing the arsonist who torched Grandma's house. A kernel of truth might lie at the heart of such a claim.

What then? Have the cop take a picture with Grandpop's camera so he could see the firebug? Good plan.

"He's ducked into the zoo." Erika refocuses my attention.

"Well, let's go visit the animals."

Erika slows to make the right turn onto Wildlife Way. We enter dense, dark territory. The two-lane road meanders through substantial forest, seemingly impenetrable when leaves cover the branches. Tonight, however, street lamps light the road and the leafless forest's skeleton sentinels. The blackness beyond the bare-branched tree line feels palpable, alive. The forest shadows don't move. They wait.

For Popcorn...or for us?

"Stop."

Erika applies the brake. She pulls into the drive

to our left, spotting the same thing I do. The gate is open. She nudges the truck onto the zoo grounds. "He led us here, didn't he?"

I nod. "I'd bet he did. Let's not keep him waiting. Or do you want to go back?"

I almost hope she'll opt to run. Given the deciding vote, I'm not sure what I would choose. Erika's raised chin and unwavering stare announce her choice. She's angry about the fire.

So am I.

We cruise into the park, eyes scanning left, right, and forward. What we leave behind us drops down the priority list. Nothing moves. Calm darkness waits for us.

To do what? Shine a light into it? That sure would be intimidating.

We roll to a stop. Erika turns the headlights off.

I push my door open, keeping my tone as even as I can. "Better leave them on."

The high beams light up the area again. Erika climbs out. I don't wait for her. I lean against the door frame and pull my crutches out from behind the seat myself.

The lights reach out far ahead of us. The beams cast the bare trees, shrubs, and animal areas in sickly bluish-white. We stand still together in the light, our shadows elongated, distorted. Silence. No breeze. No insects, of course, not in November. No traffic, either. I find this odd. We're in a deserted park between two busy streets, near enough to both Fulton Parkway and Memphis Avenue to hear something. Pearl Road runs only half a mile away, too. I hear nothing mechanical. Not even the buzz of electrical transformers reaches us. These sounds become almost subliminal, noticed only when they are absent.

Like now.

Nothing else stirs, either, nothing in nature. No nocturnal beasts. No birds. Everything sleeps in here.

Sleeps...or hides.

We stand in the deep, weird silence for what feels like ten or fifteen minutes. My watch says only a fraction of that actually passed. Erika clears her throat. "Do we wait here?"

I take a step forward. "No."

We edge deeper into the park. The light dissipates. We slow to a stop before leaving the light entirely. Our way here is not clear. Erika grips my arm, her first acknowledgement of fear.

I tense up, too. A familiar problem, a question, displaces my anger. *What will we do when we face Popcorn?* This quandary is no surprise. Once Erika and I opened Grandpop's envelope I imagined, off and on, an actual confrontation. Despite major uncertainty, I tailed him to League Park. I pondered the issue more at the hospital. But now, standing in the murk, the problem really hits home. Am I the hunter, or the hunter's imminent trophy? The stakes are higher now as well. I've got someone with me this time, someone who stands in as much danger as I do.

A yowl startles us. Primates. Gorillas, apes, whatever they are, something disturbs them in a big way. The waterfowl in the lake next to the primates flutter to life a gasp later. Disturbed by the baboons? Something thrashes violently in the water. The splashing and struggling doesn't sound much like waterfowl, not without wingspans of twenty feet or more. From dead ahead of us, comes more screeching of animals I can't identify. Now the big cats, lions and tigers, begin snuffling and roaring. The sounds travel from our left to our right, a cascading wave of disruption. Noisy unease fills the once silent night.

My gut contracts. The hairs on my arms stand on end. I try not to shake. "Are all these animals nocturnal?"

Erika's grip on my arm tightens. "I'm not a zoology major. Doesn't seem likely, though. They're not all cold weather animals, are they? Shouldn't they be sheltered for the winter by now?"

"I would've thought so. I'm not a zoology major, either."

The dim, diffused light around us flickers. We spin around. Shadows dance in front of the truck, shadows cast by no bodies. They show less of their previous aversion to light.

Erika's eyes widen. Her nostrils flare, and she doubles over. "My God, do you smell that?"

My own nose twitches. "Yeah."

The stench of ultimate corruption reaches us. Erika responds violently. She retches to the side, away from me.

My lack of gag reflex mystifies me. When the one shadow got its arm in my car the other night, I supposed my nose would, and should, self-destruct without delay. The stink in my hospital room and the one on my apartment landing were similar but distinct, the way feces, sulfur, and rotting corpses are all unpleasant, but different from one another. But the odor at the apartment affected me less than the other two. I noticed it without wanting to hurl.

Does the phenomenon somehow weaken with each encounter?

Erika straightens up. She wipes her nose with the back of her hand. Her pallid face glows.

No, they're not weaker. Am I becoming desensitized?

She inhales pointedly through her mouth only. "What are they?"

The raspy, grating answer comes from the edge of the light, from the darkness behind us where the animals stir.

"They are your legacy."

The light flickers and fades. Shadows approach from every direction, closing in on us. Popcorn, the lone figure of substance, advances from beyond our pitiful pool of light.

Putrescence thickens the air. Erika doubles over once again, but her stomach is already empty. The reek is unbearable to her. My stomach roils only a little, which disturbs me. I study the demon as he closes the distance between us. "Legacy?"

"Yes. You creatures leave a stinking mess."

"Great. An environmentalist."

Popcorn's eyes flash a bright, icy blue. He snaps his head at me and hisses, his wide-open mouth baring viper's fangs. The shadows rush at us. Only one breaks into our midst, a particularly vile-smelling one. Erika sinks to one knee, overcome by the brutal stench. I flinch but recover.

It's just a shadow. It can't do—

The shadow bends low and swings its arm, knocking my legs out from under me. I land flat on my back. The wind rushes out of my lungs. The memory of the assault on me and of the shadow's foul kiss at the hospital floods back. I forgot these things have substance. I'll remember now.

Popcorn bends over me. He yanks the knit cap from his head. Erika gasps. The demon's crew cut changes. The stubby brush of hair grows longer and thicker, winding and slithering until it becomes a foot-long, writhing, gray tangle.

His voice grates in a half-hiss, half-growl. "Environmentalist. Funny, yes. This is my environment. You are trespassers."

Popcorn's gnarled hand reaches for my throat. Before his bony claw grabs hold, he lurches forward, almost falling on top of me. He twists around. Erika straddles his back, one arm locked around his neck in a choke hold. A banshee howl fills the air. I can't tell if the shriek comes from him or from her.

The creature twists like an enraged, demented rodeo bull. Erika holds on, bashing the side of the demon's head with her other fist. Wicked, vicious shots land on his ear, his temple, his jaw.

Her assault is hopeless. I manage to push myself up to a standing position. The shadows dancing around us become hesitant, uncertain. I think they are somewhat stunned.

Good.

Popcorn's sudden spin takes Erika by surprise. She finds her face within a foot of his. He snarls at her. She composes herself enough to land a thunderous right to his nose, snapping his head back. He shakes the blow off, grabs the front of her shirt with one hand and lifts her two feet off the ground.

"Strong spirit, yes. I'll take your spirit. I'll take you. Right here. Now. In front of your little boyfriend."

The creature's head bobs slowly up and down. Low, guttural groans come from him. He sizes her up like a teenager drooling over his first eyeful of a *Playboy* centerfold. Popcorn gives her his full attention. He turns his back on me.

The notion of this thing violating Erika stirs something inside me. My anger's intensity can't be measured or held back any longer. I grasp one of my crutches at the bottom, like a baseball bat, and swing harder than I've ever swung before. It's a textbook homerun swat…weight and power transferring from my right foot to my damaged left, hips swiveling out, torso uncoiling, arms fully extended, wrists snapping at just the right time, the bat—the crutch—crashing into its target at the optimum point in its arc…

The crutch crumples, bending and twisting in my hands. Erika remains suspended in mid-air. Popcorn turns his head back toward me. His hiss drips contempt. "That's all? Hmm. Career .240 hitter, yes, no wonder."

".243."

Like a lightning strike, his free hand grabs me by the shirt. My feet leave the ground. The beast sneers at us in turn. "I'll take her now. Deal with you when I'm done."

I spit my enraged question at him. "What do you want with us?"

Popcorn lifts his chin, his eyes shining. "I have what I want. I have you. You are both mine!"

"No. They are not."

The soft voice reverberates both in my ears and on my skin, a disembodied baritone originating from nowhere, but resonating everywhere.

The sound affects us all. Erika's head swivels. She scans the area in vain for the source. Popcorn's eyes widen, and his triumphant sneer collapses. What takes its place? Contrition? Surprise? Some terror thrown in? He drops us.

I land on my left leg and crumple to the ground. My eyes search the darkness beyond us, every corner. I find nothing.

A gentle hand rests on my shoulder. "I am right here, Buddy."

I lift my eyes toward the soothing voice. A man with a calm and handsome face stoops beside me and extends his other hand, taking mine. His grip is firm and warm. He helps me to my feet.

"I am sorry for the trouble."

Anticipation and excitement fill me. I gaze into knowing, sorrowful eyes. "You're him."

His pleasant smile warms me. "Yes. I am."

CHAPTER 19

My head empties of all critical thought. I fumble for words. No experience in my past prepared me for this meeting.

But Erika takes only a moment to processes the scene. Her uncertainty gives way to her faith. She drops to one knee and bows her head in the classic worship position. I try to follow suit. My shattered leg thwarts me.

The kind face turns toward the bowed Erika. The compassionate eyes flash for an instant in an emotion I can't comprehend. He faces me again, the epitome of tranquility and peace.

And confidence?

"Here, let me help you." He pulls at one of my brace's Velcro straps.

I jerk my leg away on impulse. "Lord, I'll need the support for a while." I feel immediately stupid. I'm told he knows everything, including my every need.

"No. You no longer need the brace, or the crutches." He undoes the other straps. The brace unfolds and drops to the ground. "Stand, Buddy."

I put a little weight on my leg, forcing myself to trust. My foot presses against the ground. No pain. More weight is added, then more. The thigh muscles squeeze around my mess of a femur. Nothing. I distribute my full weight evenly to both feet. I flex my shattered knee. I can touch my heel to my butt! Dr. Hurth told me regaining full range of motion was a physical, a mechanical, impossibility.

Impossible.

I drop to my knees next to the wide-eyed Erika.

"Rise, both of you."

We stand. He glances at Erika. The connection strikes me as strange and a bit uncomfortable, somehow out-of-place. *Inappropriate?* I don't have time to dwell on the odd moment.

"You stare at me, Buddy. Are you disappointed?"

I try to gather myself. Speaking with the Savior of all Mankind, I don't dare say anything judgmental. "Forgive me for saying so, Lord, but you look average."

My observation draws a laugh. "I hope so."

"I mean, average height, average build. I doubt I could pick you out of a police line-up. God forbid you'd be in a…I mean…jeez!"

My tongue stumbles while Erika scrutinizes our savior. He raises his chin and narrows his eyes. "If you could pick a place, where would you say I'm from?"

"That's the problem, Lord. I had the same difficulty with this demon you just saved us from. He could be Asian, light-skinned African, Caucasian, Hispanic. His features fit everywhere. Like yours, except older."

You could be his son…

The gentle rumble of his voice vibrates through every muscle down to my spine, pacifying, soothing. "I must appear as everyone. I belong to everyone, just as those who follow me belong to me."

"Makes sense."

"Buddy, do you know what my plan is for you?"

My answer is quick and honest. "No, Lord. Everyone liked the articles I wrote for the school paper when I was a sophomore. A lot of people encouraged me. My grandfather told me I had a gift, so I'm doing what I do best, I guess. Or am I wrong?"

"You never sought my plan for you."

My face flushes. "No, Lord, I guess not."

He chuckles. "Do not fear. You are closer to my path than you think." His eyes wander to Erika's. He smiles but says nothing. Erika's shoulders sag. The subtle physical reaction mystifies me but, again, he gives me no time for analysis. "Buddy, you are so close. Let me show you what I want you to do. Let me point out your way."

He takes my hand, ignoring Popcorn as if the demon was absent altogether. The shadow creatures part. We walk past them and their now diminishing odor, and step beyond the light. "Let me show you my love. Let me reward you for your services to me."

Ambient light with no visible source floods the zoo as we walk. Familiar sounds fill the air. The sharp crack of ash on horsehide, and the dull thump of horsehide on leather, make me smile.

Two baseball diamonds, sandlots with chain-link backstops, materialize where the lion area should be, like a mirage in a summer haze. I marvel at the vision. A full squad of baseball players emerges. They appear to be just a bit younger than me, maybe a college team. But which team? Their uniform colors are fuzzy, indistinct.

A dozen players pair up and play catch in the outfield between us and the dirt diamonds. Some throw hard, straight rockets at each other. The others lob playful rainbows.

Beyond them on the diamond to our left, three hitters mill around a batting cage. The young men limber up. They wait their turn as a fourth batter, a lefty, takes his swings. An older man, a coach, I assume, lofts pop-ups to infielders on the right-side diamond. The mood overall is carefree, almost jovial as this team basks in sunshine that gives light but no warmth, light that shouldn't be here.

"Come with me."

Erika and I follow through the perfect, manicured, emerald outfield toward the diamonds. She watches me walk without aid, without crutches. She smiles but furrows her brow.

"What?"

She shrugs and shakes her head.

What does that *mean?*

WHACK!

The coach on the right diamond hits a pop-up too far. The shortstop runs hard toward us. He searches over his shoulder for the ball, but he'll never get to the blooper in time.

Instinct takes over. I jog forward and settle under the lazy fly ball, peeking back at my fan base of two. They seem divided. One beams like a father watching his kid catch the final out of a championship game. His smile is broad, sincere. His eyes flash, his fists clench in front of his chest in hopeful anticipation. The other appears…confused, worried, her posture stiff and tense. She cocks her head to one side, as if listening to a heckler yelling that I'm sure to drop the ball and blow the game for everyone.

I'm not dropping the ball.

An upward glance tells me my timing hasn't suffered after a half dozen years on the figurative bench. I sidestep. As soon as the ball touches my hands I swing them behind me, killing the ball's momentum. My palms still sting, but I've caught the ball.

Voices around me cheer the way ballplayers do—words of encouragement and positive reinforcement. I blush despite myself.

"Shortstop! Heads up!" I cock my arm and snap a pretty good throw off to the young infielder.

"Thanks, Coach! Nice grab!" The shortstop tosses the ball ahead of him and trots back to the infield.

I turn to my companions. They remain a combination of infinite pride in one, and minor worry in the other. My curiosity grows. I'm unable to contain it, much the way a child fails to curb his excitement on Christmas morning. "Coach?"

The voice soothes me in a way I never experienced before. It excites me, too, without losing its placid, even tone. Both my emotions and my body are drawn to the sound as I wander back to him.

"Not all players excel, no matter how much they may love the game. But not all great players make talented coaches, either. And what is a coach? A guide. A molder and shaper of lives. A teacher."

I stand next to Erika as he finishes. Something is wrong, or at least is not quite right. She edges away from the Messiah, increasing the distance between her and him, inching closer to me. She moves slowly.

Is she creating a respectful distance...or a cautious one?

My curiosity overcomes my concern. "Coaching where? At what level? I mean, I don't want to sound demanding or ungrateful."

Another gentle chuckle cuts me off. "You are none of those things, Buddy. To teach youth in my ways, you should indeed know as much as you can."

He sweeps a hand across the scene before us. The ballplayers all jog our way. Their uniforms change color as they approach, the washed-out gray and black intensifying to white and blue. A team logo surfaces on the white caps with the blue bills.

I recognize the colors and the logo. "You want me to coach at Case Western?"

"Would you be uncomfortable here?"

"They lost only six games last season. I doubt they want to make a coaching change."

"But I do."

Why would he want to make a change? I count Derrick Howard, the CWRU Spartan's baseball coach, as a friend. He has a major league-caliber baseball mind. His code of conduct is both unimpeachable and non-negotiable, but his silly, dorky sense of humor makes him far from stuffy. The combination earns him enormous popularity. True, his popularity suffered with those players he had to cut from the club for repeatedly breaking team or school rules. Derrick is strict but patient, giving all his players three strikes in the conduct department. I can't imagine this team without him any more than I can imagine myself in his place.

"Sometimes change is necessary, my son. You are concerned about Derrick, yes?"

Having my mind read unnerves me. "Yes."

"Do not concern yourself with him. Secure your own future. You owe yourself that much."

Sympathy and self-interest war with each other. My instinct shouts, *TURN THE JOB DOWN,* but my mouth has other ideas. "How far can I go?"

"How far would you like to go?"

"Big league manager?" The question is not completely serious, but serious enough to be asked.

"No, but would you like to be a bench coach? Maybe a pitching coach or hitting instructor."

"I only hit .243 myself."

"Perhaps you would like to be the third base coach on a World Series team. On Cleveland's first World Championship team in over fifty years."

The approaching squad arrives. The players surround us. They shout and laugh and slap each other on the back...and age a few years before my eyes, passing from boys to men. Their uniforms change, too. Blue jerseys darken to navy. Red bleeds into the white block-letter "Spartans" across each chest. The letters twist into the familiar cursive script "Indians." The inference is clear.

The Indians will win the World Series soon, and I can play a part!

I almost jump up and down as if I'd just had twenty years amputated from me. A crowd of fans approaches from nowhere. They mob us, a swirling sea of delirious people of every age and ethnicity united by their Tribe jackets, sweatshirts, and caps. We're on the field at The Jake now. The throng in the stands empties into the third base coach's box. Hands reach for me, bodies crush together. The joy of the city suffocates in a kind of civic *schadenfreude*. The horde jostles me, twisting, bumping, and turning me in every direction. Heads, shoulders, hands flash in front of my face.

The chaos excites and disturbs me. I can't keep my equilibrium and begin to imagine I'm being buried under still-living bodies. I'm shoved and turned again. The view twists and swirls like I'm on a speeding merry-go-round, or in a revolving door.

Popcorn and his shadows stand behind Erika. They don't attack her, but station themselves too close for my comfort, threatening to envelope her the way this crowd does me. She stands alone, unguarded and undefended.

The manhandling fans fade. They become specters before my eyes. Outlines of distant houses, trees and shrubs become more distinct. The dimming mob's touch becomes softer, less violent. Their bodies finally vaporize into a wispy smoke cloud that drifts away on a sudden, brief, gentle breeze.

But the shadows remain, notwithstanding the eerie, cold sunlight. So does Popcorn. The demon stands beside Erika, menacing but not touching her. He's waiting, but for what? He glares at me until something over my shoulder distracts him. I spin around.

The third base section of stands is still here. Two familiar faces beam at me from the second row. One face brings me tranquility, serenity, but the other stirs something else in me. My heartbeat quickens, my blood surges through my body.

Kelly's big, deep green eyes shine above haughty cheekbones, and her ruby lips form a pouting smile. She hesitates before rising. Her tentative movements suggest apology, or remorse. She folds her anxious hands in front of herself and stands on tip-toe.

The breeze carries her throaty whisper to my ears. "Buddy."

I'm tempted to run to her. I freeze instead. An irksome sense nags at me like a persistent mosquito. Something is not quite right.

Kelly unfolds her hands and holds them out to me. She pauses only to push her floppy sweatshirt's sleeves up past her wrists. I take a mental inventory of her clothing for the first time, the baggy sweat shirt, the loose and faded blue jeans.

A hand rests on my shoulder. "You two belong together."

I jump a bit at both the voice and the touch; he

was in the stands next to Kelly not a second ago. I'm not sure where he'll be from one breath to the next. That makes me nervous. I try not to let the sudden moves distract me. The nagging buzz in my head insists on focusing my attention. "She doesn't look right."

"Your tastes have changed, have they not?"

The comment seems cryptic to me, but only for a moment. Kelly never dressed down this way before. She always chooses clothes that show her model's body off to me, to everyone. But she seems ready to writhe in discomfort in these duds.

An awkward truth strikes me. I always objectified Kelly. Such behavior should have bothered me, but I didn't care. Why would I? I was with a woman who looked every inch the goddess. I enjoyed gawking in lust-filled desire at her. She enjoyed being stared at, too, often admitting as much to me. How I got to be with this goddess always escaped me. But now our higher power tells me we're supposed to be together, we are meant for each other no matter what clothes she wears, and my chauvinism is justified.

Still, she doesn't look like herself. Seeing her this way makes me think she's putting on an act.

For my benefit? Why? She doesn't look bad; she isn't capable. But if I didn't know better, I'd say she borrowed Erika's wardrobe.

A commotion grows behind me. Popcorn growls in discontent. He hangs his head, like the last kid left after the popular players have been picked. He spits and splutters.

The hand lifts from my shoulder. Its angelic owner picks his way toward the demon. He stands close to the pouting fiend and, with his back to me, says something in tones too low for me to hear. I try to keep a straight face. The scenario reminds me of a conference on a pitcher's mound after a bad outing by the staff's ace.

But since when does your manager talk to the opposing pitcher?

Erika stands off to the side, her body rigid. Her wide eyes lock on mine. I read them in an instant. Translation doesn't take much effort on my part. Fear mixes with anxiety all over her. I feel a strong urge to join her.

The truth crashes down on me. What is in fact taking place becomes clear. Not everything, I suppose, but the obvious slaps me in the head. I want to kick myself for being so stupid. My anger at myself squashes the fear I should be feeling.

I don't care whether I'm doing the right thing now or not. "Hey, Popcorn. He promised you Kelly, didn't he?"

The back facing me straightens.

Confirmation.

I spit. A bad taste coats my tongue. "I thought you were Jesus, or the Holy Ghost or something."

He turns, his tone of voice still controlled and even. "Maybe even God the Father Himself?"

"Sure, why not? You said—"

"I said nothing. You made assumptions."

"I guess I did. You're Satan."

"I have many names."

Not exactly a straight answer. More confirmation, the ultimate deceiver.

The serene composure remains. So, do the dark, handsome but vague, almost generic looks. This is him, the beast, the scourge of all mankind since the Garden of Eden. I'm unable to work up Erika's level of fear...and Popcorn's. I suppose I understand Erika's dread, even though our eternal enemy comes off as benign.

Popcorn's alarm seems odd. He wreaks havoc on behalf of the enemy of man, yet his boss's arrival on the scene unnerves him. Popcorn is no happier than Erika at this moment.

Why?

I decide to clear this up for myself by doing what I am trained to do. I shift carefully into journalist mode. "If you are—well, let's call you Satan—then who is your friend here?"

The king of the underworld throws an arm across the flinching Popcorn's shoulders. "This is...well, your tongue would not be able to pronounce his true name. How important is his name to you? What do you call him?"

"Popcorn."

"Popcorn, yes. This name amuses me."

Erika plants herself on her little spit of soil like a tomato stake. I glance at her. She's terrified, but she won't give ground. She stares at the hand I hold out to her but doesn't move.

I ask Satan's permission. "Do you mind?"

He answers with a curt nod.

She walks with as normal and steady a speed as

she can, refusing to show her horror and fear. Terror begins to creep into me now. My mind whispers to me, making only a simple observation at first.

This is the devil.

The observation repeats itself once, twice, again, becoming a constant reminder.

This is the devil.

The reminder becomes almost a mantra. No matter what his demeanor, no matter what his promises...

This is the devil. This is the devil?

"You don't look all that scary." I blurt this out. Even Erika chuckles despite herself.

Popcorn finds my observation less amusing. "My master rules. Show respect!"

"A bit late for that now. Yes, I rule. And you disobeyed me." The softness of his voice doesn't blunt the admonishment.

"Master, I did your work!"

Satan sighs, unmoved, his demon's plea falling on unreceptive ears. This confuses me. My comfort level shrinks a bit more, but not enough to keep me from voicing a guess. "Popcorn's a rogue, right? None of this was your idea."

"This was an unfortunate comedy of errors."

Erika's anger flares, no doubt kindled by Grandma's smoldering house. "Comedy? Interesting word."

Not more interesting a word than "error."

A hard slap sends Erika reeling. She rights herself and holds her fists up to defend herself from Popcorn. He glowers at me then turns, raising his hand against her.

I run at him as hard as I can, driving my shoulder into the small of his back. We tumble into a heap. Not a bad tackle for a baseball player. My fists connect with his face three or four times each. The blows deliver the same effect my crutch did. He growls and shoves me off. My hands go up instinctively into a defensive position, just as Erika's did.

He's off her at least.

But nothing happens.

I look up past my raised fists. Popcorn stands next to his master, bowing his head in sorrow, but without remorse. I don't believe he's sorry for doing something wrong. He's sorry he's being reprimanded.

Erika and I help each other to our feet. I plant myself between her and the two demons from hell, though I can't imagine what I'd do should they attack. The third base grandstands still loom behind them, but the ballplayers are gone. The clipped infield and cold sunlight remain.

Kelly stays behind, too. She leans back against her folded seat, mimicking the semi-erotic pose she struck for the picture I took at O'Leary's.

My mind reels. Scattered mental images pile up in a free-for-all. Kelly dresses to kill for Grandpop's wake and ends up with Popcorn in her ear. O'Leary's burns and Grandma's house burns harder, like the deck of the *Enterprise* after Popcorn's aerial attack. Mannion tells me the story of Helen of Troy turning men's heads and muddying their minds, and

I come back to Kelly ending up with Popcorn in her ear…

Popcorn, the common denominator. I eventually assumed he followed Grandpop home from the Pacific, but now I wonder again. Did he draw a bead on Grandpop earlier? But why would he? Did Popcorn have something to do with Helen Summers the way he did with Kelly? And is he really a renegade, or is he following Satan's orders?

An even creepier question arises. How close was he whenever Kelly and I were together?

The devil lifts his chin, appraising me, measuring me. "Your eyes consume Kelly with desire, Buddy. Of course. You cannot help but want her."

The voice comforts me less each time I hear it. "Yes and no," I say.

"She is yours for the taking. But you must choose."

Love. The word pops into my head. I wonder about the concept of "love," the difference between Erika's warmth and Kelly's all-consuming fire…Kelly's fire and a sunlight with no warmth…a demon torching my family and Grandpop's old acquaintance comforting me in a hospital room…

I snap out of my funk. Something moves deep inside me. Something I accepted as a child but silenced long ago, a buried belief, a faith, unearths itself and speaks both to me and through me.

"Where I spend eternity is more important to me than where I'll spend the night."

"As you wish."

A nonchalant wave of his arm makes the grandstand disappear, taking Kelly's apparition away, too. The sun darkens, the sky goes pitch black. The playing fields evaporate, replaced by the animal habitats that belong here. The animals' restless noises slash at the air again.

Pain wracks my leg. I crumple to the ground, almost blacking out from the agony. Erika bends down at my side. She helps me straighten my broken leg.

Satan smiles sadly, shaking his head. "Such a shame. So much promise wasted."

"I'll be fine," I gasp through gritted teeth. I sit up with brutal difficulty.

"Perhaps. I do apologize for all this."

"I'll bet." Erika's furious retort comes from behind me as she gropes along the black ground for my leg brace.

"Truly. I demand much subtler methods. They produce far better results."

Erika brings me the brace and a twisted sculpture I recognize as my mangled and useless crutch.

Satan takes the crutch from her. He holds the prop for a moment as if brandishing a rifle. His hand begins running over it, caressing it. The corckscrewed crutch untwists and flattens as he speaks. "The problem with overt action is the danger of a negative reaction. This reaction is resistance. Leaders, politicians, they understand the concept well. Resistance is a choice with consequences."

Erika lifts my leg as gently as she can. I bite my scream off. She's doing her best, and I refuse to complain in any way. She slips the brace under my leg, fastening the Velcro straps. She grunts a reply as she works. "Everything's a choice. Every choice has consequences."

"You are quite correct, Erika." Satan beckons Popcorn with one hand. In the other he holds what used to be my crutch.

Popcorn stares at the object in the devil's hand and bows his head again. He shuffles his feet, kicking at the dirt. He whines and whimpers.

The minion gets to within arm's length of Satan. The Prince of Darkness's free hand grabs Popcorn's writhing mane. The other hand slashes downward. Moonlight glints off what is now an over-sized scimitar. A whispering *whoosh* disturbs the air. Popcorn's body falls away.

Flying blood spatters both Erika and me.

Satan holds Popcorn's severed head up by the tangled hair, studying the lifeless face. He speaks as much to the decapitated demon as to us. "Consequences. Yes. Some choices baffle me. Why choose that which carries so high a cost, such terrible consequences?"

Gore drips down my forehead. I wipe my brow before the spatter drips into to my eyes. Erika does the same. The blood, a lot of blood, snarls her long, thick hair, making her clean-up efforts more difficult.

Beams of light swing toward us from behind Dad's truck. The light captures the legion of shadows. A few of the transparent creatures scatter, but most continue milling with uncertainty around the edges of the light. Satan backs away from the glare.

Perplexed, Erika raises an eyebrow. "You're not going to kill us?"

The comforting sound of his reply contrasts with the sight of the dripping head he carries. "This is between God and me. Make your own decisions, your own choices. You most often choose poorly, from His standpoint. God's glory thus diminishes, and I win. You cannot make decisions if you are dead, and I cannot then take God's glory from Him."

I begin to understand now. "We're more useful to you if we're alive than if we're dead."

"More often than not, yes." A car door slams behind us. Satan backs further into the darkness. "You may not see me again, but I am with you, Buddy. I am with you all. Always."

I spit out some burnt-copper blood. "John Francis. My Christian name is John Francis."

Satan chuckles quietly and disappears beyond our sight.

The remaining shadows turn gray. Facial features and clothing details emerge, etching themselves for a brief moment on each shadow. Heads and bodies become distinct. A tall, hulking form lingers in the light as the others disintegrate into a gathering mist. The sketchy, lone shadow smiles and nods at me. He finally loses cohesion, merging into the formless fog bank.

I recognize the face, and the nod of approval. I

raise my hand, waving good-bye to the dissipating remains of Bill Mannion.

"You gonna sit there in the wet grass all night, or just 'til the police come?"

A shadow crosses over me, but its owner is mortal and solid. Reverend Newhouse ambles to my side.

"Hey, check this out!" Erika holds her hands up. Her hands, face and hair glisten with misty water, not blood. I survey the ground around us. The dark splatter from Popcorn's beheading loses its color. We now sit on a patch of dewy, silver-tipped sod. Light fog lingers. The shadows no longer threaten us. But their aftermath reminds us of their malignant past.

Will we remember beyond tonight? What about beyond the next year, or the next decade?

The reverend helps Erika up, and then me. She hands me the crutch the devil discarded. I'll pitch it myself when we leave the park. The scimitar became a crutch again without my noticing, but the mess is a crutch in name only. No one would guess this tubular pretzel's original use. The other crutch lies here, somewhere. No one cares to search. I'll buy another pair tomorrow.

We pick our way back toward our parked vehicles, Erika and Reverend Newhouse on either side of me, assisting me. I turn to the reverend. "How's Grandma?"

"I left her with neighbors. She's a little in shock. Just lost her home."

Erika pats my arm. "She can stay with me for a

while if your dad can't take her in."

"He may not have a home either. I may not, for all I know."

Newhouse cocks his head. "How's that?"

I tell him about the blaze at O'Leary's, connecting the fiery attacks on my family tonight.

Erika interrupts my tale. "We should call your mother."

I call out Mom's number, which Erika punches into her cellular phone. We reach the truck. I pull away from the helping hands and lean back against the pick-up's hood. Erika shakes her head, grimacing. A growing sensation begins as a shiver at the back of my neck. I try to slough the tingle off. "She answering?"

Erika's face lights up as she speaks into her cellular. "Hello, Mrs. Cullen?"

Relief washes over me. I lose much of Erika's end of the conversation while trying to keep my shivers from growing into a full-body shake. I fail. She speaks to Mom for me.

The reverend roots around the bed of the pick-up. He finds a dusty old tarp and throws it over my shoulders. "Cold, huh?"

"Cold? Yeah. Tired. I'm so tired. My leg feels like sh…hurts beyond description." I note the reverend's grave demeanor, his slow nod. I barely whisper, "You know, don't you? You saw the demons, the devil and his pal."

"Didn't tonight, but I saw 'em a long time ago."

"How'd you find us, Reverend?"

"Almost didn't. Reached the Second District

Police station on Fulton and couldn't find you anywhere, so I doubled back."

"What made you pull into Wildlife Way?"

He shrugs. "This might sound crazy to you. I believe I was led here. What do you believe?"

Erika ends her call, gives me a "thumbs up," and opens the passenger door. The reverend lets me lean on his arm, helping me inside.

I settle in before answering his question. "Hamlet."

"How's that?"

Erika groans. "I made a comment I'm afraid I'm never gonna live down."

"But you were right."

"Sorry," the reverend says, "I'm a little lost."

A smile spreads across my face. "We were doing some research on paranormal phenomena. I was skeptical. Erika hit me with a line from Shakespeare's *Hamlet.* 'There is more in heaven and earth than is dreamt of in your philosophy.'" I turn to Erika, a new question nagging me. "How did you know he wasn't God, or Jesus?"

"I didn't. Not at first."

"What gave him away?"

She takes a soft, apologetic tone. "I guess I know the Bible a lot better than you. Sorry. But the more he talked, the more I heard about rewards for you in this life. Jesus promised rewards in the next life, not this one."

"Amen, young lady." Reverend Newhouse turns his gaze to me. "I ask you again, young Mr. Cullen. What do you believe?"

"I believe it's time for me to crack open that book you gave me. Time to consider things beyond my philosophy."

The reverend claps his hands. He laughs, then sobers a bit. "I wouldn't be wearing this collar without Irish Jimmy opening my eyes to a new world. The Lord knows I'll help his kin any way I can."

"I'd like to hear that story someday, Reverend."

My smile fades. I try to process what I witnessed tonight, and what I lived through this week. Good and evil, I discovered, exist separate and apart from each other, yet side-by-side. I found they can be difficult to distinguish from each other sometimes, like so many different types of fish in murky water when everything mixes together. Tonight, I met the fallen one who stirs as much dissent and conflict into the water as he can.

I also begin to understand how man, collectively and individually shuns God, giving our mortal foe a powerful ally—mankind itself.

CHAPTER 20

The foul ball crashes into an empty chair behind us. The sizzling hiss passing my ear makes an impression on me, but not until the ball's impact on the chair. Stunned spectators in our section sit frozen in their places. All are too surprised to duck for cover, let alone try for a souvenir. Several faces on the field show surprise as well. Mouths drop open while eyes widen.

"Jumped off the bat pretty quick, didn't it? That pitcher brings some heat," Reverend Newhouse says.

"Whew! You're not kidding." My voice shakes more than I like.

A mental red flag flutters. My eyes scan the grandstands. I keep watch with more diligence than I used to. I must. I met the devil in the zoo a decade ago. He took my naiveté and my complacency away with him that night.

Reverend Newhouse, Erika, and I sit together near the third-base dugout in Classic Park, the home of the minor league Lake County Captains. The sun bakes us as if we were in a convection oven. This July day seems hot enough to please Satan himself. He may well be here in the ball park—he or one of his minions.

The idea disturbs me, but only a little. Our enemy walks the earth with us, always. He told me so himself. Mankind knows Satan as the consummate liar, but I have no reason to doubt him on this point.

If anything, there's been too much proof to support his claim.

I learn to live with the knowledge. For example, I enjoy simple pleasures, like a well-played ball game, unhindered by such concerns on days like today.

A battle of wits, skills, and wills takes place on the field. The young left-hander on the mound wipes his brow with the back of his hand. His adversary is also a lefty. The batter paws at the loose dirt around home plate with his cleats. Neither the pitcher nor the batter takes his eyes off the other as they duel in the sun, hurler against hitter, player against player.

Man against man.

Reverend Newhouse squints at his score card. "This kid who's up…"

"Anderson," Erika says.

"Anderson," the reverend repeats. "This kid's in a slump. He's gonna strike out."

Erika munches on a kernel of popcorn. The corners of her mouth turn up in a mischievous grin. "I'm not so sure, Reverend. I think he's due."

A loud *plop* turns our heads back toward the diamond. The umpire hesitates behind home plate. I'd bet the pitch's speed took him by surprise. He lowers his right hand and calls, "Ball!"

Reverend Newhouse snorts. "Guess that pitch didn't sound enough like a strike. I know he couldn't see it." He twists in his seat and raises his voice. "Mrs. Cullen thinks Anderson's gonna get a hit. What do y'all think?"

A dozen children around us, the Fellowship Baptist Church youth group, raise a chorus of conflicting opinions.

I can't hide my own smile. "She's been right four batters in a row, Reverend. Anderson's not the one in a slump."

A boy wearing an over-sized Indians cap jumps up from his seat. He climbs over a succession of his cohorts' knees and makes his way toward us. Our tow-headed seven-year-old, Michael, climbs into my lap. "Mom's right again, isn't she, Dad?"

"Maybe, Michael. Maybe."

"Not sure?"

"No. I'm not."

My arms encircle him. The moment reminds me of the picture of my own father and me, the shot taken at Municipal Stadium. I wish Dad was here now.

The doctor told us in August of '01 that the stroke didn't kill Dad. The light pole he wrapped his truck around while having the stroke killed him. Dad was on his way to work, to O'Leary's. He restored the place with determination and care after the fire. O'Leary's was his place, after all, the place where he belonged. We held his wake in the old pub, just as he held his own father's there. Dad willed the business to me. I appreciated the gesture but had no interest in running a tavern. I sold O'Leary's to an investor a month later, a restaurateur who saw big dollar signs in a Warehouse District address.

The investor folded the business within six

months. The place just wasn't the same without Dad. The space in the Burgess Building remains empty, another basement where the dust falls on half-forgotten and ever fading memories.

Mom cried at Dad's funeral. I hadn't caught her in that kind of emotion since I was about my son's present age. She and I grew much closer after Dad's death. She refuses to talk about him. Is this remorse or guilt or anger? I doubt the last, but since she won't open up about him, I'll never really know. We're not as close as I'd like, but still, closer than ever. I'll take that.

Mom's also connected more with Grandma, who we all visit at her Westlake retirement community. Gram spoils Michael at every opportunity, usually with a scoop of Neopolitan ice cream that she never used to keep on hand but now, mysteriously, always does. Worsening arthritis keeps her from attending weekly Mass. Reverend Newhouse visits her every Sunday after his own church services. Their bond, their faith, inspires me.

My hometown and its beloved baseball team continue to mirror each other. The Indians had an impressive run from '96 up until a few years ago. The city itself enjoyed a resurgence of sorts over that same span. Shiny new buildings popped up, historic ones were cleaned and renovated, and nightlife thrived in the Flats and the Warehouse District. Then everything fell apart on all fronts. The Indians were sold, Jacobs Field got a new name, and the whole city began emptying again.

Kelly was one of the many who fled. She took a

job in Seattle in '98, disappearing from our lives almost without a trace.

Erika and I married a year almost to the day after our walk in the woods. I made a comparison that night, Kelly's bright burning flame versus Erika's steady, ever-present warmth. Grandma's house fire comes to mind. After an intense blaze goes out, the cold seems somehow colder than before. But Erika is capable of turning up a considerable flame herself. She always warms me. *Always.* Michael, who arrived a year into our marriage, warms both of us.

RJ and I still get together every few weeks to shoot darts and down a few beers. He still beats me every time. Some things never change, I guess, but some things do. We talk about everything except Popcorn. Our conversations never felt superficial before. Now, they do.

Another foul ball, another laser shot into our midst. The ball clatters off the seat my son just vacated. Everyone in the reverend's youth group gasps. The pitcher and the umpire gape into the stands at us, impotent concern etched on their faces.

Anderson, the batter who launched the foul ball at us, turns our way, too. His expression lacks the others' concern. The trace of a sneer takes its place. His eyes narrow when they meet mine. Those eyes make me uneasy.

Erika grips my arm. She reads the darkness in Anderson's eyes, I guess. She takes Michael on her lap. His own eyes are as big as dinner plates.

I reach under my seat for a rumpled paper bag.

"What do you think?" I ask my adult companions. "Too soon?"

Erika shakes her head. "He's old enough to think about stuff besides what's on TV."

"Hmm. Wait 'til he's old enough to surf the internet."

"Ten years ago," Reverend Newhouse says, "they'd have made you leave your bag at the gate. How'd you sneak it in?"

I pull Grandpop's camera from the bag. "I didn't. Why keep anyone from bringing a camera in? Most fans here have cell phones with cameras anyway."

Michael sizes up the camera with scrunched eyebrows. "Is that yours, Dad?"

I take Michael back on my lap. "This belonged to your great-grandfather. I'll tell you the story after the game. You want to hold it now?"

Our son's face lights up, his body goes rigid. His excitement keeps him from forming actual words.

I put the precious antique in his small hands and pull the camera's viewfinder up to his eye. "You just look through there. Then you press this button."

I peek past the viewfinder toward the batter, Anderson, who angles his head for a final glare at us. To anyone else, he might appear to be checking on our welfare. But the sneer curls into a scowl.

CLICK!

Anderson faces the pitcher again. Michael turns to me with questioning eyes. I vow to teach him to keep those eyes open wide.

ABOUT THE AUTHOR

Marty Roppelt was born and raised in Cleveland, Ohio. His original profession was acting, on stage, in local commercials and training films, and in film. This means that he has experienced life through a wide variety of day and night jobs, from barista to waiter and bartender to security guard, amongst many others. He lives in Illinois with his wife, Becky, and their eccentric cat, Fritz. *Mortal Foe* is his debut novel.

www.ingramcontent.com/pod-product-compliance
Lightning Source LLC
Chambersburg PA
CBHW021314250626
47155CB00002B/529